THE SAVAGE

THE SAVAGE

ROMAN REPUBLIC SERIES BOOK TWO

PENELOPE SKY

This is a work of fiction. Names, characters, organizations, places, events, and incidents are either products of the author's imagination or are used fictitiously. Otherwise, any resemblance to actual persons, living or dead, is purely coincidental.

Published by Montlake, Seattle

www.apub.com

EU product safety contact:
Amazon Media EU S. à r.l.
38, avenue John F. Kennedy, L-1855 Luxembourg
amazonpublishing-gpsr@amazon.com

ISBN-13: 9781662539251 (paperback)
ISBN-13: 9781662539244 (digital)

Cover design by Caroline Teagle Johnson
Cover image: © Michelle Lancaster PTY LTD

Printed in the United States of America

For Lenny.
I'd take a bullet for you too, babe.

Prologue I

Constantine

Bright and early in the morning, I worked in the kitchen of Rosticceria Da Cristina and prepared the dough for the pizzas and the fillings for the arancini. The pizza dough took the longest, requiring adequate time for the yeast to activate and for the dough to rise at the right temperature. I turned on the music from the sound system, cranking it up because I was the only one in there, singing along to the parts I liked because there was no one there to judge me.

Then I saw my mother through the window. She used her key to unlock the door, but when there was no resistance, she realized I'd left it open and she walked inside. "What did I tell you about locking the door, Con?" she shouted over the music.

"What do you think's gonna happen? Someone is gonna jack our pizza?"

"Why is this so loud?" She marched to the sound system and aggressively pushed the buttons until the music abruptly ended. "Jesus Christ, it's seven in the morning."

I rolled my eyes and got back to work.

"Roll your eyes at me again, and I'll smack them out of your head."

I smirked as I rolled the dough in the flour. "Sorry, Ma."

She gave me a gentle smack on the ass before she headed into the office. She did the books while I continued to prepare the store to open. I turned the music back on, keeping it at a reasonable level so she wouldn't yell at me again.

A couple hours later, she joined me in the kitchen. "Everything ready to go?"

"Like always, Ma." Working at the family business wasn't exactly glamorous, but it'd been in our family for generations and we were all proud of it. The restaurant had become a famous tourist spot for everyone who visited Taormina. Sometimes I wondered what life would be like if I left the island and made my own way on the mainland, but I had too much to leave behind. My family was everything to me, and if I ever decided to move, my mother would be devastated. She smacked me a lot, but I knew she did it out of love.

She rubbed my arm before she gave me a gentle pat. "That's my boy."

"Your boy has been a man a long time."

"Yes, I'm reminded every time I stand next to you." She glanced up at me, a foot and a half shorter than me. "So how are you? How are things with Issy?"

"Good," I said with a smile. "We were at the beach yesterday."

"She's a nice girl, Con."

"I know."

"And nice girls don't wait around forever . . ." She shot me a look before she started to place the trays of arancini and pizzas inside the glass-covered display case where the customers could choose what they wanted.

"I know they don't. Which is why I'm going to ask her to marry me."

"Wait too long and all the good ones will be taken, Con." She clearly hadn't heard what I said, obviously drowning in her anxiety that I wouldn't marry and have two kids before I turned twenty-five. "They will have another man's babies, and you'll be sorry."

"Ma?"

"Hmm?" She finished loading the last tray into the glass case, then shut the door. She came back to me, dusting her palms from the flour that was always sprinkled throughout the place.

"I'm going to ask her to marry me."

She blinked once, and then her face hardened like she didn't understand. Her hands flew to her mouth as she silenced a gasp she didn't realize she'd made. "Con, do not mess with me right now. I'm not in the mood for one of your jokes—"

"I would never joke about that, Ma."

"So, you're serious?"

"Yes."

She smacked both of her hands onto the counter, probably hard enough that it hurt, but she then threw her arms in the air and hopped up and down, moving with an enthusiasm she hadn't shown in . . . forever. "Oh my god, my boy is getting married. I can't believe this. I just . . . I have to talk to your aunt Chiara. She's going to be so excited—"

"Ma, let's keep this between you and me, all right? People can't keep a secret. Honestly, I probably already blew it telling you."

"I would never say anything!"

"You were just about to tell everyone in town. I don't even have the ring yet. I just need to save up a few more checks. I found the one that I want, but it's a little out of my price range. So the jeweler said he would hold it until I come up with the rest of the money."

"Con, I'll open the safe right now and give it to you." She was already headed for the hallway.

"Ma, *chill*."

She turned back to me. "Money is just money, Con. Take it."

"No."

"Do not be stubborn like your father!"

I released a short laugh. "I'm stubborn like *you*, not him. And I don't want money I haven't earned. I'm not buying my wife's ring with a handout. That's insulting to her and insulting to our marriage."

"Con, you can pay me back."

"What's the rush? I'll ask her in a couple months. Not like she's going anywhere." I grinned before the alarm went off and the next batch of pizzas was done. I pulled them out of the oven and set them on the counter so they could cool. "You're the only person I've told. So you need to keep it together, all right?"

"You're going to make me wait months? Con, I could drop dead—"

"Well, now you have a reason to stay alive." I grabbed the pizza roller and sliced each pizza into slices. Our bestseller was the Bronte pizza, which was sliced mortadella piled on top of a sprinkle of mozzarella cheese with pistachio pesto sauce drizzled over the top. I had a couple of slices myself when it came out fresh from the oven. "This stays between us." I pointed back and forth between her and me. "Got it?"

She gave a performative sigh before she rolled her eyes.

"Did you just roll your eyes at me?" I teased.

She started to march back to the office. "I'm your mother. I can roll my eyes at you all I want!" Then she slammed the door as hard as her little body could manage.

~

My mom hosted her weekly dinner on Sunday evening, and the small house was packed with pretty much all of Taormina. Friends, family, neighbors, the door was open to everyone. My mom, aunt, and sister cooked most of the food, but everyone brought something to help out. No other way seventy people were going to get fed without a little assistance.

Isabella and I sat together on the patio. My arm was draped over her chair while I drank a glass of wine and chatted with my friends and cousins at the little table we were crammed into. "We should all take a trip to Rome," Antonio, my cousin, said. "I've never been, and it's just an hour flight."

"Because no one ever leaves Taormina," I said. "And for good reason. We've got the best food, the best wine, and . . ." I turned to Isabella beside me and kissed her in front of everyone. "And the most beautiful women."

Her lips didn't just melt for me, but her eyes did as well.

"That's the lamest line I've ever heard," Antonio said.

"Hey, it worked," I said before I raised my glass and took a drink.

"It worked because you're six five," Francesco said.

My glass was empty and so was hers, so I left the guys and walked to the table under the patio where all the booze was set up. I opened a new bottle, let it breathe for a second, and then poured the glasses.

That was when I noticed my brother Edric step onto the patio. One hand was tucked into the pocket of his jeans, and he had a swagger so distinctive, it made it obvious which twin he was. He either didn't notice me or wasn't in the mood to talk, because he moved to the patio and the sea of tables. He didn't say a word before he took a seat.

I recorked the wine before I took a drink out of the glass, pivoting my body to look at the sea of people gathered around to enjoy the festivities. My mother knew how to bring everyone together. She said her mother had been the same way, a quality that had been passed down through the generations.

Antonio joined me. "Any wine left?"

"Yeah, just opened a new bottle." I looked at my brother again, about to walk over and talk to him, but he wore the hardest look I'd ever seen.

And when I followed his gaze, I saw it landed right on Isabella.

And she stared back . . . with the exact same look.

I felt my chest tighten as I watched them, witnessing an unspoken conversation pass between them, in a language no one else in that room could understand.

It went on and on, and I waited to see who would look away first.

But it took nearly a minute for Isabella to drop her gaze, to cross her arms over her chest like she was cold or uncomfortable.

And Edric continued to stare on . . . like she might look at him again.

When I got to Daiquiri, Edric was already there, sitting alone at a table for four, his drink in front of him, along with appetizers he hadn't touched. He lounged back, arms crossed, examining one of the nearby trees.

I walked up and took a seat. "Hey."

His eyes flicked to me, but his body remained in place. "Hey."

I grabbed the menu and browsed. "Might get a piña colada."

"Are you a girl on vacation?"

"I like the fruity drinks here. Makes me feel like I'm in Turks and Caicos."

"You haven't been to Turks and Caicos."

"And this is probably as close as I'm going to get." I closed the menu. "What's your problem?"

"I don't have a problem."

"You're being weird."

"How am I being weird?" he asked.

"You aren't being yourself."

He gave a slight shake of his head, then took a drink. "You're paranoid."

"And you're trying to gaslight me." I'd always had it, a remarkable intuition. I could read people like an open book. I'd known Edric my entire life and knew his behaviors and his tells. He'd been different the last few weeks, and I still hadn't figured out why.

Edric stopped participating in the conversation.

I tried to change the subject, sticking to the restaurant. He worked at the other location we had, the one that was only takeaway.

A couple minutes later, his eyes latched on to something in the distance and didn't pull away.

I glanced over my shoulder and spotted Isabella, out with some of her friends for a drink. Naturally, my eyes lit up at the sight of her in that little dress with her sexy thighs, and I swooned as always.

But her eyes were on my brother instead of me—and she was white as a ghost.

Her eyes finally made contact with mine and she smiled, but it was strained.

She and her two friends headed over. "Hey, what are you doing here?"

My hand went to her hip, and I pulled her onto my lap. "Get that fine ass over here. Ladies, take a seat."

The girls occupied the two open chairs. Her friends were cute, so I assumed Edric would be excited by this easy proposition, but he was standoffish to both of them.

"What are you guys up to?" I asked, inching my hand up Isabella's dress to the point where she had to shove it away before she flashed everyone.

"Just getting drinks and dinner," she said. "What are you guys doing?"

"Just talking about work."

She nodded but didn't say much else.

The three of us used to hang out all the time, have dinner together, and we'd felt like a threesome, but now everything had changed. The air was constantly sucked out of the room. The energy was . . . tense. "Did something happen between you guys?"

Edric's eyes shifted to my face with lightning speed.

And bumps immediately formed on Isabella's arms.

"Did you have a fight?" I asked. "Did Edric say some shit to you? Because I'll throw him down the stairs over there if he did."

"No," she blurted. "No . . . everything is fine."

Edric shifted his eyes elsewhere. "Yeah, we're good."

The awkwardness continued, and there was no explanation in sight.

~

"You think she's hooking up with Edric?" Antonio asked as we walked to the back of the truck, grabbed the boxes of supplies for the restaurant, and then carried them down the alleyway, into the store, and all the way into the storage room in the back.

Our town was quaint and cozy, a perfect spot for travelers because everything was walkable with no cars, but when it came to deliveries, it was always a bitch. "No."

He walked back with me to the truck, slightly winded. "Then what else could have happened?"

"I don't know, but she wouldn't do that."

"If he was an ass to her, wouldn't she have told you?"

"I don't know," I said as we passed underneath the Rosticceria Da Cristina sign and headed up the alleyway toward the truck. "Maybe he said something really stupid and she's afraid I'll never speak to him again."

"But why would he do that?"

"I don't know. Why does Edric do anything?"

"But what if—"

I stopped before we got to the truck. "She would never do that to me. And as much of an asshole as Edric is, he wouldn't do that either. All right?"

Antonio raised both of his hands and backed off. "All right."

I let myself inside my mother's front door and entered the house. I'd gotten caught up with work, and then I had to help a friend with a shipment for his family's business, so I'd lost track of time. I was almost an hour late to dinner, but even if the food was cold, my mom's cooking was still better than anyone else's piping-hot food.

Before I entered the kitchen, I turned to the patio. It'd been raining all day, so the party would be held inside, probably in the living room with all the furniture pushed up against the walls. But under the awning, I saw them together.

Isabella and Edric.

They were a solid three feet apart, and her arms were crossed over her chest, but the looks on both of their faces made it clear their conversation was serious. Whatever they spoke about was as grave as death, judging from the paleness of their faces, the hardness in their gazes.

I shouldn't spy on their conversation, but I couldn't pull my gaze away. My heart was beating hard in a way it never had before. It pounded with dread and anxiety—and I never had anxiety. Antonio's words came back to me, an accusation so lethal to my heart I couldn't even entertain it, and I pushed it away.

I always worked the morning shift at Rosticceria Da Cristina. Prepared everything for the day so the day crew could come in and run the store while I went home and took a nap. Otherwise, I'd be asleep before eight. I got there early, usually before five, so the dough had adequate time to rest.

I'd just finished putting everything in the glass cases when the day crew arrived to run the show. I made small talk with the guys before I left my apron in the break room and headed out.

The second I stepped out the door and turned into the alleyway, I ran straight into Edric. "What are you doing here?" He worked the other location because it was easier having a set of eyes on each place. My sister Beatrice wasn't quite old enough to be working the way we were.

He started to walk with me back in the direction he'd just come. "Wanted to run something by you."

"Yeah? What's up?" I continued up the slight incline until we made it to the road. Tourists were already out discovering the town because it was almost noon. I saw a group of them head for the restaurant to order fresh arancini and make a bunch of videos about it for social media. It didn't annoy me when people pulled out their phones when they ordered. Free marketing, right?

"Let's go to your apartment."

"Why can't we just talk here?" I asked.

"Because." That was all he said. "Come on, let's go."

My heart started to pound again. That sickening anxiety that I still wasn't quite familiar with hit me hard. Dread was a sensation I wasn't all that familiar with either, and now it hit me like a ton of bricks. "This is about Isabella."

His gaze shifted away to break the contact between our eyes.

That was my confirmation, because my brother was an arrogant son of a bitch who didn't have an ounce of humility within him—but he looked downright ashamed. "Come on." This time, he took the lead, forcing me to follow him, down several side streets and for minutes of painful silence.

I felt like I was going to black out from the anticipation.

What the fuck was he about to say?

She wouldn't hurt me. She wouldn't lie to me.

She would never betray me.

I couldn't even remember taking the stairs to my upstairs apartment. Couldn't remember getting the key in the door. Everything that took place in the last five minutes was immediately scrubbed from my memory.

I stepped into the place that was home, but now it felt like a prisoner's cell.

I moved to one of the couches but didn't take a seat. I turned to my brother and waited for him *not* to say what I was terrified he might say.

He slid his hands into his pockets and released a painful sigh. "Look, I wasn't gonna say anything, but it's fucking eating me and . . ."

I couldn't fucking believe it. It was like he punched me in the throat with a fucking hammer. "Just say it." My voice came out so calm, it sounded like someone else had said the words. Because I wasn't the least bit calm.

"It's a long story . . ."

I stared him down and waited for him to get on with it. Waited for him to destroy my goddamn world. To take that hammer he'd put to my throat and use it to shatter my heart. "Just get on with it, Edric. Otherwise, it's gonna be even longer before this shit conversation is over." I didn't have a clue how I sounded so calm and rational—when I felt nothing of the sort.

"All right, all right." He slid his hands into his pockets. "A couple weeks ago, I ran into Isabella in town . . . and I kissed her. I'd been drinking a lot, and I'm not sure what came over me. She thought I was you . . . so she went for it."

Now my temper roared. "Why the fuck would she think you were me?"

His eyes shifted away again.

"Edric."

"Because . . . I made it seem like I was you."

"How?"

"Wore a long-sleeved shirt to hide that I don't have tattoos . . . did the walk and the talk . . . smiled."

"So this was completely premeditated."

"Not really," he said. "I saw an opportunity, and I just took it."

"What the fuck is wrong with you?"

"I told you I'd been drinking . . . and you know I've always had a thing for her—"

"I've been dating her for over a year, and you *still* have a thing for her? Or do you still have a thing for her because she is mine and not yours? You always do this shit, Edric. You always go for the same girls, like it's some kind of sick competition."

"I swear I don't. We just have identical taste in women—which makes sense since we're fucking identical."

"You're going to blame this on genetics?" I asked incredulously.

"And like I said, I'd been drinking."

"Or it's because you're a worthless piece of shit. You chase a girl until you get underneath her skirt, and then you find some reason to dump her and chase someone else. Over and over. Doomed to repeat the same mistakes forever because you're a shit human being, Edric."

He stared with stoicism, but his throat shifted when he swallowed.

"You will never be happy. And then you'll be a middle-aged guy bitching about the fact that all women suck, when you're the one who sucks. Blaming them for the fact that you're alone, when the reason you're alone is because you can't be happy with anyone since you aren't happy with yourself."

"Wow. So that's what you think of me?"

"It is now, yeah," I snapped. "I point-blank asked what was going on, and you gaslit me. Told me I was paranoid. I'm the one who just got cheated on, and you're flipping the narrative to make me look like the asshole. Straight from the narcissist playbook. Well, that shit won't work on me, Edric." My mom always excused his bullshit because he was her son. I got it. My dad did too. But I saw a lot more that they never witnessed.

"I didn't have to tell you this, Con. But I wanted to—"

"Because you want me to dump Isabella so you can have her. And then you'll pump and dump."

He stepped back as the most wounded look he'd ever worn came over his face. "Jesus Christ, Con. She doesn't want me. She wants you. I couldn't have her even if I wanted to. The only way I could was when she thought I was you for sixty seconds."

"Then what the fuck has been going on between you? I saw you talking on the patio. Saw the way you stared at each other across the room. If you didn't want me to know, you sure made it pretty fucking obvious."

He pulled his hands out of his pockets and crossed his arms. He looked at the floor before he found my eyes again. "She was obviously pissed off when she realized I wasn't you. Slapped me and shoved me."

"I would hope so, because that's fucking assault, Edric."

"I didn't assault her—"

"She thought you were me, so that wasn't consensual. Your face will be broken before you leave this apartment, Edric." I wouldn't let him get away with what he did to my girl—even if she wouldn't be my girl anymore when this was over.

He didn't argue, accepted the punishment like a man. "And then there was tension between us because . . . I think she started to feel attracted to me."

I felt fucking sick.

"We talked a couple times, and she said she just wanted to forget what happened. I wanted to tell you, but she said you would never forgive her so we needed to take it to the grave."

Never forgive her when my brother kissed her?

"And I thought I could do that . . . until every time I had to look at you. I was a stupid asshole, and I would give anything to take it back. Hand to God, I feel like fucking shit—"

"Don't you dare bring him into this."

"Con, I truly feel horrible for what happened. I can't sleep. I can't eat. I can barely breathe. I've never felt so shitty for anything I've ever done in my life."

"Well, you can continue to feel terrible, because I don't forgive you."

His shoulders dropped at the blow. "Con—"

"I was going to ask her to marry me. Still haven't paid off the damn ring."

He took a step back, truly looking horror struck, like he might vomit in the middle of the living room. "Oh Jesus . . ." He cupped his mouth with his hand before he covered his eyes. It didn't look like a performance but a true reaction.

"And now it's over." Just like that. Done.

"Con, come on." He dropped his hand. "She didn't do anything wrong."

"What she did was worse than what you did."

He took a few steps toward me. "No, no, no. Do not throw this away because of what I did."

"She lied to me, Edric. And she told you to lie to me."

"Because she was scared how you would react. Scared you wouldn't forgive her. Scared it would destroy our relationship—"

"I don't care what the reasons were," I barked. "If she'd just come to me, I would have broken your nose and your arm and dropped you off at the hospital, and we would have moved on. But she fucking lied to me. The one person I'm supposed to trust without question fucking *lied* to me."

"Con, I get you're upset right now, but dumping Isabella is not the answer."

"That's not the kind of woman I want to marry."

"You love her."

"And I'll probably always love her, but we're done."

"You're reacting exactly the way she was afraid you would react."

"I told her all I want in a relationship is honesty. Instead of giving that to me, she lied to me and told you to lie to me. When I saw you two together multiple times, not once did I assume either of you would betray me. When Antonio suggested it, I told him to fuck off. That was how unwavering my trust was in both of you. But knowing you two were playing me like a damn fool . . ." I shook my head, humiliated that I'd put my trust in the wrong person. "Honestly, if you two hooked up and she told me about it right away and begged for my forgiveness, I probably could have moved forward because that's how much I love that girl. But this . . . no."

"Con, come on."

"No."

"Don't throw away the best thing that's ever happened to you."

"She *was* the best thing that ever happened to me. Now she's the worst."

I didn't need to confront Isabella, not when Edric told her everything and she came straight to my apartment.

I'd been sitting there for an hour, ice over my knuckles, watching the light change as the shadows shifted in the living room.

She pounded on my front door. “Con!”

“It’s open.” I dreaded the conversation because I’d already had it in my head, so it would feel like a repeat. She’d beg for me to stay, sob until she couldn’t breathe, get on her knees and plead—and it wouldn’t change anything.

She burst inside with a look of sheer panic that masked her beauty. “I didn’t know what to do—”

“Tell the truth. That’s always the right answer.”

“I—I didn’t know how you’d react.”

“Then you obviously don’t know me very well.” I tossed the bag of ice on the table and stood up, making her take a step back. “You really think if you’d told me what happened, I’d leave?”

“I—I didn’t know—”

“I think the real reason you didn’t tell me is because you felt something.”

She turned pale, as if she lived in the Arctic Circle instead of the Mediterranean.

“And you were afraid I’d pick up on it—which I would have and which I already have.”

Still in shock at what I’d said but also pained by the truth, she took another step back. “Con—”

“I would have understood, Isabella. We’re twins. Most people can’t tell us apart. How can you be attracted to me and not him?”

“You look the same, but you’re nothing alike.”

“But you still felt something when he kissed you—when you thought he was me—and I would have understood. I wouldn’t have liked it, and I would have been livid about it for a while, but I would have understood. But lying to me and choosing to lie to me for the rest of our lives . . . that’s just fucked up.”

“I’m sorry.” She started to get teary. “I’m so fucking sorry. I was scared and I panicked and I didn’t know what to do. I didn’t want to ruin your relationship with your brother. I didn’t want to risk losing you. I had so much more to lose by telling you than not telling you.”

"When we were at Daiquiri, I asked both of you what was going on—and you lied to me." I slammed my fist into my chest. *"To my fucking face."*

"I'm sorry—"

"I heard you the first time, and I don't care. You let me walk around looking like a fool. You should have heard me when Antonio suggested you were fucking around with my brother. I nearly punched him in the face. Now I owe him a big fucking apology because he was right on the money and I was too fucking dumb to see it."

"I did not fuck around with your brother."

"The fact that you both lied about what happened and continued what I can only describe as an emotional affair feels like you did."

"We did not have an emotional affair."

"I saw you stare at each other across the room. I saw you together on the patio. It doesn't matter that you were three feet apart. Something happened between you two, and you continued it right in front of me. You took advantage of my trust and mistook it for stupidity."

"I never thought you were stupid—"

"We're done, Isabella." We could go around and around, but no amount of arguing would change the facts.

"No . . ." The tears came so fast, it was as if they'd been there the entire time. "Con, no. I love you."

"And I fucking love you, but that doesn't matter anymore."

"It always matters."

"I took a loan out on the ring so I could ask you to marry me—and while I was doing that, you two were sneaking off together or texting when I wasn't around. God, I feel like the biggest idiot alive."

This was obviously a surprise to her, because she gasped like I'd punched her in the stomach. "It wasn't like that, I swear. Con, please don't do this." She brought her hands together like she was about to kneel and pray. "We're meant to be together. I've known it since we were kids. Please, don't ruin this."

"I didn't ruin it, Isabella. *You did.*"

"I didn't cheat on you."

"You lied directly and by omission. You lied and lied and lied and would have taken that fucking lie to the grave buried beside me. I'd roll over in my coffin if I'd known who I'd married. Who'd mothered my children. Someone who could keep a secret of this magnitude from me. *Who the fuck does that?*"

She sobbed her heart out. Released a flood of tears that should run her ducts dry. She moved into me and grabbed on to my arm like it was a life raft and she was lost out at sea. "No. You're the love of my life. Please, I'm sorry. I promise I'll never keep anything from you again."

I pulled away from her grasp as gently as I could. I didn't want to be touched by the person who'd ripped out my heart. Just because I didn't shed a tear didn't mean I wasn't fucking devastated. "It's done."

"Give me another chance." She latched on to me again.

I continued to step out of her hold. "You should go."

"No!" Now she screamed, falling to her knees at my feet. "Please don't do this to me, please don't do this to me, don't do this to us . . ." It was an ugly sob, her face so beet red it was like she'd run a marathon. A thick vein popped in her forehead I'd never seen before. She was always calm and collected, but she'd completely lost her mind.

I knew she wasn't going to leave.

So I had to go.

I felt her try to grab me again as I walked past her, but I forced myself forward and onward, moving for the door, doing my best to drown out the sound of her cries and walk out.

Chapter 1

Constantine

I walked into the Temple, and my boots hit the sand. The heater below warmed the sand just like it was in ancient times, from the forges below and the sun beating down from the sky, making it even harder for the gladiators to handle the heat—especially barefoot.

"Drop him." I turned to the men behind me—the ones who carried Timothée's unconscious body.

They dropped him on his back in the sand.

"Thanks, boys." I could have carried the kid myself, but as the emperor, I didn't carry anyone. Well, except my woman when she needed a ride from the couch to the bed or a ride from the bed to my lap.

Timothée began to stir, probably because the heat had started to warm his clothes.

Rocco called from the stands, "Let's have him fight a lion."

"We don't have lions," I replied.

"Yeah, but that'd be fun."

I chuckled quietly. "Not for the lion."

"I think it's something we should do. Make it like the real Colosseum. The guys would love to watch."

"I'm not doing that to a lion."

"Come on, the lion would win."

"And in the meantime?" I asked. "He's just sitting in a cage. Come on, fuck that."

"Didn't realize you were such an animal lover."

"I'm just an asshole." I turned back to Timothée.

He blinked a couple of times as he looked up at me, still not understanding the predicament he was in.

"Rise and shine, asshole." I kicked him hard in the leg.

He gave a strained moan, his throat still not working properly after being knocked out cold. But the sudden sense of pain made him alert, and after he hugged his knee to his chest, he crawled backward across the sand to get away from me. The panic really set in when he looked around and realized where he was. "What the fuck?"

"Remember me?" I winked at him.

He finally got to his feet to run away, but when he looked and saw all the armed guards with machine guns, he changed his mind.

I whistled to get his attention.

He whipped back to me, out of breath from the panic rather than the exertion.

"Listen up." I pulled out the dagger identical to the ones used in ancient times, where the handle weighed just as much as the blade, making it a remarkable weapon for the slaves who weren't meant to win. "You were paid to profile victims for Vladimir, and as Emperor Constantine of the Roman Republic, I sentence you to fight in the Temple. If you survive, you walk out of here as a free man." I held out the blade to him.

He glanced at the dagger, then at me, like he couldn't believe this. "You're fucking crazy."

"You didn't realize that when I broke down your front door and put my boot against your head?" I smirked before I spun the blade in the air and caught it by the hilt. Then I threw it down hard into the sand—the hilt up by his feet. "Good luck." I walked off to the stands where Rocco was seated.

I could tell that Timothée had picked up the knife and started to rush me from behind. I knew it even before Rocco made a gesture with his hand for me to spin around.

I ducked before he could strike me, the blade and his arm flying by.

I righted myself again, then kicked him in the back so he hit the sand. Then I stepped over him and slammed my boot so hard into his knee that the socket popped.

"Ahhhhhh!"

"I think you just hurt your chances." I continued my walk to the stands, then up the stairs to join Rocco. I whistled for the show to get started, the doors rising and the armed guards coming out to cut Timothée into pieces.

He continued to hug his knee and shriek in pain as he looked at the two men coming right for him.

Rocco turned to me. "Get anything out of him?"

"Nah," I said. "He was paid in cash, stashed in electrical boxes behind buildings. And the number he would call has been deactivated. So Vladimir connected Aurelia to Timothée and got ahead of it."

"Damn."

"But hey, it's still fun." I put my feet up on the chair in front of me and watched Timothée try to get away from the guard carrying a full sword, about to hack him to pieces. "So, at this point, I think we need to call Luca. He owes me anyway."

"For what?"

I shook my head from side to side. "Eh, long story—"

Timothée screamed when he was stabbed with the sword right in his chest cavity.

"Well, that didn't last long," Rocco said.

"Eh. Could have given him a gun, and it'd still be over."

Rocco chuckled. "So what's the status with you and Aurelia?"

I gave a shrug. "It's water under the bridge now."

"Good."

"I don't know what it is about her, but I just can't stay mad. She's got these beautiful green eyes, man. They get me every time."

He released a loud laugh. "I don't think it's her eyes, man."

I laughed too, knowing he had me dead to rights. But I wasn't going to tell him about her killer pussy. "I thought about it, and if the situations were reversed, if she barged into my place because she knew Isabella was there and threatened her and barked at her and all that . . . I don't think I'd stick around."

He gave a nod. "Yep."

"So yeah, I fucked up."

"You did."

"I just admitted it. You don't gotta keep repeating it."

"Just want that message to sink in so you don't fuck it up again."

"Why do you care if I fuck it up or not?"

"Because."

"Because why?" I nudged him in the side.

"Because she makes you happy." He nudged me back.

A smirk moved on to my lips. "Aww, that's kinda sweet."

"Shut up," he said. "Don't make it weird."

"Maybe I like weird."

"Okay, let's change the subject before it gets any weirder. When am I going to meet her officially?"

"I don't know. You want to meet her?"

"She's your woman, isn't she?"

"Damn right she is." She was all mine, not one foot halfway out the door. And it was fucking glorious. No bullshit. No second-guessing.

"Then yeah, I should meet her."

"All right, I'll set it up. But try not to stare, all right?"

He turned to look at me hard, one eyebrow raised.

"Because she is *fiiiiine*."

"I've already seen her."

"Yeah, but that was chaos. Not her natural environment. So you can look a little bit." I brought my forefinger and thumb together, the tips almost touching. "But that's it. Just a glance."

He gave a quiet chuckle. "Thank you for your generosity."

I pulled my phone from my pocket. "I'd show you a picture but, you know, none are exactly PG . . ." I'd taken pictures and videos of her sleeping, going down on me, a picture of her ass when she rode me reverse cowgirl. All just for me. I found Luca's name in my contacts and called.

It rang a couple times before he answered. "Luca."

"Constantine."

There was a pause before he spoke. "It's been a while. Need something?"

"Yes, in fact, I do. I've got a guy down here who keeps evading my net. Thought you might be of some help."

"Not sure why."

"Because it seems all his cronies are French."

"Ah, I see. What's he dealing?"

"Illegal transplants. Organs on the black market. Shit like that. Targets young people, and they just disappear. Every time I get close, he changes the tactics of his operation. None of his men roll on him because he doesn't let them know anything."

"Then he must pay them a lot not to ask questions."

"Yeah, probably," I said. "All I have is a name. Vladimir."

"Last name?"

"Nope."

Luca was quiet for a while. "I'm sure you heard about the commotion we had up here?"

"You'd have to live in North Korea not to know about it."

"Well, Bastien is out. I'm the First French Emperor now."

"Congratulations."

Luca paused over the line like he wasn't sure if I was being genuine. "Give me some time to figure it out."

"Great. Thanks."

"Yeah." He hung up.

Chapter 2

Constantine

I texted Aurelia. Let's have dinner tonight.

The three dots popped up, and her message appeared right away. Alright.

I loved how easy this was. Good, I want you to meet Rocco. Well, Rocco wants to meet you . . .

Well, I met him that night . . .

Eh, doesn't really count. I'll pick you up at 7:30, sweetheart.

Okay, see you then.

After I slept a couple hours, I arrived at her apartment and watched her open the door in the sexiest black dress. It had one strap over a shoulder while the other was bare, and it was tight and so short she'd definitely struggle to sit without her ass popping out.

So it was fucking perfect.

I was all over her as always, my hand getting a nice grip on her ass right there in the doorway, yanking up that dress so I could squeeze her ass and touch the little G-string that barely covered anything.

The heat of our embrace was like an anchor that dragged me to the bottom of the ocean, and I felt myself fall as I guided her back into her apartment, kicking the door shut with my boot, then lifting her into my chest.

"Aren't we going to be late?" she asked between breathless kisses, like she had absolutely no desire to stop.

I carried her into her bedroom and laid her across the bed. "Trust me," I said as I popped open my jeans and yanked them down. "He'll understand."

When we walked into the restaurant, Rocco was seated at a table with a drink, but he wasn't alone. While I was nailing my girl, he'd picked up a *friend* to keep him company. A petite blonde with a lot of boobage popping out—exactly his type.

"Told you he wouldn't mind," I said as I guided Aurelia to the table with my hand on her waist.

She wore a mischievous little smile on her lips.

A smile so mischievous it made me grab her by the ass.

Rocco cast a quick glance at me before he wrapped things up with his new side piece. Pulled out his phone and got her number before she left the table.

I smirked as we took our seats across from him. "I would apologize for being late, but it seems like we did you a favor."

Rocco ignored me and extended his hand to Aurelia. "Rocco. Nice to meet you . . . under better circumstances."

She shook his hand. "Thank you for everything you did that night. Scariest night of my life."

He gave a slight nod. "Yeah, that was pretty shitty."

"Did you guys end up getting the guy?"

"I handled Timothée," I said. "He didn't cough up anything good. But we know a guy who might be able to help us track down Vladimir. We're leaving for Paris tomorrow to meet with him."

"Paris?" she asked.

"Yeah. I'll be gone just for a day and a half."

She seemed surprised and a little taken aback, but she didn't say anything.

The waiter came over, and we ordered our drinks. Rocco was still working on his.

When her disappointment continued to fill the air, I outright asked her what the problem was. "Is that okay?"

"Of course it's okay," she said with an awkward laugh. "You don't have to ask my permission."

"Then why are you being weird?" I put her on the spot in front of Rocco because I didn't care what he saw. I was always fully transparent with him—except for the intimate stuff.

"She's scared," Rocco said. "Which is pretty obvious."

I turned to look at my friend across the table, my eyebrow cocked.

"She just said that was the worst night of her life, we haven't caught the guy yet, and now we're both leaving." Rocco took a sip of his wine. "You're good at reading people, but you aren't always good at understanding them."

I just got schooled by my friend. I turned to her and silently asked if that was the problem.

She wouldn't look at me. "It was a gut reaction. Just being paranoid."

So, she was scared. Scared that I wouldn't be there to protect her if she needed me. It was untrue, because I could deploy my men to protect her the second she needed something. "Stay at my place until I get back."

"What?" she asked quietly.

"Medusa would love to have you. But I gotta warn you, she likes to cuddle." And she was a big dog who needed to stretch out across the entire bed like it was her house instead of mine.

"Oh, that's okay—"

"Would I offer if I wasn't being genuine?"

"Why don't you talk about it later instead of putting the poor girl on blast right in front of me?" Rocco asked. He looked at Aurelia. "He means well. He just doesn't get it sometimes."

"Ganging up on me now?" I questioned him.

"Yep," he said before he took a drink. "It's nice to have someone to team up with."

Aurelia gave a quiet chuckle, like she found our relentless back-and-forth banter humorous. "How long have you two known each other?"

"Years," Rocco said. "What is it? Five?"

"Six, asshole," I said. "Glad it's meant as much to you as it has to me."

"You want to celebrate an anniversary too?"

"I wouldn't *hate* a box of chocolates."

She chuckled again before she drank her wine. "You guys are cute."

"Cute?" I asked incredulously. "You think two arguing six-and-a-half-feet-tall guys who weigh two hundred pounds are cute?"

"Um . . . yeah?"

Rocco smirked slightly before he changed the subject. "Con says you're a photographer?"

"Yeah . . . I love it."

~

Aurelia left and headed downstairs to use the restroom, so it was just Rocco and me alone at the table.

"So, what do you think?"

"Does it matter?" His arms were folded across the table as he sat there, leaning forward slightly. "If I said I hated her, it wouldn't change anything, right?"

"You hate her?"

"No," he said quickly. "But we both know my opinion doesn't matter."

"No, it doesn't change anything. But I still want to know."

"So, it does matter."

"A little bit." I shrugged. "Okay . . . maybe a lot. Tell me what you think."

He wore a slight smirk. "She's cool."

"That's it?"

"What do you want me to say, Con?"

"The truth."

"Trust me, you don't want the truth."

"I asked, didn't I?"

"Jesus, fine." He threw his arms up quickly before he crossed them over his chest. "She's out of your league."

The smile that crept over my face made my whole body flush with heat. "Yeah?"

"A thousand percent."

The smile just grew and grew, unstoppable. "She is, isn't she?"

"I think she's gonna be around for a while."

I held up my hand, showing my crossed fingers. "That's the plan, man."

"And you can tell she's really into you."

"Fuck yeah." I slapped my hand on the table. "That's what I want to hear."

~

Aurelia sat on the couch with Medusa seated beside her. She ran her fingers through Medusa's fur, watching her with the same sappy eyes I wore whenever I cuddled with my dog on the couch. She was definitely a dog person.

I threw my bag over my shoulder. "I'll be home tomorrow afternoon. Call me if you need anything."

"All right. Are you sure it's okay if I stay?"

My answer was a cold stare.

"Okay, message received." She left Medusa on the couch and walked up to me, still in the little black dress and heels she'd worn to dinner. She hadn't brought a bag because she'd come straight here. She would head home after she woke up because she had shoots scheduled.

My hand moved to her ass under her dress, able to look her in the eye because she wore five-inch heels that made her height comparable to mine. "I love how tall you are." I wasn't picky when it came to women, but I loved that I could actually look her in the eyes with ease, that I could slide my hand to her ass without having to hang down low.

Her eyes flicked away briefly, clearly caught off guard or uncomfortable by the comment. "It's funny that you say that, because I've always hated it. Most guys are my height or shorter."

"Then it sounds like you needed to find the right guy." I dipped my head slightly and kissed her, squeezing her ass at the same time. I'd always been an ass man—and her ass was a fucking summer peach. "Good night, sweetheart."

"Good night."

~

Luca gave me a call to update me on the situation. "I asked around, and Bastien remembers a man named Vladimir from about fifteen years ago. His father dealt with him . . . giving up his workers who refused to comply. He couldn't let them go, and he couldn't get them to work, so . . . may as well make some money off it."

I was appalled, but I kept my judgment to myself as I held the phone to my ear.

"I suspect that is the man you seek."

"Yeah, sounds like it," I said. "He's committing his crimes in Rome to avoid violating the laws of the Fifth Republic. So he's obviously a lot more afraid of you than he is of me."

"Perhaps," he said. "Or perhaps he's just smart enough not to shit where he eats. Give me a week or two, and I'll extradite him to you."

“I appreciate your cooperation.”

“And I appreciate your cooperation in the future.”

An eye for an eye, but I wanted an allyship that was deeper. “The Roman Republic will always stand with the Fifth Republic. We’re allies in our mission—and we will always answer your call for aid if you need it.”

Luca said nothing.

“And I hope that the Fifth Republic feels the same.”

An even longer stretch of silence passed. “As long as that commitment is equal in quantity and substance—then yes.”

Chapter 3

Constantine

I'm back in Rome. I texted Aurelia when I returned to the city, just so she knew I was there if she needed me for anything. With my casual liaisons and my flings, I barely gave them the time of day because I didn't give anyone more than my body. But I gave Aurelia all of me, laid my cards on the table, checked in with her, never let her wonder where I was or if I was thinking of her.

How was your trip?

Good. I'm optimistic.

She didn't ask for the details.

How'd you sleep?

Took a second to get used to Medusa, but other than that, slept like a rock.

Forgot to tell you she snores.

Yeah, I figured that out pretty quick. And she kept stretching her paws toward me and pushing me farther across the bed like I was in her way. By the time I woke up, I was barely on the edge. 😂

Yep, that's my girl.

Imagine when it's the three of us. 😂

I smirked when I read that message. You aren't going to kick her out?

Isn't it her bed?

Now I really smiled, because I loved that answer. My other guests wanted Medusa on the couch or in the other room. They petted her and showed her affection but were mostly disinterested in her. But Aurelia seemed to genuinely care for her. Damn right, it's her bed.

I'm sure we'll figure it out.

I loved the attitude. I'd wanted *we* since the day I met her. Wanted *us*.

Will I see you tonight?

Ooh, she was starting to get a little needy. I liked it. I've got a lot of stuff to take care of the next couple days. I'll see what I can do.

Alright, talk to you later.

She was needy at the right time and patient at the right time. Perfect combination. Bye, sweetheart.

The second I walked into his office, President Barsetti went for my throat.

"What the fuck, Con?" He jumped up from his chair behind the desk.

I already knew what this was about. "Look—"

"Don't *look* me." He came around the desk in his tailored suit, lean and toned but with broad shoulders that filled out the jacket well, like he worked out instead of sitting on his ass all day, signing papers. "You made a scene down the street from the Pantheon."

"Not the first time blood has run down the streets of Rome."

"You think this is funny?"

"No, not funny." I helped myself to one of the armchairs. "But definitely satisfying."

He swung his arm as he turned, like he needed to punch the air instead of me. "You set people on fire."

"Assholes. I set *assholes* on fire."

"Machine guns were blazing. The military almost moved in, but I told General Farina to stand down because I knew it was you."

"If he'd gotten there, he would have done the same thing—trust me."

He stopped in front of me, arms crossed over his chest, eyes livid. "You're insane if you believe that."

"These are the netters from the black market. They catch the prey and neutralize them before they deliver their bodies. They were about to take another innocent woman, and I stopped it. You're fucking welcome."

"You've saved lots of people without making a scene. So why was this fucking chaos?"

Because it was personal—damn personal.

He continued to stare at me as he waited for an answer.

I didn't want to lie. Honesty was like marrow in my bones, the foundation of who I was. "Because . . . they picked the wrong girl. My girl."

He released a heavy sigh before he dragged his fingers down his face. "Jesus Christ—"

"She's okay, thanks for asking."

"You caused a panic throughout the entire city, Con."

"I protected this city."

"So that means you finally caught Vladimir?" He leaned up against his desk and crossed his ankles.

Goddammit.

Judging by his pissed-off expression, I could tell he already knew the answer.

"I'm close."

"You're close?"

"I met with Luca Fornier—"

"Who the fuck is Luca?"

"The new First French Emperor of the Fifth Republic. Says he knows a guy that used to know the guy, like fifteen years ago. He'll find him and hand him over to me. We'll put a stop to this for good."

President Barsetti wasn't the least bit reassured by that. He continued to stare me down like I was a terrorist against my own country. "How long will it take?"

"He said a week or two. Crow, come on, you know me. You know I'll take care of this. It's taken a little longer than I'd like, but you know I always do my job."

He dragged his hand down his face and over the stubble of his jawline as he looked out the window to the left. He ignored me for several seconds, lost in thought, and then he came back to the conversation. "We did our investigation into Antoine's arms business. One lead led to another, and we've figured out the arms are coming from Florence."

A slab of bricks fell right on top of my chest and cracked my sternum.

"And you know what that means . . ."

The Skull King.

"Nothing happens in Florence that he doesn't know about," President Barsetti said. "So, he's either a part of it or doesn't give a shit that it's happening."

I knew where this was going. "No."

"Con, it's your job."

"It's *my* job? Last time I checked, you were the president of Italy."

"But it falls under your jurisdiction. And we both know he won't say a word to me."

I shook my head, my throat full of flames I wanted to unleash.

"I get it's shitty—"

I released a loud, painful laugh. "Shitty . . . that's putting it mildly."

~

"We had an agreement." Lorenzo launched out of the chair and almost flew across the table at Marco. "But you fucking pissed on that because you thought I wouldn't find out." Then he pulled out a knife, and all hell broke loose as he climbed over the table toward Marco.

"Gentlemen," I said from my seat at the head of the table.

Lorenzo swung the knife at Marco and backed him up into the wall. "Thought you could take a cut of my business and I wouldn't find out, you fucking weasel!" He cut down Marco's arm, and he let out a muffled scream. Blood dripped and splashed on the wall.

I nodded to one of my men. "Break up the schoolgirls."

Lorenzo was pulled away and forced back into his seat. The knife was yanked out of his hand.

Marco squeezed the long cut on his arm to stop the bleeding.

I nodded to one of my other guys, who put a bottle of scotch on the table along with a roll of gauze. "The jurisdictions throughout the city are distinct. Marco, don't act like you don't know exactly what they are." I didn't just police the crime, but I also handled the disputes between the different gangs and disciplines. At the end of the day, they were all criminals, so of course they continued to try to undercut one another. And it was my job to keep everything fair. "You'll pay Lorenzo twenty percent of your profits for the last thirty days—"

"Fucking bullshit," Marco said as he splashed the scotch on his arm.

"Excuse me?" I cocked my head.

He kept his eyes down and started to wrap the gauze.

"Yes, did you say something?" Lorenzo pressed.

I turned to Lorenzo and gave him my signature *I'll fucking kill you* stare.

Lorenzo immediately looked away.

Marco secured the gauze around the cut. "Lorenzo has been cutting his product with fentanyl, making his prices so cheap no one can compete."

"Is that true?" I turned back to Lorenzo.

"Of course it's not true," he said, already red in the face.

I continued to stare him down.

"It's not," he repeated.

"You do realize all I have to do is try your product, right?" I was a great judge of character, and I could see right through the sweat on his forehead.

My phone started to vibrate in my pocket, so I pulled it out and glanced at the screen, expecting it to be someone I could call back later. But it was Aurelia. "I have to take this. Lorenzo, take this time to think about how you want to handle this—because we both know how much I fucking hate liars." I left the room, heading down the hallway as I put the phone to my ear. "Hey, sweetheart."

"Hey . . ."

"Everything all right?"

"Yeah. Are you busy right now?"

I glanced back down the hallway and saw Lorenzo sitting in his chair and sweating like a pig, knowing he was a dead man. "No." I continued farther down the hallway. "How was your day?"

"Had a couple of shoots. Been working on edits all day."

"You spend more time behind the lens than in front of it."

"Yeah," she said with a little chuckle. "Seems that way sometimes. How are you?"

I'd been bombarded with one thing after another at work. Bullshit on top of bullshit. I didn't have as much time for her as I had before.

But I knew I was invested in this relationship, so I had to make the time. "A lot of stuff has been happening with work. Hasn't been fun."

She didn't ask for details. She never asked. "Yeah, I figured. Well, I'll let you go. I—I just miss you . . ." Her voice faltered at the end, like she was embarrassed by what she said before she even finished saying it.

I was not gonna lie. I loved seeing this vulnerability from her. Dropping her for a week had been the hard lesson she needed to learn. "I miss you too, sweetheart. Pack a bag and stay with me a couple days."

"A couple days?" she asked.

"Yeah. I'll be in and out, taking care of business, but at least we'll see each other when I'm home."

There was a pause, and this was where she would distance herself and say she didn't want to bother me or burden me or some other bullshit. But instead, she said, "Okay. I miss Medusa too, so . . ."

Just like that, it wasn't complicated anymore. So fucking simple. So fucking easy. She was my woman, and I was her man. "I'll have my guys pick you up in an hour."

It was almost midnight when I got home. I'd settled the dispute between Lorenzo and Marco. Marco's accusation had been correct. Lorenzo had been cutting his product with fentanyl to lower the costs, but he'd put in such a trace amount that it didn't have a drastic impact on his customers. But that didn't matter—because he'd still violated the laws of the Roman Republic. So Lorenzo was shot and burned in a furnace, and Marco got to absorb his business.

My job was done.

I walked through the enormous thirty-foot doors, entered the entryway with my statues from Egypt, and strolled past the sculpture of the Eye of Horus before I moved into the second entryway, where the stairs were located.

Elio emerged to greet me, always knowing when I was home because my security team alerted him the instant I approached the property. "Good evening, Your Highness."

"I'd like dinner in my chambers—for two."

"Of course." He gave a slight bow.

I headed up the flights of stairs until I reached my private corridor of the residence. It was blocked by a set of mahogany doors outlined with gold. None of the staff was permitted to enter the corridor without Elio's supervision. As a result, whenever I was home, I didn't have to see or speak to anyone as long as I stayed within that part of the villa. The hallway had other guest rooms, a private gym, one of my collection rooms, and my office.

I walked down the long corridor and found the double gold doors that led to my primary suite. The doors were heavy, and that was by design—because no one was getting in there if they weren't welcome.

When I stepped into the entryway, I heard Medusa run from the other room and beeline for me.

"Hey, baby girl." I knelt down and let her climb up me slightly as I greeted her with lots of pets and a kiss on the head. I stood up, then pulled my gun from the back of my jeans and left it on the round table next to the vase of flowers.

When I moved to the open doorway leading into the next section of the suite, Aurelia appeared in nothing but one of my T-shirts.

God, that was sexier than the finest French lingerie. I felt the grin lift into my mouth as I walked over her, my arms circling her as I pulled her into me, significantly shorter without her five-inch heels to give her some lift. I pulled her flush against my chest and kissed her, my mouth melting against the warmth of her lips, immediately sucked into this magnetic chemistry we had. I slid my hand into her soft hair, grazed the delicate skin of her neck, and I kissed her with a gentleness I didn't know I had.

Fuck, this woman did some shit to me.

I was dead tired after all the stuff I'd had to handle today, but all of that left my mind at the sight of her. I lifted her into me, her long legs hooking around my waist, and I carried her to the big bed I normally only shared with Medusa.

I laid her back, rolling on top of her, loving how loosely my shirt fit her lithe body. Her makeup was gone, like she'd already been in bed when I walked in the door, and that natural look was a turn-on for me. Not just because she was so damn beautiful she didn't need makeup, but because it felt . . . intimate. She wasn't a woman who was gone before the morning light hit the windows. My bed was her bed, so she helped herself to my clothes and my bathroom and made herself at home.

That turned me the fuck on.

I lifted up her shirt and found her little thong, pulling it off her sexy legs that I could stare at for days. Then I bent her legs back and dropped my face between her thighs to kiss that perfect little pussy.

She inhaled a deep gasp when she felt me come for her hard, with my lips, tongue, and even a bit of my teeth.

The urge to have her, eat her, and inhale her came over me, and with my hard dick pinned between me and the mattress, I went to town on her flesh. It wasn't something I normally did, not when my conquests were mostly transactional and purely physical, but with her, I wanted to drown in it. In her smell, her taste, her softness.

Her fingers dug into my hair, and she gently rocked into my face. She pulled up her shirt to expose her tits like she was warm from the flush of heat that burned her flesh. She ground and moaned, and even when I didn't mean to make it happen, she came with a whimper like the rush was as pleasurable as it was painful.

I could eat her for fucking dinner, but my dick was about to throw a tantrum. It wanted to slide through the cream of my labor. I lifted my body and yanked my shirt free before I got my boots and bottoms off. My dick was so fucking hard it hurt. I moved over her, pinned her like the flexible doll she was, and shoved my hard dick inside her with a moan that made my spine shiver.

I nailed her into the mattress, pounded into her like she was a whore instead of my woman, so desperate for her I couldn't control myself. I felt like a boy instead of a man, desperate to come inside that pussy as many times as her little body could take.

Chapter 4

Constantine

When I stepped out of the shower, she was still in bed where I'd left her, her thong on the floor where it had landed after I tossed it aside. Her eyes were closed, and my shirt was like a comfortable dress.

I pulled on a clean pair of boxers. "Hungry, sweetheart?"

She opened her tired eyes and looked at me. Then she gave a slight nod.

"Dinner is in the dining room."

"It is?"

"Elio uses a different door to get to it."

"Oh . . ." She pulled on a clean thong, then joined me in the dining room, a ten-seater table with a table runner and low centerpieces. We sat across from each other, and when I removed the silver lids, I revealed a meal of steak, greens, and potatoes for me, while she had a piece of salmon with rice and white asparagus.

For the first few minutes, we ate in silence. I could tell she was tired because she wasn't normally up this late. But for me, I was wired. "Where were your shoots?" I asked.

"I had an engagement shoot in the afternoon and then a kid's birthday party in the evening."

"Fun."

She shrugged. "I don't care for the birthday ones, but they pay the bills."

"Have you worked on your art photography?"

She sliced into her salmon and took a few bites. I could tell she liked it when it was on our salad the other day. She preferred seafood to steak, that was for sure. "Honestly, haven't really had time. Haven't been inspired either. So many changes in such a short amount of time. I'm still getting settled."

"Have you spoken to Enzo?"

"No," she said. "I highly doubt I'll ever hear from him again."

Not unless he wanted a broken nose.

"You think he and Luna will make it?"

She released a quiet laugh. "I doubt it. He might stick it out for a while because he sacrificed everything to have her, but who knows. Truthfully, I don't care. I don't think about him anymore. I'm either too busy with work or too busy thinking about you."

I grinned before I took a bite. "Yeah?"

"Come on," she said with a laugh. "Don't play dumb."

"What do you think about exactly?"

"I don't know . . . stuff."

"Ooh . . . I like *stuff*."

Her cheeks started to flush, so I knew exactly what kind of *stuff* was on her mind.

"You think about me when you touch yourself, sweetheart?"

She stiffened at the question like she couldn't believe I asked. "What about you?"

"I don't jerk off."

"Right. Sure, you don't."

"I don't," I said seriously. "That's why I pay for sex sometimes. I prefer the flesh of a woman instead of my own. I grew out of that in my early twenties and never went back."

She seemed to believe me, seemed to remember that I was always honest with her because I didn't care enough to lie about anything. "So, when we weren't together . . . were you with other women?"

"No." The thought didn't cross my mind. I'd been too pissed off to get hard. "Were you?"

The relief that spread into all the delicate features of her face was so distinct, it was obvious it'd been on her mind but she was too scared to ask—or too scared to hear the answer. "No."

"So then let's circle back to my previous question. Do you think of me when you touch yourself?"

She was flustered all over again, beet red.

"Come on, tell me." I already knew the answer, but I wanted to hear it anyway.

"You're such an ass."

"You were the one talking about that OnlyFans of yours."

She released a self-conscious laugh.

I cut her some slack because she truly seemed embarrassed by it—for a reason I didn't understand. "Record yourself and send it to me."

"Oh wow . . ."

"Come on, I'll be your number one subscriber. A top-paying customer."

"Like I'd ever take your money."

"Then do it for free." I grinned.

The flush in her cheeks was so intense she looked the same as she did in bed, like she was about to come. She sliced her fork through her salmon and focused on her dish like that was whom she had a conversation with. "What's been going on at work?"

"Do you actually want to know, or are you just trying to change the subject?"

"You really are an ass, you know that?" she said with an uncontrollable smile on her lips.

"Yes, I'm aware." I smiled back.

"And yes, I do want to know."

"I spoke with Luca Fornier, the new First French Emperor of the Fifth Republic, and he said he'll find Vladimir for me and extradite him to Rome. There've been whispers of an upcoming terrorist attack on the EU, and unfortunately, arms moving to the east are coming from Florence—and most likely the Skull King. And then I had a couple turf disputes I had to handle today, and some asshole was boosting his profits by cutting fentanyl into his product. No one died from the contamination, so he really worked his magic to make it safe. But that's not the point."

She stopped eating and stared as she listened to all of that. "I'm sorry . . . French Emperor? Skull King? Who are all these people?"

I chuckled because I forgot she wasn't fully a part of my world—yet. "The French Emperor is the French equivalent of what I am here in Rome. Bastien used to be in charge, but he's retired and now Luca has taken his position."

"Oh . . ."

"Yeah," I said, moving on. "And the Skull King is a crime boss in Florence—and we don't get along. Italy is divided into two halves. I have the north, and he has the south. We've agreed to a truce, but the tension continues to simmer beneath the surface."

She stopped asking questions, but absolute confusion was written on her face.

"It's a lot," I said. "Don't worry, you'll catch on."

"Um . . . the way you talk. It's like we're living in the fifteen hundreds."

Because regular people who aren't tied to power by connections or inheritance didn't have a clue what went on behind the scenes. They were glued to their screens and their apps, too busy trying to get by to care about archaic institutions and battles for power. "It may seem like the world has evolved and modernized, but some things never change."

~

When I woke up, I hit my private gym, showered, and because Aurelia was still asleep, I worked in my office.

When she woke up, she texted me. Where are you guys?

Medusa was asleep on one of the couches in front of my desk, where she liked to hang out when I was in there. But I loved the fact that Aurelia included Medusa in *us*, because she was more than just my dog.

She was family to me.

In my office across the hall.

A couple minutes later, she stepped through the open door and immediately looked up at the ceiling, seeing the painted frescoes there in the same style as the Sistine Chapel. She stared at it for several seconds before she looked at me and the rest of the room. My desk was the size of a king-size bed, but it was still a thumbtack in comparison to the enormousness of the room, the floor-to-ceiling bookshelves with old tomes I hadn't touched. There was another side table that had a couple books on it and a large seating area that could easily accommodate twelve people comfortably.

Like always, she was humbled in every room she entered. With other women I slept with, they looked at what I had with the gleam of greed and a hint of resentful envy. They tried hard to make something serious happen with me, but I could see right through their motivations.

But Aurelia simply felt unworthy.

I came around the desk and kissed her. "How'd you sleep, sweetheart?"

"Good. Until I noticed you were gone."

My arms hooked across her lower back above her ass, and I squeezed her to me. I loved her height, but I loved her petiteness too, the deep curve in her lower back, the muscles in her ass, the little divot over her spine. I kissed her, lowering my head to meet her lips when she was barefoot. "Hungry?"

"Always."

I gave her ass a playful smack. "Attagirl." I turned back to the desk. "I've got to take care of some things. It'll be a few hours." I wanted to blow off everything for her, but unfortunately, I didn't have that luxury.

"That's okay," she said. "I have, like, a million edits to do. Can I bring my computer in here?"

She didn't skirt away. Didn't assume I didn't want her around. And that made my chest feel warm. "Of course, sweetheart."

She retrieved her bag and sat on the edge of the couch. Then she pulled out her laptop and her cameras and got to work.

Medusa opened her eyes from the other couch and decided to join Aurelia instead. She curled up next to Aurelia on the couch, her chin almost on her thigh.

Aurelia smiled and petted Medusa on the back of the neck, that affectionate warmth in her eyes. She grabbed her camera and then changed the lens before she pointed it down at Medusa. "Look at me, honey."

Medusa tilted her head back and looked right into the lens.

The camera clicked when she got the shot. "Wow, you're a natural." She smiled, then gave Medusa another rubdown before she set the camera aside.

I should be focused on my laptop, but all I could do was stare at the two of them.

My girls.

~

We worked together in comfortable silence for hours. When Elio brought breakfast, we worked while we ate. I usually had an egg-white omelet with my coffee, and all she had was coffee and a side of fruit.

Elio returned to retrieve Medusa for her afternoon walk, and then it was just the two of us in my study.

I closed my laptop and joined her on the couch. "Show me what you've been working on."

"Oh, I don't think my kids' birthday party is that interesting," she said with a chuckle. "No French emperors or Skull Kongs there."

"Skull King," I said with a smile. "But I think I like Kong better." I patted her thigh. "Show me some of your recent favorites."

"Well . . ." She closed out of the photo she was working on and moved to her desktop, where she had folders and more folders. Folders within folders. She was definitely organized. She opened a folder labeled **Favorites** and then clicked on the first picture there. "I feel the best photos are ones where the subject doesn't know they're being photographed. I'm not exactly sure what was going on with this couple, but it looks like she got cold feet and he came to talk to her. They didn't know I was still in the room." It was a picture of a young couple, him in a suit and her in her wedding dress, and she was sobbing. An ugly cry. But he looked at her like she was the most beautiful thing he'd ever seen. Just pure love in his eyes. "The way he looks at her . . . I can't even describe it."

"Yeah, I see what you mean."

She clicked on another. It was an older woman who looked sick and emaciated and had lost all her hair. She stood at the open window with the sunshine pouring through, highlighting her pale skin. It looked like she could barely remain standing, clinging to the ledge with twig-like fingers.

I immediately knew who she was.

Aurelia swallowed as she looked at the picture. "I came down the hallway to check on her . . . it was the first time I'd seen her stand in a long time. She could have fallen and broken something, but . . . I just let her have her moment instead. It's the last picture I took of her. She was gone the next day." She swallowed again, her eyes starting to tear up like the wound was still raw. Then she quickly clicked on the picture and minimized it, as if she couldn't look at it anymore.

I could feel the ache of her pain like it was my own. Feel the weight of loneliness she carried on her shoulders. We were two different bodies, but it felt like we had the same soul for that moment in time. "Sweetheart." I pulled her into me and pressed a kiss to her hairline. I let my lips linger there as I held her close, as I tried to take away her pain in whatever way I could.

She took a slow breath and blinked back the tears. "Some days I'm okay . . . and then other days I'm not."

"Yeah, I know how that goes."

"But when those bad days come . . . they're a lot easier with you."

~

After I climbed the steps and pushed through the mahogany doors, I saw Medusa run at a full sprint toward me.

And then I noticed the green tennis ball she was chasing.

She pulled off a full stop with ease and then wagged her tail at the sight of me, jumping up on her hind legs and putting her paws to my chest. She was well trained and knew not to do that with anyone else—but with me, it was okay.

"Hey, baby girl." I gave her a rubdown and then looked down the long corridor to where Aurelia stood in jean shorts and an orange blouse that showed her stomach and the little piercing at her navel. "Playing fetch?" I asked with a laugh.

"I bought a couple balls for her when I was out earlier," she called from the other side. "Hope that's okay."

I grabbed the ball, squeezed it to make it squeak, and then threw it back to Aurelia.

Medusa took off at a rocket-speed sprint and chased down the ball in the other direction.

I headed over, and a minute later, I made it to Aurelia.

"Are you mad?"

I hugged her and squeezed her ass in both my hands before I kissed her. "Do I look mad?"

"I was careful not to hit anything."

"All I care about is my girls getting along." I kissed her again.

"Your girls?" she asked with a smile, like she was happy to be Medusa's equal rather than offended by it.

"Hungry?"

"Just assume I'm always hungry until told otherwise."

No one made me smile more than she did. Whether she was being playful or just herself, it always made me feel . . . something. "Good, I'm starving. How does pizza sound?"

"Pizza always sounds good."

We left the house, and I drove us to my favorite spot, a little hole-in-the-wall place visited only by locals. We were given a table right away in the back, and when the waitress came over, I ordered our drinks without asking what Aurelia wanted.

She never complained about that, so I assumed she liked not having to make decisions, that she liked being in a relationship with a man who took the lead so she didn't have to. After fighting for a dead relationship, it was probably nice to be chased, to have someone order for her, to have someone drive her everywhere.

Someone to take care of her.

"How's Cindy?" I asked.

Her good mood immediately soured at the thought of Timothée. "Devastated. She thinks he took off to Paris and ghosted her."

I didn't pity Cindy. Not when I'd done her a huge fucking favor.

Aurelia didn't ask what I'd done to Timothée.

I spared her the burden of the details.

"I spent a couple days with her. She was there for me after Enzo, so I was happy to help her."

I still hated hearing his name. Not because I was jealous or threatened. I just fucking hated him for how he'd hurt her. She was fucking gorgeous head to toe, and he decided to treat her like a plastic bag stuffed in a garbage can. "She'll find someone else."

"Of course. She's gorgeous."

"And find someone better."

"Yeah, but she'll be heartbroken awhile."

"Then maybe you should tell her the truth so she won't be."

"I don't know," she said. "I don't know which is worse, honestly. And if I tell her the truth, she may not like you."

I shrugged. "I don't care if she likes me or not."

"Well, I'd like my friends to like you."

"I don't care what mine think of you."

"You don't?" she questioned. "Because you seem to care what Rocco thinks."

She had me and she fucking knew it—and I liked that. "I guess I care a little."

"So . . . does he?"

"He said you were cool."

"Cool?" she asked.

I shrugged. "He's not a wordy kind of guy."

"I was afraid he wouldn't."

"Why the hell wouldn't he?"

"I don't know." Her eyes flicked away to another spot in the restaurant.

"Why wouldn't he?" I repeated, knowing she was hiding something from me.

Her eyes came back to me. "Well, I didn't make a good first impression. Got mixed up with a couple assholes, let one spike my drink, left the restaurant with him . . . I looked like the biggest idiot in the world. And then I'm sure you told him Enzo left me for a woman almost a decade older than me with two kids. It's just not a good look."

This drop-dead gorgeous woman with a heart of gold was in front of me, but she talked about herself like she was the most worthless human being on the planet. "Why are you so unkind to yourself?"

"I'm not. I just know how the world works. I know how people think."

"Maybe assholes, but not people. Because Rocco never once thought any of those things—and neither have I. What happened to you was a crime. Those assholes have run that same skit before, because it's worked before. And Enzo is a dumbass. Stop judging your own worth based on how a prick treated you." My arms folded on the table, and I came closer to her. "This is the actual story. Some dumbass miraculously gets the perfect woman but fucks it up because he was too stupid to know what he had. It's his story—not yours. His mistakes are not a reflection of your worth, sweetheart. And I promise you." My hand tightened into a fist, and I gave a slight thump on the table. "He regrets it now, and he'll regret it forever."

Her eyes flicked away again, like she couldn't accept my kindness.

"And now that perfect woman is mine—and like hell am I gonna fuck it up."

She hesitated before she looked at me again. There was a shine there, not from tears, but emotion. "I don't understand how you're real, Constantine. Because you could literally have any woman you want, and you're the one saying the nicest things no one has ever said to me." Her eyes dropped again like her emotions were volatile—and about to ignite.

All the anger and resentment I'd felt toward her were long gone. So absent, it was as if it'd never been there in the first place. Whenever I looked at her, I saw my whole world in a single person. There was still so much we didn't know about each other—our time together had been so brief—but I just . . . felt so much for her. "Because I'm the man who's meant to say them."

Chapter 5

Constantine

Because it was the fucking pope, I had to check in with security just like everyone else. I never showed up to the Vatican with any weapons because no one was permitted to carry anything in his presence except his private security team.

I was family, and that still wasn't good enough.

While all the tourists and visitors entered the grounds and then the papal gardens before they began their tour of the museums and the Sistine Chapel, I was escorted through Saint Peter's Square and to the right of the basilica next to the museum and the Sistine Chapel. Pope Zephyrinus occupied the Apostolic Palace, and I was escorted directly into his study, the back of his desk underneath the large window that had a breathtaking view of Saint Peter's Square.

I took a seat and waited for him to join me.

"Constantine."

I immediately rose to my feet at the sound of his voice. I turned to him with a big smile on my face and extended my hand to his. "Your Holiness."

Two guards were in the room, lingering a short distance away.

He was in his seventies, his skin wrinkled in many places but still tanned from being outdoors or from the illumination of God's light. He wore glasses on the bridge of his nose, and his red robes distinguished his power. He turned slightly to the guards behind him, then made a single gesture with his hand, dismissing them from our presence.

The guards left and the door shut.

I was one of the few people in the world who could speak to the pope in complete privacy.

Call it nepotism.

He beamed at me like I was his own son, his energy full of so much warmth and vitality. Very few people looked at me like that, except my family and Medusa—and now Aurelia.

"How are you, my son?"

"I'm well, Father. And you?"

"I'm always well." He gestured to the armchairs in front of his desk.

We sat together, me across from him.

With his hands together in his lap, he waited for me to speak first. When I couldn't find the words, he took the reins—as always. "You're troubled by a weight I can't see, Constantine."

"Yes."

"Share your burden."

"There's so much going on lately, and I feel like I've barely been able to keep up with it all."

He nodded in understanding.

"President Barsetti is disappointed I haven't caught Vladimir yet, but I'm close. And he's upset about the commotion I caused last week. I'm sure you heard about it."

He nodded. "As did everyone, Constantine."

"I lost my temper . . . may have taken it too far, but I feel no remorse."

He nodded again.

"What does that say about me, Father? That I burn men in the streets . . . and feel nothing."

The silence dragged on and on. His eyes left mine, and he seemed deep in thought, truly thinking about the words I shared with him. "I'm not here to pass judgment on the choices of others. All I can do is guide you closer to God. But I will say . . . we're two leaders in two different kingdoms. You in the kingdom of men—and me in the kingdom of God. Men are more corrupt and more readily tempted. They're flawed and easily misled. To excuse or pardon the crimes of the guilty is to condemn the needy, the poor, and the vulnerable. Perhaps you feel nothing for those who cause pain because you're too busy protecting those who have received that pain. And the fact that you come to me to share these burdens tells me you're a humble man before the eyes of God."

That was always how he spoke, and I'd gotten used to it over the years. Whenever I felt at my worst, his presence seemed to bring the light back into my darkness. "It's come to my attention there may be an attack on our country and our people, and the Skull King is probably indirectly responsible for it. Selling arms to our enemies in the east."

He gave a nod in understanding.

"I need to speak to him, but I'm afraid I'll kill him."

With eyes that held no judgment for anyone on this earth, he continued to listen to me.

"You're the only man he respects and reveres." Because everyone in this country, and the world, revered the man before me. Whether you were a civilian or a criminal, it didn't matter.

"It's not my place, Constantine. All I can do is bring him closer to God."

"But perhaps I can speak to him here—so I'll behave and so will he." Because all I'd want to do would be to pull out my knife and carve his mouth from his face, his eyes from their sockets. I couldn't think of the man without my heart racing, without my blood pressure skyrocketing. Every fiber of my being wanted him dead, and I'd want him dead until I was dead myself.

After another round of packed silence, Pope Zephyrinus addressed my request. "My service is not only to God, but to my fellow man, to the people of this country, and to this world. So yes, I will mediate your meeting."

"Thank you, Father."

He gave a nod in acknowledgment. "How's your family?"

"Good. Living their idyllic lives in Taormina."

"And the restaurant?"

"Business is good. Too good, honestly."

He gave a quiet chuckle. "It's been a long time since I've had your mother's arancini."

"You're always welcome for a visit, but we understand you have bigger obligations." Like being the head of the Catholic Church and the most famous man alive.

"Maybe someday, Constantine."

"Yeah, maybe someday." We both spoke of it like it was a dream that would never come true.

"What else is new with you?"

I was the busiest I'd ever been at work. But that ebb and flow was typical. There was a reign of peace between the wars, and even though that period could be long, it felt so brief. "Well . . . I've met someone." The smile that came on to my face was impossible to restrain. There had never been anyone in my life who made me as happy as she did . . . at least not in nine years.

"That's wonderful, Constantine. Tell me about her."

"Her name is Aurelia."

"Gilded. Noble. Beautiful name."

"Yeah, I like it too," I said. "She . . . means a lot to me."

"It's been a long time since you've had someone."

A long time since Isabella. "It has."

"I wish the two of you the best." He rose to his feet, his hands together and hidden under the long sleeves of his robe.

I rose to my feet as well.

He came to me and blessed me. "God be with you, Constantine."

"And with you, Uncle."

Prologue II

Constantine

Six months had passed since I'd ended things with Isabella.

I took the ring back to the jeweler and lost a few thousand, but I was relieved to have it out of my home.

Out of my life.

Taormina was a small place, everyone knew each other, so while I had offers left and right from women who had shot their shot before, I kept to myself. I didn't just do it out of respect for Isabella, but I wasn't ready. I'd spent almost two years with her, and I'd really believed she would be my wife. The mother of my children. And the idea of being with someone else after such a committed relationship . . . nearly felt like infidelity. I had to move on at some point, but today wasn't that day.

I still wouldn't speak to my brother. Didn't give a damn if he was my flesh and blood. He had stabbed me in the back and sabotaged a relationship he would have fumbled if it'd ever been his. He hadn't actually tried to talk to me, like he understood an attempt was pointless.

I worked in the kitchen at Rosticceria Da Cristina in the morning, prepping everything for the day. I used to listen to music while

I worked, but I hadn't done that in six months. Silence was my companion of choice these days.

My mom opened the unlocked door and walked inside. "What did I tell you about locking the door, Con?"

My eyes stayed down, and I continued to work. "Didn't know you were coming in today."

"What does that matter—"

"I'm not in the mood for this." I picked up the rack of arancini and slid it inside the oven so it could bake. I put all the other trays inside and then set the timer before I worked on the next batch. Keeping my eyes on my hands, I waited for my mother to walk into the office, but she just stood there.

"Constantine."

She never called me by my full name, so I knew whatever she had to say was heavy. My head lifted to meet her gaze.

Her eyes shifted back and forth between mine. "This isn't you, son."

My face remained steady and stoic. Even though her words were painful because they rang true, I felt nothing. I had become an empty vessel that would shatter if I hit the floor.

"You need to reconcile with Edric."

"I don't need to do anything."

"You're brothers—"

"We were brothers when he kissed Isabella, so why don't you remind him of that?"

"I have," she said. "I just visited him in Palermo, and he said he knows you don't want to speak to him."

"And he's right."

"Con, it's been months—"

"And I don't want to speak to him for the rest of my fucking life."

"Constantine."

I piled the arancini on the tray, then shoved it into the other free oven. "I said what I said—and I fucking meant it." When I came back to the steel counter, my mother looked like she was on the verge of tears.

She never cried. She was tough and resilient and never gave in to despair.

"Family is everything, Constantine. He's not just your brother, but your twin."

"The only reason you care is because he moved to Palermo." It was a two-and-a-half-hour drive, and the distance was too much for my mother. She wanted all of us to live right here in town forever. To have lots of grandchildren and spend our days working at the restaurant and our nights cooking for our family. "You only want us to reconcile because it's what *you* want. You don't actually give a shit what he did to me. You just want me to get over it so you can have your happy family back together. If this were a friend, you would tell me to stab him with a knife, but because it's Edric, I'm just supposed to brush it off."

Her face started to tint slightly, but not with anger, just raw pain. "Yes, I want my sons back together. The boys I grew in my womb and birthed five minutes apart. The only men I love more than your father. Yes, I admit that. But Con, it's not good for you to carry anger like this. It's been six months, and you aren't you anymore."

"Well, being betrayed by your brother and the woman you thought you would marry does that to you." I stepped away from the table and ripped off my gloves, no longer interested in prepping for the day. I tossed them in the garbage and leaned against the other counter, far away from my mother.

"I'm sorry this happened to you, Constantine. But even the best people make the worst mistakes."

I crossed my arms over my chest and looked out the window. The sea was quiet, the sky clear. Fishing boats were already out there looking for their catch to bring to the village, the dinner that would be on everyone's plates that evening.

"You think you know everything right now, but in ten years, you'll look back and realize how young you were. And you'll wish that you'd pardoned your brother instead of losing all that time you could have spent with him."

"I highly doubt that."

"I wish you understood how sorry he was."

"Isabella and I would have been planning our wedding right now." I cocked my head. "Doesn't that bother you? That in six months we would have married on the cliff where you and Dad got married, and our families would have finally been united in marriage. You've said we were meant to be together since we were five years old. And all of that is gone because my asshole brother wanted what I had."

She held her silence, but her breaths increased with the weight of my words.

"And yet you look at me like I'm the asshole."

She gave a slight shake of her head. "I love Isabella like a daughter, and yes, I'm devastated that this isn't going to happen. But I don't think you should lose your brother over this too."

"You act like it's up to me to save the relationship, when Edric is the one who chose to destroy it. I didn't ask for this. I'm the victim in all of this, but somehow the responsibility to salvage the relationship has fallen to me."

"How is Edric supposed to fix it if you've blocked his calls? If you won't open your apartment door for him? If you won't come to family dinners if he's there? What is he supposed to do, Con?"

"Fuck off, that's what."

The tears finally burst from her eyes. "Constantine, please. I can't live like this . . . it hurts my heart. I can't sleep. I can't eat."

I looked away, not wanting to see my mother cry, not wanting to be responsible for her tears.

"Please, I beg you . . ."

I still wouldn't look at her, but hearing the echoes of her sobs bounce off all the ovens and steel counters was like torture.

"You don't smile anymore. You don't joke anymore. Hold on to this hate, and it'll consume you until there's nothing left. I don't want to lose my son—and I'm not talking about your brother." She continued to sob, the sound splitting my ears. "I'm so proud of who you are, and I don't want to watch that disappear. I don't want you to fade into another angry man in the crowd. I don't want you to die from bitterness and resentment. I don't want the strain on your heart to kill you, like it did your father."

"Ma . . ." I found the strength to look at her—and that was a mistake.

She was a mess of tears, her makeup destroyed, her skin puffy, her eyes . . . like death. "Please." She came to me, grabbed both of my hands, and squeezed them tight. "Please, I beg you."

I'd never felt so shitty in my life. I'd made my mother bawl harder than she did at my father's funeral. I'd broken nothing, but it was my responsibility to fix it. To suture the wound. To realign the broken bones. "Okay, I'll talk to him, Ma."

She yanked me into her and buried her face in my chest, sobbing against my apron and getting flour all over her clothes and hair. "Thank you, Con." She sobbed and sniffed and squeezed. "My son."

I took a drive down to Palermo.

It was on the other side of the island, a popular tourist spot in its own right. He'd moved there a couple months ago when the rift between us was the worst it'd ever been. When I didn't come to the family dinners he attended, he seemed to think it was best to bow out altogether.

I had no idea what he did for work or how he spent his time. I didn't know him at all anymore, and in a lot of ways, I felt like I'd never known him in the first place. My mom had given me the address, and when I pulled up to the villa, I double-checked her text to make sure I'd found the right place.

It was a beautiful building, with lion statues erected in front and a doorman posted outside. I had a two-bedroom apartment in Taormina, and it was nice but not flashy. But this place . . . seemed a little flashy.

I parked the car several blocks away, checked in with the doorman, and then took the elevator to his floor. It seemed like a renovated building that had kept its Sicilian charm. There were paintings in the hallways along with sculptures in the corners. When I made it to his door, I took a second to breathe, to question whether this was the right move.

I was certain my mother had already told him I was coming, so he wouldn't be surprised to see me on his doorstep. If my mother hadn't guilted me into being there, I would have been content with never speaking to him again. I knew she'd manipulated me into coming here, but after watching her bend over backward for all of us our entire lives and doing it alone, even before my father was gone, I knew I owed her everything. She never asked for anything—except for this.

So I'd give it to her.

I didn't knock on the door, but Edric answered it as if I had.

Yep, he knew I was coming.

He stared at me, eyes shifting as he took in my appearance like he'd seen a ghost. There was no smirk, no joke, just a serious stare. And I could see emotion there, below the surface, simmering like a pan about to boil.

Then his eyes started to smart, the emotion splashing over the edges of the pan and extinguishing the flames beneath. He moved into me, then gripped me in his arms, squeezing me tightly, clapping me on the back as he took a heavy breath.

Caught off guard by the only display of emotion I'd ever seen my brother make, I stood there and let him hold me. And piece by piece, the anger started to fade. My arms eventually encircled him, and I gave him a gentle pat on the back.

"I'm sorry," he said in a hoarse voice, tears about to break.

I patted him again, this time harder. "I know."

We sat together at his dining table. He'd placed a bottle of wine there along with two glasses, but neither one of us drank. He had a nice apartment with luxurious furniture, but I didn't pay much attention to it, given the circumstances.

We were silent for a long time, like neither one of us knew where to start.

"I'm really fucking sorry," he said abruptly.

I gave a nod.

"I felt bad after it happened, but in the months since, I've felt so much worse. Like an infection that's slowly spread to the rest of my body, it's taken its toll. The guilt. The shame. The heartbreak."

I watched my brother pour his soul out to me.

"But what I feel the worst about . . . is the fact that you two aren't together anymore."

The mention of her made my chest tighten, like always. "Yeah, it's been rough."

He stared at me for a while, the unspoken words about to fire off from his eyes. "It's not too late, Constantine."

Isabella continued to text me, but I told her that I didn't want to hear from her anymore. That we both needed to move on. And when she continued to do so, I threatened to block her if she didn't stop, and I didn't want to do that. I still wanted her in my life . . . someday . . . when I was past this. So we hadn't spoken in a while, about two months. "I'm done."

"You love her."

"Love isn't enough."

"You're being too harsh—"

"Edric, if I wanted your opinion, I'd ask for it."

He retreated, pulled back the neck he'd stuck out for her.

"She's not the one. It's done."

He stared at me like he wanted to say more but decided to stay on my good side. "I feel so fucking bad."

"You should," I said. "But we're done because of her actions, not yours. If anything, you did me a favor. Now I know her true character."

"Isn't there a difference between someone's character and a mistake?" he asked. "Because I don't think she'd make a mistake like that again if you gave her another chance. She's still a good person, Con."

"Never said she wasn't. She's just not my person."

He gave a painful sigh.

"I'm done talking about her."

He gave a nod in agreement, then stared at the wine bottle. "I'm really glad you came down here."

"Well, Ma made me, so . . ."

He didn't look offended by that, just grateful for whatever made me face him.

"Sobbed her heart out to me, so what the fuck was I supposed to do?"

"Yeah."

"But she was right. I'd lost myself. Lost myself to the anger and the grief, and I didn't like who I was."

"That's not your fault, Con. Isabella and I are responsible for that."

"It's been six months. I thought I'd feel better by now."

"Might take years."

"Yeah." Six months had come and gone, and I felt exactly the same as the night everything unfolded. It was as if no time had passed at all.

"Everything you said before . . . you were right." He lifted his eyes from the wine bottle. "I'm not happy with what I have, and I'm even less happy when I have whatever made someone else happy. And then I hate myself for being so fucked in the head."

I'd said the harshest thing you could say to another person, but I wasn't sorry about it.

"I've always had a crush on Isabella. Didn't understand why she was drawn to you instead of me."

"I asked if you were cool with me going for her."

"I know, I know."

"And you said yes."

He nodded. "I know. I assumed I would move on, but I never really did. Thought I'd make a move after you broke up, but you never did. I felt like she and I made more sense than you two ever did, but you're right. I would have gotten bored in a couple days and would have dumped her, like I do with all the others. I keep waiting for 'the one' to walk through the door, but even if she did, I'd probably pump and dump . . . like always. But the truth is, there's no 'the one' for someone like me. I blame my unhappiness on everyone else, but in truth, I'm just a shit person. Could find a billion euros on the street, and I'd still be depressed."

It was the first time he'd ever been this vulnerable with me, showing me all of his colors . . . including all the ugly ones.

"Everyone loves you because you're charming and charismatic and all that, and I'm . . . nothing." He gave a painful chuckle. "It's funny that we're twins but nothing alike. You're happy and healthy, and I'm just fucked in the head."

I didn't dismiss anything hc said. Didn't say it wasn't true, because it was one hundred percent true. "You don't have to end where you start, Edric. You can change all those things if you want to."

He crossed his arms over his chest and sank into the chair. "Maybe. Or maybe people never change."

"I think they can if they want to."

He gave a noncommittal shrug.

I let the silence pass for a while, let the heft of the conversation wane before I changed the subject. "So what are you doing here in Palermo?"

It took him a moment to leave the previous conversation and join the new one. "I've always liked it over here. Picked up a job as a cook in one of the restaurants."

"And you can afford this place?" I asked bluntly. I'd barely seen any of it, but it had a separate dining room, a full kitchen, and the living room had space for at least twelve people. Major step up from his old place.

"Well . . . there's more to the story." A little smirk came on to his face. "The restaurant is owned by one of the Cosa Nostra guys. He took a liking to me and started having me do other things for them."

"As in, the Mafia?"

"Yep."

He'd gotten himself into trouble in Taormina, and now he'd come to Palermo and gotten himself into deeper trouble. "Does Ma know this?"

"God no."

"What kind of stuff do they ask you to do?"

"You know, deliver certain kinds of packages, tail some of the other guys to make sure they're doing their jobs, eavesdrop on conversations, stuff like that. It pays well. Like, *really* well. Sure beats making pizza and arancini."

"Only you would get into this situation."

He gave a shrug. "Right place, right time."

"Then what are you going to do?"

"What do you mean?"

"When you come back to Taormina."

He stared at me blankly for a couple seconds like he didn't understand. "I'm not coming back, Con."

The finality of his words struck me like a blow to the stomach. "What?"

"I originally came here because I knew you didn't want to see my face. Wanted to stay out of your way. Didn't want to make family dinners awkward for everyone. But I've been with Cosa Nostra for a couple months now, and I like it."

"It's the *Mafia*, Edric."

"I know, I know. But it's not like what you see in the movies. I mean, sure, it *can* be. But I like the guys, and I like the work. I like being a part of it."

"Until you piss someone off and get a bullet in your skull."

He gave a slight shake of his head. "It's hard to explain, but it's not like that. They're good guys, as crazy as that sounds."

"It sounds crazy because it is crazy." I should have listened to Ma and come sooner. Now Edric was mixed up in bullshit that would get him killed.

"Look, it's nice to do something different from working in a kitchen all day. It's nice to be respected. It's nice to get paid well. It's nice not to smell like tomato sauce all the time. And the women . . ." He shoved his closed fist into his mouth. "Goddamn . . ."

"There are beautiful women in Taormina."

"Sure, but Cosa Nostra has their own women . . ."

"What does that mean?"

"Like how a famous band has groupies? Well, they have their own groupies."

"Edric, you've never had a problem getting laid."

"I know, but these women are *unbelievable*. You need to see them to understand."

"Edric, trust me, you don't want to get mixed up with these guys—"

"Trust me, *you* don't know what you're talking about."

My brother was at it again, chasing something shiny and new that he'd regret later.

"You used to talk about leaving Sicily. Traveling to Rome and Paris. Seeing the world. Doing something different from slaving away in a kitchen all day," he said.

"Yeah, but that was before—" *Before I fell in love.*

"You gave up on those dreams because you chose to settle down. But now that you and Isabella are done, maybe you should reconsider what to do with your life. Because I know making arancini isn't your calling."

"And stealing from people and killing people is yours?" I asked incredulously.

"Whoa, you've got it all wrong." He held up both of his hands like he wanted me to back up. "Cosa Nostra kills people—but only people who deserve it. They aren't out killing people for being in the wrong place at the wrong time. And we don't steal from people. Well, except the government . . . because we ain't paying taxes. We just run our business the way we want without an audit or interference. Pay off people who get in the way. Bribe people to look the other way. Infiltrate businesses to do our bidding. And if someone tries to infringe on our territory or compete with our businesses, then we *might* kill them."

He talked like he was one of them. He was already that deep in this cult. "Ma will never let you stay here."

"What's she gonna do?" he asked as he threw his arms up. "Fight my boss?"

"Yeah, she might," I said seriously.

He chuckled. "Honestly, Ma would be perfect in Cosa Nostra. That woman doesn't flinch."

"You can't really see a long-term future with these guys."

"Why not?" he asked.

"You're going to want to do this when you're married with a family?"

"Why not? A lot of the guys have wives and kids. And who knows if I'll ever clean up my act enough to settle down. I'm not going to base my decisions for today on a future version of me I may never know."

"And what if you want to leave? They'll kill you."

He released a loud laugh. "Another thing from the movies that's just not true."

"Really?"

"Really," he said. "Come down with me and let me show you around."

"You're out of your mind."

"Why not?" he asked. "Come on, aren't you just a little bit curious?"

All I could do was stare because I couldn't honestly say I wasn't curious.

He grinned. "Knew it."

Prologue III

Constantine

Edric drove me to an enormous villa behind an iron gate. No one was out front, monitored instead by a series of cameras, but once the gates opened and we made it inside, we saw the militia of armed men in the courtyard. All carried rifles and shotguns, smoking cigars as they leaned against the cars and waited for their shifts to finish.

I'd never been around guns before, but for some reason, it didn't bother me.

Edric took me in, and the guards at the front did a double take when they looked at the two of us.

"My brother, Con," Edric explained.

We headed inside, and the main room was full of round tables, which were all occupied by men gambling and drinking.

"What in the actual fuck?" Some guy in a pin-striped suit walked up with a lit cigar hanging out of the corner of his mouth. He took a look at me, then Edric, and then me again. "What am I looking at right now?"

"Oh yeah, I'm a twin," Edric said. "Guess I forgot to mention that."

"There's two of you?" he asked in disbelief. "Like the world needs that." He broke out into a loud laugh.

Edric did the same—like they were well acquainted.

"Take him to Tommaso," the guy said. "He'll get a kick out of that."

Edric walked off with me in tow and headed away from the room where everyone gambled.

"Who's Tommaso?"

"The boss. Mr. Boss Man."

I saw my brother in a new light, in a new world where he seemed to fit in perfectly. "And he's going to want to meet me?"

"Yeah, we're cool." He crossed the villa to another set of double doors, which were closed and guarded by two men. But Edric knew them too, because they all exchanged hand embraces before Edric said, "This is my brother, Con."

"You have a twin?" one of the guys said.

"Yep—and I'm the better-looking one. Tell Tommaso I want to introduce him."

One of the guys entered the double doors to relay the message.

"You sure we aren't going to bother him?" I asked, not understanding how a crime boss could care about my brother being a twin.

"Yeah, it's cool," he said. "Don't be nervous. No one will shoot you, because they'll think you're me."

"Or they'll shoot me *because* they think I'm you."

Edric chuckled and gave me a playful jab in the side.

The guard returned. "The boss will see you." He stepped aside so we could pass through the doors into the other room.

The next room was a study, a large hearth against the wall, a sprawling living room set and a wet bar. The villa itself was like a palace, and the mammoth size of it was intimidating on its own. Cosa Nostra obviously had more money than they knew how to spend.

A man with jet-black hair stood there, suspenders over his shoulders, a stiff drink in his hand. He finished speaking to one of the guys in a hushed tone before he dismissed him with a flick of his hand. Then he turned to us, stopping to glance back and forth between the two of us. "Now we've got two pretty boys." He came forward and sized me up like I was a pig he was about to butcher for meat. "But this one has ink. I like it." He took a drink, then shook the ice cubes in his glass. "We can use him."

"I had the same thought," Edric said. "Now I can be in two places at once. Perfect way to set up one deal and take down another."

I had no idea what that meant. "I'm not looking for a job."

"Oh?" Tommaso asked. "Then what do you do?"

"Work at my family's restaurant in Taormina."

"Oh, I see. So you're already making the big bucks," he said with a slight chuckle. "Mr. Moneybags, huh?"

"No one is richer than a man who doesn't care about money."

His chuckles subsided, and a serious expression came onto his face. He shook his glass again before he took a step closer. "And a man who says he doesn't care about money is a man who's never had money. If I put twenty in your hands every month, you'd be singing a different tune—preferably Sinatra."

Twenty what? Twenty thousand? "A bit clichéd, don't you think?"

Edric turned to me, gave me a look, and mouthed, "Chill."

Tommaso examined me again, like he didn't know what to make of me. "You look exactly alike, but it's obvious you're nothing alike. What brings you down here from Taormina?"

"Trying to get my brother to come home."

"But he doesn't want to?"

"Unfortunately," I said. "He's always been like a balloon . . . drifts off easily."

"And you're the rock. I can see that." He moved to the couch, then addressed one of his men. "Make my new friend a drink." He got comfortable, crossed one of his legs, and then gestured for me to take a seat.

I complied.

Edric remained standing like he wasn't part of the conversation.

"Edric has spoken of you often—just left out the twin part."

"Yeah? What has he said?"

"That he fucked up things pretty badly between you two. But it seems like you've made up. How sweet."

I glanced at my brother, realizing he really did feel terrible if he mentioned it to strangers. "Yeah, we're good now."

"Trust me, pussy is never worth it. My brother and I fought over a woman once. I regretted winning right away because she wasn't that great in bed. Kicked her out, and five years later, we were friends again. Glad you two didn't take as long." He took a drink from his glass, then set it on the table.

One of the guys put the drink on the coaster in front of me before he retreated to the edge of the room.

I didn't touch it.

Silence passed for a while as he continued to stare me down. "You say you don't care about money, but you're in the presence of the wealthiest men in Sicily. You say you want your brother to come home, but instead, you've ended up here with me. So, what do you really want, Constantine?"

I didn't have a clue. For the last six months, I'd nursed my broken heart. Spent my nights alone in my apartment. Stopped going out with my friends because all I wanted to do was be alone. When I didn't think about how much Isabella had hurt me, I thought about how much my brother had killed me. Now I didn't know what direction to take in life . . . if I belonged in Taormina anymore. "Honestly, I don't know. I planned to settle down with a woman, until she broke my heart."

"I'm sorry to hear that. But sometimes the worst things that happen to us end up also being the best things that ever happen to us." He finished off his glass, then lifted it in the air until one of his men retrieved it and made another. "You're far too young to be married. You aren't old enough to know what life really is. Haven't had enough pussy to know which pussy you really want for the rest of your life. So may I suggest you take the time to figure that out . . . and make some money along the way."

It was the quickest job offer I'd ever received. "You're offering me a job when you don't know me?"

"I'm offering you an opportunity. What you do with that opportunity determines where you end up. I am a great judge of character, and I can tell you're as smart as your brother but not as impulsive. Keep making your little rice balls at home if you want to live in a cramped apartment for the rest of your life—or expand your horizons and explore something greater. The choice is yours. But don't wait too long . . . because my generosity has always been fickle."

~

I worked in the kitchen at Rosticceria Da Cristina in the morning, preparing the restaurant for the morning crew. It was the same thing every day since we were open every single day of the week. I never had a day off because I just had to be there a couple hours every morning. We could hire people to come in and do the morning stuff, but my mom didn't trust anyone alone in the restaurant except for family.

Something caught my eye in the window, so I looked up—and saw Isabella walk to the front door.

The front door that I left unlocked. "Fuck." I should have listened to my ma.

She burst in the door with a wild look in her eyes.

I already knew what this was about. I took off my gloves before she even came behind the counter.

"You're moving to Palermo?" She yelled when she didn't need to, not where there was no music or other conversation to talk over. "What the hell is this, Constantine?"

I'd expected a conversation to happen at some point, but I didn't expect it like this.

"Your restaurant is here. Your family is here. Why do you need to move three hours away?"

"Because there's more to life than this little town."

"This *little* town?" She stepped back. "Or you're too good for us now?"

"That's not what I said, and you know it."

"This is your home. This is where we decided to settle down—"

"I had other plans before that. I wanted to move to Rome or Florence, see some of this big, beautiful world. But I stayed here because I fell in love with you, and I wasn't going to leave you. I gave it all up to settle down and be a husband and a father. But then we know what happened after that . . ."

She flinched like I'd struck her with the back of my hand. Cut her deep with my words.

"So there's nothing keeping me here anymore."

"Nothing?" Her voice cracked from the tears. "I've given you space like you asked, even though it nearly killed me—"

"I didn't ask for space. I asked you to let me go." Big difference.

"I hoped something would change in the last few months. That you would forgive me and we would find our way back to each other, but now you're leaving—"

"I do forgive you, Isabella. I don't hold any ill will toward you."

"Then stay. Give us another chance."

"No."

"Con, please—"

"I'm leaving because it's time to move on. And I can't do that in this little town where I have to see you all the time. It's been a really shitty six months, and I need to be away from here." I needed to live in a city where everything wouldn't remind me of her. Where I could eat at a restaurant and not think about our first date. Where I could go to the beach and not remember how pink her nose was after she got sunburned. I needed to be free of her, and this was the only way I could accomplish that.

"So . . . you aren't over me?"

No other woman had my attention. I got offers left and right, but I behaved like I was still in a relationship. Was committed to her even when she hadn't been committed to me. She'd made me feel like a fucking fool. "Of course I'm not."

She sucked in a big breath as her eyes watered. "Then let's—"

"No."

"Con, come on."

"No."

"You seriously can't let this go? How can you love me and not be over me six months later but still not let this go?"

"Because you aren't the one, okay?"

She winced again, this time her hand flying to her mouth.

"Because if you were, none of this would have happened."

She sniffled and blinked back her tears as best she could. "You're an asshole."

"Yeah, I'm the asshole. I'm the one who kissed your twin sister and lied about it and carried on an emotional affair with clandestine meetings and texts late into the night. Yep, all me."

Her eyes started to water again. "How can you do this to my family? To your mom? Just leave her like this?"

"Because she understands that I need to go. She understands that life has been fucking unbearable for me and it's time to leave. Because she actually gives a shit about me, and all you care about is yourself."

"All I care about is myself?" she asked incredulously. "I fucking love you, Constantine. Your brother is the one who intentionally pretended to be you, and I'm the one who gets all the blame for this—"

"Trust me, you both got the same treatment."

"But I'm the one who loses you. He still gets to keep you as a brother."

"And you get to keep me as a friend—someday."

"I don't want to be your fucking friend!" she screamed through her tears.

Footsteps sounded from the back, and then I realized it was my mother. I'd completely forgotten she was there, that she'd gotten in hours ago to do some work in the office.

Isabella spotted her first, quickly stopped crying, and wiped her tears away.

I felt humiliated that my mother had heard a very private conversation.

But of course, my mother was a loving woman, and she came to Isabella and held her. Held her like she was her own daughter. Stroked her hair like she was a child who'd just had a bad dream. "Shh, I know this is hard . . ." She continued to hold Isabella while I stood there. "Hard for everyone."

"Please talk some sense into your son," she said through a shaky voice. "We're meant to be together. I just made a mistake, and I said I'm sorry . . ."

Now I was about to be ganged up on—*great.* My mom and her mom were best friends. Isabella really was another member of our family. My mom had watched her grow into a woman, and when I told her we were together, she'd never looked so happy. She'd been crushed when I'd told her we were done—and then she was crushed again when I told her I was moving.

My mom pulled away when Isabella seemed to have recovered. "Isabella, I know that you are sorry. And I know that you love my son. But he's made his decision, and we all have to respect the way he feels."

Isabella was so shocked she couldn't even hide it. She'd expected my mother to take her side in a heartbeat.

But I was even more shocked.

"Of course I was sad when he told me he wanted to move to Palermo. But I've seen him wither away here in Taormina. He doesn't listen to music anymore. He doesn't smile when I walk inside. He's always so charming and funny and warm . . . and he's become a shell of a man. This is what he needs to heal—and we should all support him."

I have the best fucking mom.

My mom continued to stroke Isabella's hair. "My heart breaks for you, honey. I know you're a good person who just made the wrong choice. I wanted you as my daughter-in-law, but make no mistake, you're still my daughter. Still a part of this family, whether you marry my son or not." She started to rub her back. "I know it doesn't seem like it right now, but it's going to be okay."

Isabella sniffed, then blinked quickly to stop the next wave of tears. She gave a nod before she wiped her eyes again. Then she turned away, and without a word to either of us, she walked out and left.

The second she was gone, I felt the stress leave my shoulders.

My mother stood across the counter from me, looking at me with the kind of love only a mother could give. "You okay, baby?"

I nodded. "Yeah."

She watched me for a moment longer before she read the lie in my words and came around the table to hug me. She could only reach my chest, but she seemed to cocoon me anyway.

I didn't know how much I needed that hug until she gave it to me. I rested my chin on her head and closed my eyes. "I love you, Ma."

"I love you too, baby." She pulled away, then gently patted both of my cheeks with her palms. "I agree that she's not the one for you. Because you deserve someone who would never make you feel like this. Someone who would never suck your soul from your body. Take the light from your eyes and leave you in the dark."

"I really thought you would try to convince me to take her back." It came as a complete surprise to me when my mom accepted the news and stayed out of it. Never tried to persuade me either way. It wasn't like her at all to take a step back, especially when it came to family matters.

"No." She shook her head. "You're the most exceptional young man, Constantine. I'm not just saying that because you're my son. You deserve the absolute best, shouldn't have to forgive and forget, shouldn't have to tolerate a mistake. The woman who's meant for you is out there somewhere—and I can't wait to meet her when you find her."

Chapter 6

Aurelia

I pulled up to the gates on my motorbike. The gate was the same height as the wall that surrounded his property, at least seventy feet high. Trees were visible over the top, but all the branches that should have extended over the wall had been sawed off so no one could climb over. The wall was also like the one that surrounded the Vatican, angled slightly outward so no one could climb it even if they wanted to.

His security team knew who I was at this point, so they let me inside. I drove my little bike down the driveway and around the fountain in the front, seeing the group of armed men stand there and stare at me.

I smiled awkwardly. "Hi." I left my motorbike there and hooked my helmet on the handlebar. The second I was behind the walls, the noises of the city were muffled. You could hear the sound of birds in the trees, the falling water from the fountain. It was like an oasis in the middle of the desert.

When I made my way up the stairs to the entryway with the double doors, they parted simultaneously, his staff opening the doors for him so he could walk out. He was dressed in jeans and a T-shirt, but his wealth and power made him look like he wore a crown and a cape.

That big smile was on his face—as always.

A smile that could make every inch of me melt into a puddle.

"Hey, sweetheart." His arms hooked around me, and he pulled me in tight, giving me a kiss in front of his entire staff. "You look cute on that motorbike." He gave my ass a playful smack before he took the bag from over my shoulder. It was bright pink with white flowers, but he didn't hesitate to take it.

"Thanks."

"I worry about you driving it, though." He took my hand and walked inside with me, into the palace decorated with priceless pieces of human history. The front entryway room was always a spectacular view.

"I've been driving a motorbike a long time. I'll be fine." I stopped before the Eye of Horus and admired it. "Is everything in this room . . . real?"

"It is."

"Even those?" I pointed to the enormous statues of Anubis.

"Yep. I see it so often, I forget about it sometimes."

"That's wild."

"You know what else is wild? The Romans were obsessed with Egypt because it was the only civilization that felt ancient to them. Just as the Romans feel ancient to us. And someday, we'll be ancient to some other civilization."

"Yeah. That's deep."

"Come on," he said as he nodded toward the next room. "I want to see you naked."

"Wow, right to the point, huh?"

He grabbed my hand again, and we walked up the several flights of stairs until we reached the mahogany door that separated his wing from the rest of the villa. Then we moved through the enormous gold doors until we were in the sanctuary of his palace.

He carried my bag to the closet.

"Where's Medusa?"

"On her evening walk." He came back to me, focused intensity in his eyes, and he immediately scooped me up like I weighed nothing and held me to his chest, kissing me like it was all he'd thought about all fucking day.

I hooked my arms around his neck, and I fell into the abyss of his kiss, my fingers digging into his short hair, feeling the thick slabs of muscle of his shoulders and arms. I'd been picked on in school for being the tallest girl in the class. I'd heard every mean name in the book. Sometimes I had a crush on a guy who was shorter than me, and he acted like I was a freak. Constantine was the first man who made me feel . . . small. Enzo couldn't have picked me up like that if his life depended on it.

Constantine carried me to the bed, then slipped off my flats and got me undressed, yanking my dress over my head, unclasping my bra so my tits came free. He leaned over the bed and kissed me everywhere, kissed my stomach and then my tits, squeezed me to him like all of me still wasn't enough.

What the hell did I do to earn a man like this?

I pulled his shirt over his head and finally felt his searing-hot skin. Gripped his enormous arm muscles, the strength that could crush me in an instant.

He pulled away to kick off his boots and get his bottoms off. When he was stripped naked, six and a half feet of muscle on muscle on muscle, with cuts through the flesh to separate all the different layers of strength, he came to the bed and moved over me, his fat dick anxious for me like I was something to be anxious for.

He pinned me like he always did, opening my hips wide, bending me like a plastic doll, conquering me like a city underneath a king. He guided himself inside me, then sank deep into my flesh until there was nowhere else to go. "This pussy makes me fucking crazy." He planted my foot against his shoulder, while my other leg rested in the crook of his arm. Then he pounded me relentlessly into his mattress and headboard, giving me the best dick a woman could ever ask for.

~

We had dinner together in his dining room, and then Medusa was returned after her evening walk. We all sat on the couch together and watched TV before bed. When I slept here alone, it felt like a hotel. But when I slept here with him, it felt like home.

All three of us piled into the bed together, and of course, Medusa had to get the spot between us.

"Medusa," Constantine said with a slight tone.

I laughed because her jealousy and desire for attention were cute. "It's okay, I don't mind."

She closed her eyes like she wanted to pretend not to notice Constantine's look of admonishment.

"Baby girl." He sat up and patted the end of the bed by our feet. "Come on." He gave a quick whistle.

She opened her eyes but continued not to move.

"Con, she's fine. I really don't mind."

"I want to sleep with my woman."

"Well, she was your woman before I came along. It's hard for her."

He gave a humorous sigh before he rolled his eyes. "You two could at least switch places."

"I don't think she's going to move."

He gave Medusa *that* look.

She closed her eyes.

I chuckled before I got comfortable, turning on my side to face him, the sheets to my shoulder. "It's fine. Let's go to bed."

He gave a growl before he turned off the lamp on his bedside table, then turned to face me. "Maybe I didn't plan on going to bed just yet . . ."

"Well, I'm pretty sore now, so . . ."

He grinned. "Told you that pussy makes me fucking crazy." He lay still, then continued to stare at me, the smile slowly leaving his lips the longer he looked at me. His eyes became relaxed but serious, just looking at me with his dog in between us.

I could look at him forever. He had a jawline as sharp as a knife, cords up his neck so taut they might pop, coarse scruff along his jaw that slightly scratched my skin whenever we kissed . . . or he kissed me between my thighs. He was so handsome, I wondered if I had hallucinated all of this because Enzo's abandonment gave me a dose of psychosis. I made up this whole thing so life would be bearable.

"What are you thinking?" he said in the quiet.

The corner of my mouth quirked up in a smile. "That I'm experiencing psychosis . . . because there's no way you're real."

The corner of his lips kicked up in a smile too. "Wouldn't be sore if I weren't real."

Medusa started to snore.

He rolled his eyes. "Fifty bedrooms in this place, and she's gotta snore right here."

"Her life doesn't have to change just because I'm here. I would never want to replace her."

"No wonder she likes you so much."

"She's a sweetheart. She likes everyone."

He released a quiet scoff. "Trust me, she doesn't like everyone. She's pretty standoffish."

"Fooled me. Have you ever taken her to Taormina?"

"No."

"Aww, she'd love your family."

"Yeah, she would. She'd love the beach too."

"You have to take her."

"All right, next time we go."

"*We?*" I blurted.

His eyes narrowed. "Fuck yeah, *we*."

My tummy did that thing where it got all nice and warm. Where a garden bloomed and butterflies soared.

"If I went back without you, Ma would kill me."

"I'm glad she likes me."

His eyes turned serious once more. "She loves you, sweetheart."

"I get the feeling she's just a loving person."

"Yeah," he said with soft eyes. "She's pretty great. I definitely look up to her."

I'd never heard a man say he looked up to his mother. It was refreshing. "I notice you don't have much to say about your father, really." Nothing nice to say, at least. He spoke about his childhood like he'd been raised by a single mom.

He was quiet for a while, crafting his answer in his head before he shared it. "Even when my father was present, he was absent. He always preferred the company of his friends to his family. He used to fish with his friends all the time, and the only reason he taught me was because I asked him to. I'm not saying he was a bad guy or anything, but I just don't think he ever wanted to be a father."

I didn't realize it until now, but Constantine and I had something in common. The only difference was his father stayed, while mine ran. I wasn't sure which was worse. To have a father stick around out of obligation . . . or care so little that he just left.

"I don't judge him for it. Parenthood isn't for everyone."

"Is it for you?" I asked without really thinking about it. I always assumed this had an expiration date, so I didn't think about the future much. But now, I thought about it more.

"Honestly, I could go either way. I could easily never have kids and be perfectly fine with that. But I could also have them, and it'd be great. People, particularly women, worry about it way too much. Because they have a timetable, they think about it more, which I get, but I think it causes stress and makes them jump to a decision they might not have made if they didn't have that stress. My philosophy is, whatever happens, it'll be fine."

I could take several pages out of his book. "Yeah . . ."

"What about you?"

"I don't know. Not having my mom anymore kinda kills any desire to have a family. It's not really about her not being able to help me . . . it's just . . . I don't really have a reason to do it. I've been alone for so long that I'm fine being alone."

He continued to stare at me like he hoped I might say more.

"I can see why someone like you would want a family, because it's like adding another person to your team. But starting the team from scratch . . . that doesn't seem like much fun."

"But it wouldn't be from scratch," he said. "Because you're doing it with someone else."

"I guess," I said. "But I guess I also have the perspective of being raised by a single mom. And it looks pretty fucking hard."

He was quiet for a while. "I think you're overthinking it. And I can totally see you being a mom—a good one."

"Why do you say that?"

"The way you took care of your mom. Being a caretaker is a burden, but you never resented her for it. Loved her to the end, still love her now. And then there's this big-ass dog here . . ." He stopped when she gave a particularly loud snore. "Most of my guests want her out, but you want her here."

"Well, it's *her* house."

"The fact that you care about her perspective shows your emotional intelligence and empathy for others. Two important traits when it comes to parenthood. It's totally fine if you don't want to have kids—a lot of people don't—but don't eliminate yourself from the possibility because you think you wouldn't be good at it. That's just not true."

"I didn't say I thought I was unfit . . ."

"No, you didn't," he said. "But I can tell that's how you feel."

How did he do that? How did he know things?

"Your dad took off because it wasn't for him, so maybe it's not for you. I get it. I've had the same thoughts about myself." He propped himself on his folded arm, Medusa still between us and snoring quietly. "But if I ever became a father, I know I'd do the best I could."

~

"I want to show you something." He led the way out of the bedroom and into his office, the place that felt more like a library than a study for a single person. He crossed his arms over his chest and looked up at the wall.

It took me a second to realize what had changed.

There was a large opening in the wall above the back of his chair. Some other painting had been there before, but it was gone. The space must have been ten feet by five feet, a spot that still looked tiny compared to the sheer size of the room.

"You got something new?" I asked.

"No, but I have a vision." He turned to me and clapped his hands together before he massaged his palms. "Boudoir photos of you. One front and center right here. The only other people who come into this room are the maids, so it would just be for me."

It took me a second to process what he said before I gave a laugh. "Uh . . . you're mad."

"Why?"

"Because." I gestured to all the artwork and collectibles he had in this room. "This place is a museum of history, and you're going to have scandalous photos of some woman next to it all?"

"*Some woman?*" he asked. "Oh sweetheart, you aren't just some woman. Let me teach you something about private art collections. They're not for viewing—they're for feeling. Their purpose is to project power, status, and wealth. Have you ever been to the Vatican Museums? The pope doesn't keep that stuff to enjoy it. It's to remind every single person who steps into his domain that he's the most powerful person in the world. The same is true here." He turned back to the empty spot on the wall. "And there's nothing that makes me feel more powerful than you."

Oh Jesus, this man . . .

"So?"

"I—I don't know."

"Why not?" he pressed.

"Because I think you have a distinct vision of what you want in your head, and I'm just not *sexy*."

He released a booming laugh like I was a goddamn comedian.

"You know what I mean. I can't turn toward a camera and flip my hair and look all sexy."

"You look sexy *right now*. You're doing it *right now*."

"Look, I'm supposed to get half naked and do poses and stuff, and I'm better behind the camera rather than in front of it—"

"This is what I want."

"Well, just because it's what you want doesn't mean it's what you get."

He smiled at me, but it wasn't that boyish, charming smile he wore most of the time. It was that sinister, deadly one that I'd seen a handful of times. Like the emperor entered the room and Constantine left. "You said Maximillian Cattaneo was the greatest photographer of your generation, did you not?"

"Yes, but what does that have to do with this?"

"Because I hired him."

"He's booked out like a year . . ."

"Not for me." He continued to wear that hardened gaze, like I'd been outmatched by an opponent who could squash me with the snap of his fingers. "You say he's the best, but you don't trust him to do you justice?"

"I'm just not one of those girls."

"What girls?"

"Someone who can pull this off."

"There's no fucking way you don't know how beautiful you are. I'm not buying this."

"I'm not saying I'm not beautiful. I'm just saying I'm not model material. Not the kind of woman who needs to be blown up and put on this big-ass wall."

"Listen to me." He continued to speak to me in that authoritative tone, like I was one of his men who wouldn't follow his orders. "You're the single most beautiful thing I've ever seen. I saw you across that bar, and my heart was already lodged in my goddamn throat. That other woman came to the table, and I didn't give a damn about the easy lay, because I wanted you. I don't know what the fuck you see, but I see a fucking empress. You're mine, you're one of my collections, and I want to see you up there every time I walk into the room. I want you next to my Michelangelo because you're equal. So don't tell me no again, not unless you have a legitimate reason."

"What's a legitimate reason?"

He stared me down for a while. "You don't trust me. You don't think this is going to last, so you don't want me to have a piece of you. Something intimate, personal, and, frankly, sacred. That's a legitimate reason." His eyes started to withdraw their hostility, like he was afraid that was my reason all along.

I wanted this to last forever, but it seemed too early to say something so serious, so I said something else instead. "Can I see the photos first and then decide if I'm comfortable with them on your wall?"

The disappointment passed like clouds in the wind. He came back to me, the light returning to his eyes, a ghost of a smirk on his lips. "Sure, sweetheart."

~

He sat behind his desk, taking care of phone calls and emails. I didn't understand a lot of what he spoke about. He said a lot of people's names and issued quick orders without details.

I stayed on the couch and worked on my laptop, going through all the edits I thought I would never catch up on. I used to love my work, but now I was working all the time to keep my head above water, and it was starting to kill the passion.

He took another call and seemed to be talking to Rocco, judging by the way he spoke to him differently from everyone else. "Yeah, yeah, yeah, he said that last time." He leaned back in the chair and shifted his eyes to me.

I felt his stare, so my eyes moved to him.

He continued to stare at me, Rocco talking to him about whatever was going on.

I looked back at the computer, but even after I finished an edit, I could still feel him. So I looked back—and his stare hadn't changed.

"Tell him if he doesn't make the switch by midnight, I'll pay him a visit." He hung up the phone and tossed it onto the desk. Then he was on his feet and coming toward me. When his hands reached behind his head and he yanked off his shirt, I knew what that stare had been about. "Get your ass over here."

I'd barely put the laptop on the coffee table when he grabbed me by the ankles and tugged me down the couch. I was in a little sundress, and it immediately rode up when he yanked me toward him.

He undid his jeans and pushed them down enough for his hard cock to spring free. Then he yanked off my thong and pressed me into the corner of the couch before he shoved himself inside me without giving me even a minute to prepare for it. "You think you can sit there in that little dress and not expect me to fuck your brains out?" His hand slid into the back of my hair, and he gripped it hard before he slammed into me, nailing me right on the couch like he hadn't fucked me this morning.

It was hard and rough and fast, and I finished in less than a minute or two. It was just so unexpected, and he was so dominant . . . and a little crazy. He gave a moan when he finished, giving me all of his length even when I winced, like the primal urge took over and he couldn't control it.

He abruptly withdrew from me, pulled his jeans back on, grabbed his shirt from the floor, and started to put it on as he walked back to his desk—like nothing happened. "Now I can fucking focus." He sat behind the desk and grabbed his phone again.

I fixed myself up, put my underwear back on, and then sat there and wondered if my panties would be strong enough to stop the dam inside me from breaking free. I put my laptop back on my lap and tried to find the strength to focus, when I heard Constantine take a call.

"Hey, Ma." He was his jovial self—as if he hadn't just fucked me like an animal. "You know, same ol', same ol'. How are Beatrice and the little ones?" He listened for a while before his eyes flicked to me. "Yeah, she's good."

I knew she'd just asked about me.

"Medusa has really taken to her." He listened again, relaxed in the chair, eyes still on me. "You want to talk to her yourself? She's right here."

I could actually hear her gasp from the phone all the way over there.

"Yeah, she's here. I'm working in my office, and she's doing her photography stuff. Hold on." He stood up and headed around the desk toward me.

Oh my god, oh my god, oh my god.

He stopped in front of me and handed me the phone. "Ma wants to say hi."

I felt my eyes get so big they were about to burst out of my face.

He smirked then mouthed, "You'll be fine."

"I'm scared."

"You'll be fine." He made a fist and put it to his chest just the way he did on the rock in Taormina—telling me to be brave.

I took the phone with a shaky hand. "Hello?"

"Aurelia! Aww, dear, how are you?"

"I'm good," I said with a shaky voice, still unable to believe I was talking to her. "How are things in paradise?" I suddenly drew a blank, having no idea what her name was. I'd just referred to her as Constantine's mother. "What's her name?" I mouthed.

"Sofia," he mouthed before he sat beside me on the couch.

"It's beautiful, but the tourists are rampant. We have a line out the door the second we open—fifty people in line!"

"Oh wow, that's good for business, though."

"Yes, but it's crazy all day until we close. Beatrice has been helping me out so much. She's a great daughter."

"Yeah, that's great."

"But enough about me," she said. "I want to hear about you."

"Um . . . just been doing my photography. Shoots here and there."

"What kind of photography, dear?"

"Weddings, engagement photos, events, stuff like that. I like it, but I've been working a lot lately."

"Oh, I bet my son doesn't like that," she said with a slight chuckle.

"Actually, he's been pretty busy too. But it's okay because we both have stuff to focus on."

"Sounds like a match made in heaven."

"Yeah . . ." Jeez, she was so nice. I felt like she liked me the second I walked in the door. I didn't have to do anything. I was just accepted without conditions. "I miss Taormina. I love Rome, but I fell in love with your town."

"Because it's where you fell in love," she said affectionately. "It'll always be special to you now."

My heart gave a jolt in fear, afraid Constantine heard that, afraid that I made it so obvious that I was utterly spellbound by this man. "I think it's special because of you too."

"Aww, you're so sweet, Aurelia. I can't wait for you two to come back for a visit. But this time, stay longer. At least a month."

"I'd love that."

"Do you mind passing me back to my son? It was nice talking to you, dear."

"Of course. You too." I handed the phone back to Constantine.

He took the phone and put it to his ear. "I'll see when we can come down for a trip—"

"She's a lovely woman, Con." Her voice was loud and clear.

Which meant Constantine heard her comment about me falling in love with him in Taormina. Would he assume she was right? Or think nothing of it at all?

He grinned. "I know, Ma."

"I like that she works, has her own thing, you know."

"Yeah, I like her passion."

"Work is important, but it's never more important than the people in your life. So don't neglect her, Con. When she calls, you answer. Doesn't matter what you're doing."

"I know, Ma."

"All right, I'll let you go, baby. Love you."

"Love you too."

She hung up.

He ended the call, then held the phone between both of his palms. "She really likes you."

"I have no idea why."

"She knows you're important to me. I wouldn't have brought you to the house otherwise."

My eyes moved to the side of his face, holding on to what he said. "Yeah?"

He slowly turned to look at me, eyes locked on mine. "Yeah."

The garden in my stomach bloomed even more. The butterflies grew to the size of dragons. My heart suddenly felt weak. "You said that was a casual thing."

"It was." Then a smile lifted the corner of his mouth. "But I still wouldn't have brought you unless I thought it would be more than casual . . . at some point."

Chapter 7

Aurelia

Constantine picked me up and took me to the Hassler Hotel. At the top of the building was a spectacular rooftop bar, and we had one of the tables right at the edge, the entire city of Rome in view.

"Wow, I've never seen the city like this before."

"Yeah, it's pretty great." He wore a button-up shirt with his sleeves rolled to his elbows and dark jeans. He'd combed his hair a little differently and shaved his jawline, so he cleaned up really nice.

We ordered our drinks, and then we were given a plate of appetizers, warm bread with tomato ragù, green olives, and potato chips. He was relaxed in his chair, the tables behind him full of people who were completely oblivious to the man just as powerful as the president and the pope.

He looked through the glass balustrade and studied the city—as if it was all his.

"What do you like more? Rome or Taormina?"

"What a fucked-up question," he said with a laugh. "That's like asking my mom which one of her children is her favorite. It's me, obviously, but who's gonna make her say it outright?"

I chuckled. "You really think it's you?"

"Oh, one hundred fucking percent."

I laughed, even though I wasn't sure if it was a joke or not.

He finished off his drink. Took his phone out of his pocket and left it on the table. "Gonna use the restroom, then we'll head to dinner."

"All right."

He left the table and walked out of sight—and I stared at his muscled figure until he left.

How in the fucking hell was this man mine?

I sat there and admired the view of the city, wanting to pinch myself because my reality was every woman's dream. A man who fought crime with crime, who could have any woman he wanted, but he was satisfied committing to me—

His phone vibrated on the table, and my natural instinct was to glance at it. My phone always went off with texts from clients asking for their photos or asking to schedule a shoot. Even though I knew it was his phone instead of mine, my eyes still went there.

And I would have looked away immediately if it weren't for the name on top of the screen.

🖤🍆Lila🍆🖤

He put her name with emojis?

And then her message read, Are you free tonight?

I was sick to my stomach. Like, gonna-throw-up-my-drink-all-over-the-table sick. A minute ago, I was living the high life, and now it came crashing down like the meteor strike that killed the dinosaurs. I wasn't just jealous. I was . . . out-of-my-mind pissed off. Not at him, because I didn't know the context of the conversation or why her name was decorated with emojis, but it made me irate.

I had to remind myself not to ruin this by throwing out accusations. Needed to give him the benefit of the doubt, because he'd become my moon, sun, and stars. But fuck, I felt low. They were obviously close if she had fucking eggplant emojis around her name, and he obviously hadn't mentioned me to her if she texted him that.

Chill, girl. Fucking chill . . .

Constantine made his way back to the table, and when he took a seat, he made the check gesture to the waiter. He opened his wallet and pulled out a hundred-euro bill and left it on the table—probably as a tip. Whenever we went anywhere, he tipped like crazy, even in a culture where people didn't tip.

When the waiter brought the bill, Constantine stuffed several bills inside, leaving the hundred on the table. Then he looked at me—and he knew.

I forced a smile, and it took all my strength to pretend like everything was fine.

It must have been a pretty bad smile, because he cocked an eyebrow. "You look mad as hell."

Was I red in the face? "No, I'm just hungry."

He continued to stare at me like he didn't believe a word I said. "Sweetheart, what happened in the two minutes I was gone? Someone say something to you?"

"No, nothing is wrong—"

"Don't lie to me." His tone turned callous in a heartbeat. "I don't lie to you. Don't lie to me."

"Fine. I don't want to talk about it. Now let's go."

"Why don't you want to talk about it?"

"Because I don't."

"So you're just gonna be pissed off for the rest of the night?" he asked incredulously. "You're obviously angry at me. Otherwise, you would just tell me. So give it to me straight." His elbows moved to the table, and he leaned closer to me, his hands coming together.

I was about to ruin this, but I was so insanely jealous I couldn't think straight. "You got a text."

"A text?" He said it like he couldn't believe something that popped up on his phone prompted all this. He tapped his finger on the screen, and right at the top was Lila's text . . . with the eggplant emojis. "Ah, I understand now."

"What's with all the emojis?" I shouldn't ask, but the words were out of my mouth before I could restrain them.

He smirked slightly. "She's got a dick-sucking fetish. And she's pretty good at it."

I really was going to be sick.

"She and I have had a long-term casual hookup, booty-call type of situationship."

"Oh." I wanted to grab his phone and chuck it over the edge.

He studied my face. "Sweetheart, don't ask questions if you don't want the answers." He opened the message box and turned it around so I could read their conversation.

I didn't look at it, eyes still on him. "You don't need to show me."

"I have nothing to hide." He tapped his fingers on the table to get me to look down. "I told her about you when we met in Taormina. She texted me and asked to hook up, and I told her I was seeing someone."

I still wouldn't look at the screen, too embarrassed.

"Sweetheart, look."

I crossed my arms over my chest. "I'm not going to violate your privacy."

"The only people who ask for privacy are people who have shit to hide. I love the opportunity to clarify and explain, because I live an honorable life. Ask me anything, and I'll tell you. My passcode is 2425. You're welcome to go through my phone whenever the fuck you feel like it. It doesn't bother me."

"But doesn't that imply I don't trust you?"

"If you don't trust me or you feel insecure, then that's entirely on me. If you feel that way, then I fucked up. Don't ever let anyone make that argument to you, because that's just fucking gaslighting. The second you suspect them of foul play, they make you feel like the asshole for suspecting them—when they are the ones lying and sneaking. The second you ask to see their phone and they say you're a shit person for needing to look, then they have something to hide. Because any honest person would jump at the opportunity to show you how honest, loyal, and committed they are."

"You talk like . . . you've been cheated on."

"I haven't been cheated on," he said calmly. "But my ex-brother-in-law pulled all the tricks on my sister, and she didn't listen to me. Now she's a single mom, and he's doing god knows what." He set the phone in front of me, then relaxed in his chair. "I fucking hate cheaters and liars. They destroy lives."

I looked down at the phone again and then scrolled back. He did text her a month ago. Thanks for the offer, but I've got a woman now.

Yeah? Tell me about her.

He never texted back.

Then she texted him again just now, out of the blue.

I returned the phone to the center of the table so he could take it.

"I think she texted today because she assumed it had fizzled out by now." He grabbed the phone and typed a message and sent it before he put the phone back in front of me. It's gotten serious, and I'm fucking crazy about her. Don't text me again.

I felt embarrassed, but I was more relieved than ashamed. A little PTSD from Enzo coming to the surface. "I'm sorry—"

"Don't you dare apologize." He extended his hand. "Give me your phone."

I blinked several times before I reached for it in my purse and handed it over.

He grabbed his phone and put them side by side on the table.

I had no idea what he was about to do.

Then I watched him share his location with me and had my phone share my location with him.

He returned the phone to me. "Ready to go? I'm starving."

"Yeah . . . me too."

When we stepped into his corridor, I came to a halt.

"I'll die if I walk any farther in these." I bent down to undo the little straps on my stilettos. They were so cute, black, and sparkly, but god, they hurt like a bitch.

I was suddenly lifted off the floor, scooped into his arms like he was a caveman, and then he carried me down the hallway with my ass peeking out from underneath my dress. "That works too."

He carried me into his bedroom. Medusa was already asleep on the couch, but she came over when he carried me inside. He didn't stop to pay attention to her like he normally did. He took me to the edge of the bed and placed me on the mattress before he pulled my thong free.

Got right to the point.

He hooked my legs over his shoulders to prop them up as he unbuttoned his shirt and dropped it to the floor. Then he undid his jeans and lowered his bottoms until they fell to his knees. His big hands adjusted me into position, and he sank into me, taking up all the space inside me as he moved farther in.

I gasped when he hit the end, when I felt the fullness no other man had ever given me.

His fingers moved around the back of my neck, and he gripped me as he started to thrust into me, quick and even, his eyes possessive and maniacal, like he was the one who'd seen an old hookup text my phone. He slipped his thumb into my mouth over my tongue while his other arm held my leg in place. "Why the fuck would I want anyone else when I have you?"

Chapter 8

Aurelia

When he stepped out of the shower, he got dressed in a hurry. "Free on Sunday?"

"I have a shoot in the morning."

"Cancel it."

"Sorry, what?"

"The pope is holding a special mass on Sunday. I want you to come with me."

"You're—you're invited?"

"Yes."

I thought only world leaders were invited to that sort of thing. "Uh . . . are you sure?"

"Am I sure I'm invited?" he asked with a slight smirk. "Yeah, I'm pretty sure."

"No, are you sure you want me to come with you?"

"Of course."

"What—what am I going to wear?"

"Stick to black and you're set."

I felt like I was about to burst with excitement and utter terror.

"Why are you so nervous?"

"Because it's the fucking pope."

He gave a laugh before he slipped on his watch and clasped it shut. "He's human just like everyone else, sweetheart."

"How do you know him again?"

"Well, one of my responsibilities is to protect him."

"Doesn't he have his own security team?"

"He does, but who do you think gives them intel?" he asked before he pulled on a T-shirt. "And who do you think is the reason people are too scared to fuck with him?" He jabbed his thumb into his chest. "And he's also my uncle."

"What?"

"Many, many times removed," he said. "But that's just how Roman families are . . . always connected."

"Jesus Christ."

"Sweetheart, don't overthink it. He knows what I do and he still likes me, so he'll sure as hell like you." He came to me and gave me a quick kiss on the lips. "I've got to go. Come over Saturday night so we can leave for mass together in the morning." He gave me a smack on the ass. "Bye, sweetheart."

"Bye."

I went shopping and found a modest black dress and a jacket to wear for mass. It went down to my ankles and was by far the most conservative outfit I'd ever bought. But the last thing I wanted to do was embarrass Constantine. I knew he preferred my dresses that barely covered anything, but this was probably more appropriate for mass on a religious holiday.

On Saturday night, I drove my motorbike over, and as always, he met me out front. He wore that boyish grin that always made me weak in the knees. His eyes lit up like it was Christmas . . . and I was the biggest present under the tree.

Even when Enzo and I were happy together, I wasn't sure if he'd ever looked at me like that.

"Hey, sweetheart." Constantine kissed me, then took my bag out of my hands. "Ever think about driving a car?"

"I used to," I said as I walked with him. "But I was late to every appointment. I mean, literally every single one."

He chuckled and walked with me inside. "You look so damn cute riding around on it, but I worry every time you head over here."

"I'll be fine, Constantine."

"My driver can take you wherever you need to go."

As ludicrous as it sounded, I knew it was a legitimate offer. "I'm okay."

"Rocco is coming over for dinner. Bringing a *friend*. Is that okay?"

"Of course it is." He didn't need to ask my permission to have someone in his house. "Who's the friend?"

He shrugged. "Could be anyone."

"Is he coming to mass tomorrow?"

"Yeah."

"You think he's bringing this friend of his?"

"No," he said as he shook his head. "Mass with the pope is more of a serious-relationship type of event."

I loved hearing him describe us as serious. That he wasn't afraid to show his cards, that he didn't play games, that he just told me where he stood instead of making me have to guess. Most guys would try to keep it casual as long as possible before they were forced to slap on a label. Not Constantine . . . at least with me.

We made it to his bedroom.

"Find something to wear?" he asked.

"Yeah." I pulled out the dress and jacket from my bag and hung them up in the closet.

He stared at it, cocked an eyebrow, and then looked at me. "*That's* what you're wearing?"

"What's wrong with it?"

"You look like a nun."

"Well, it's the pope. There's a strict dress code in the Vatican."

"Sure, but this dress goes to your ankles. And a jacket? It's ninety degrees outside."

"The dress doesn't have sleeves—"

"You just need to cover your shoulders, not your whole arm."

"Look, I spent a lot of time trying to find something appropriate, so this is what I'm wearing. Deal with it."

He smirked. "Yes, Sister."

I gave him a playful smack on the arm.

"Never fucked a nun before . . . that's a first."

"Oh, shut up," I said as I smacked him again, trying not to laugh.

"Well, to make up for it, I want you to dress slutty tonight. Lots of ass and boobage."

"You want my tits hanging out in front of your friend?"

"Yep. I'm proud of those tits."

I rolled my eyes, but there was something endearing about what he said. "Would you say Rocco is your best friend?"

"No."

"He's not?" I asked in surprise. "Then what is he?"

"What do you mean, what is he? He's Rocco."

"Okay . . . is he your closest friend?"

"What does it matter?" he asked.

"It doesn't. But I think he's your best friend, but you won't say he's your best friend for some reason."

"Because guys don't talk like that, sweetheart."

"Since when have you been most guys?" I asked.

He pulled out his phone when he got a text. "He's downstairs. The girl's name is Becca."

"All right, let me get changed." I hung up the rest of my stuff in his closet and found a little black dress that had a little lining over the chest to hide my nipples so I wouldn't have to wear a bra. The dress went up higher on one side than the other, showing more of my right thigh than my left. I slipped on my black heels to go with it, and I would ask

Constantine to carry me downstairs so my feet wouldn't kill me fifteen minutes into the night.

When I was finished getting ready, he stared at me. Stared at me hard. "Can't wait to fuck you in the ass, sweetheart."

I heard what he said but didn't take in a word of it. "Excuse me . . . what?"

That smug smirk moved over his lips. "You heard me."

We had dinner outside on his terrace, farther into the yard and away from the main part of the villa, hidden from the world in a perfectly manicured garden. The light left the sky, but the outdoor lighting made it plenty bright.

We had dinner and wine, and Rocco and Constantine did most of the talking. Becca was quiet, but she was touchy-feely with Rocco, her hand either on his arm or on his thigh under the table. I could tell by the way she leaned into him.

The subject of mass came up. "You should see the dress Aurelia wants to wear tomorrow," Constantine said. "She looks like a fucking nun."

I shook my head. "It's the fucking *pope*. You're supposed to look like a nun."

Rocco gave a chuckle. "I look forward to seeing it tomorrow."

"Where's the restroom?" Becca asked.

Constantine put his fingers in his mouth and gave a quick whistle. One of the staff came over like she knew what that whistle meant. "Could you escort Becca to the bathroom? It's too complicated for directions."

Becca left with the staff member, and then it was just the three of us.

"Becca is really pretty," I said.

"Yeah," Rocco said noncommittally.

"You guys together or . . . ?"

He gave a shrug. "Just a situationship. Sometimes we see each other, sometimes we don't." He took a drink of his wine. He was a lot more closed off than Constantine. Said very little. Showed almost no emotion.

"I asked Constantine if you were his best friend, and he said he didn't want to put a label on it."

Rocco's eyebrows furrowed like he was about to laugh, then he looked at Constantine. "That true?"

Constantine moved his hand to my thigh under the table and gave me a playful squeeze. "Thanks for throwing me under the bus, sweetheart."

Rocco continued to stare him down. "Answer the question."

"Of course you're my best friend," he said. "Jesus."

Rocco switched his gaze to me. "You know how many times he's told me I'm his best friend?"

"Just trying not to sound like a pussy in front of my girl," Constantine said as he shook his head. "Jeez."

"Well, I think it's cute if you call him your best friend." My hand moved to his thigh under the table, purposely close to his happy place.

"Yeah?" Constantine asked with a grin.

"Yeah."

"We did shower together that one time at the gym," he said.

Rocco released a loud laugh. "Wow, you're really going to tell her about that?"

"Ooh, I want to know *everything*." Two sexy naked dudes in the shower together. Goddamn.

"It was years ago," Constantine said. "We worked out together, but all the showers except one were broken, so . . ." He gave a guilty shrug. "It was one of those rooms where there're shower heads everywhere."

"Like in prison?" I asked incredulously.

"Yeah," he said with a chuckle. "You could say that."

"Oh my god, that's so hot."

Constantine wasn't the least bit offended by or jealous because of the comment. "Yep, definitely best friends after that."

"We'd have to be to pull that off and still talk to each other," Rocco said.

"And not fuck each other." I smirked as I looked at the two of them.

"Con is a very good-looking man but not my type," Rocco said before he took another drink of his wine.

"Becca is a lucky woman, but yeah, I definitely prefer you." His fingers started to slide underneath my dress to my panties beneath. "All that ass and boobage . . . and those eyes are killer."

"Did you mean to say eyes?" Rocco teased. "Or something else . . ."

Constantine rolled his eyes but didn't rise to the taunt.

I was certain they talked about me when I wasn't around, but it didn't bother me. Even if Constantine shared every little detail describing my body and our intimacy, it still wouldn't bother me.

Becca returned from the bathroom. "So what did you guys talk about while I was gone?"

"The time that Constantine and Rocco showered together," I said.

Her eyes snapped wide open, and she looked at Constantine and then at Rocco. "Got any pictures or . . . ?"

~

The car pulled up outside of Saint Peter's Basilica, and Constantine helped me out of the back seat. Despite my conservative outfit, I still wore my sky-high stilettos to give my ass a little oomph. It was all cobblestone here, so I'd have to hold Constantine's arm if I was going to make it without breaking a leg. He couldn't carry me here and flash my ass to all the spectators who'd come to participate in mass.

We were guided to a separate entrance into the basilica and then placed in a line before we were allowed to enter. I'd been in the basilica before on a tour, but it was a long time ago and full of tons of tourists who'd come from all over the world.

It was not an event like this.

Constantine stood with me, his arm around my waist.

I recognized people in the line ahead of us, the prime minister of England, the vice president of the United States, the president of France, people who had come all the way here on a holiday.

I felt completely out of place. "I have never been so nervous in all my life."

He started to rub my back. "I'll do all the talking, all right?" He brought me in close and kissed my temple. "Just stand there and look pretty."

One by one, people were ushered inside, probably to meet the pope one-on-one before the ceremony began.

I couldn't believe I was in this line at all.

The prime minister went next, and then shortly after him the vice president of the United States.

"I told him about you."

"Who?" I asked. *"The pope?"*

"I told my uncle about you."

"What did you say?"

"That I'd met someone. Told him your name. He said he was happy for me." He took a step forward after the president of France entered the basilica. "He's not the kind of man that says a lot, as I'm sure you can imagine."

"What else do you guys talk about?"

"Work, mostly."

"So, he's aware of what you do?"

He nodded.

"And he . . . supports that?"

"He understands there's a separation of church and state. And he understands he wouldn't have the freedom of being the pope if there weren't an emperor protecting him and his people from the evil forces in this world. Basically, I get my hands dirty so he doesn't have to wash his."

One of the security guys waved us forward.

"Showtime." He took my hand and walked with me inside, and then the shade of the basilica covered us and the air was cool on my skin. I felt the hardness of the tile underneath my heels, felt all the blood rush into my heart with dread.

I saw the pope ahead, standing in his beautiful robes and his hat, smiling with his eyes as he squinted through his glasses. Behind him was the altar directly above Peter's tomb down below, covered in black and gold.

Pope Zephyrinus extended his hand to take Constantine's. "My son, how are you?"

Constantine took it with a firm grip. "Hello, Father. This is Aurelia."

He extended his hand to me.

I almost gasped right in his face. The pope extended his hand to me, and I'd never been so floored in all my life.

He continued to smile, like he was used to everyone he interacted with being affected by his connection with God.

I finally took his hand.

He placed his other on top of mine. "May God be with you, Aurelia."

I took a second to find the words, my hand encompassed by his. "And you, Father."

He blessed me before he blessed Constantine.

Constantine took my hand and guided us to our seats—right in the front row. Thousands of chairs went back through the basilica to the door that led to the square outside. People were already seated there, including Rocco.

We sat down, and it was good timing, because my legs were about to give out from the thrill.

"You did great." Constantine's hand moved to my thigh.

"I don't think I can ever wash this hand again . . ." I stared at the hand he'd touched, my fingertips numb like he'd zapped me with electric current. I'd been blessed by the freakin' pope. I felt like I could survive a plane crash with that blessing.

He gave a chuckle. "Please do . . ."

Once mass concluded, everyone rose from their seats and started to mingle.

Constantine knew everyone. And not just superficially, but intimately. He asked the prime minister of England about his kids, walked right up to the Prince of Wales and talked about football for a few minutes, spoke with the prince of Denmark about some gambling app that just launched . . . I couldn't believe it.

Then another man walked up, and I knew right away he was different from all the others. Something about the look in his eyes, the way he carried himself, the aura around him.

He was just like Constantine.

When he stopped before Constantine, he didn't shake his hand, but he didn't seem hostile either. There were no greetings or pleasantries or talk about sports. "I have Vladimir." He spoke in Italian but with a distinct French accent. "Brought him along, and he's ready for the exchange."

Vladimir, the man who ran the operation that had almost gotten me killed. It was the first time I'd witnessed a conversation like this, watching Constantine work in real time. He took phone calls around me, saved my life on the street, but I'd never seen him interact with someone like this.

"Thank you, Luca."

"Keep your friends close but keep your allies closer."

"Aren't friends and allies the same?"

He gave a slight shake of his head. "Not at all." Then he walked off, sliding his hands into his pockets, and headed for the door that led to the square.

"Who was that?" I knew he wasn't a president or a diplomat or a senator.

"The First French Emperor of the Fifth Republic."

So, I was right—he was Constantine.

He turned to me. "Let's go. I have work to do."

Constantine

It was three in the morning when I texted her. I hadn't been able to wind down after all the shit that had happened to get ready to deal with Vladimir. I'd gone home, but I'd sat in my study, trapped in a rage that continued to make my heart pound like I hadn't gotten my vengeance. Now I was sitting in my Range Rover outside her apartment. Sweetheart?

To my surprise, the three dots popped up, and then a message appeared. You okay?

Yes.

Then what is it?

I would have gone to her door, but I didn't want to scare her in the middle of the night. I know this makes me sound like a dick, but I just want to fuck you and go home. Don't want to talk. It's the only thing that helps me wind down sometimes. And this night had been packed with violence and rage and so much adrenaline that my heart couldn't pump it out of my system. I would have stopped by a brothel, but there was only one woman I wanted to take my dick these days.

The dots appeared, and I expected many questions. But then her quick response came through. Door's unlocked.

"Yes." I left the Range Rover on the street, headed up the stairs to her floor, and then let myself into her apartment. The lights were off because she hadn't bothered to turn them on. I made it to her bedroom and found her naked in bed, the covers pushed to the side, her eyes sleepy like she'd been knocked out cold when I texted her.

I was fucking hard at the sight of her and dropped my clothes at record speed. I joined her in the small bed, moved on top of her, and bent her the way I liked, and then I sank into the warm flesh of a beautiful woman. I felt the softness of her skin every time I thrust inside her, felt how wet she was when she'd just been asleep minutes ago. I didn't kiss her like I normally did, just fucked her, hard and fast, my hips working like a piston in an engine.

She came with a whimper, not one of those drawn-out moans she normally made, probably because she was still half asleep. It was like morning sex, when she wasn't quite there, when she didn't react with the same enthusiasm because she was in a dreamlike state.

I'd been ready to go when I'd sat outside her apartment, so it didn't take much for me to finish, filling her little body with my seed, releasing my adrenaline through my sweat and arousal, finishing off a violent night by finding peace between my woman's legs.

When I was done, I didn't lie beside her. Immediately, I pulled out and put on my clothes so I could head home.

She turned toward the wall, pulled the sheets to her shoulder, and seemed to go right back to sleep.

I watched her as I continued to dress, expecting her to say something, but she didn't.

I smirked, then walked out. "Night, sweetheart."

She didn't say anything back—so she really was asleep.

Chapter 9

CONSTANTINE

Rocco and I entered the villa, a handful of guys with us, while the rest remained outside and at the Temple, ready to be deployed when we were ready. Luca had texted me the address where his men were holding Vladimir. All I had to do was pick him up, like a kid at day care.

"He asked for nothing in exchange?" Rocco asked as we stepped through the double doors into the entryway.

"No."

"You sure about that?"

"I told him a symbiotic relationship would be mutually beneficial. Can't do everything alone."

"He seems like the kind of guy that *only* does things alone."

We approached the next set of doors and came across Vladimir tied and bound to a wooden chair, his face already beaten badly because he'd tried to run—or Luca just didn't like him.

A dozen of Luca's men were there, all carrying automatic weapons in case someone in Vladimir's camp knew where to find him. "Thanks, boys," I said. "We can take it from here."

One guy walked up to me and snapped a photo. "Handoff complete." Like a food delivery driver, he took a receipt to send to Luca in case shit went south and I tried to blame it on him. They all left, and then it was just the three of us.

I pulled up a chair and sat across from Vladimir.

He focused on the floor, too afraid to look at me . . . or stupid enough to ignore me.

"You know how this goes, Vladimir. And I've got a lot of shit to do, and I'd rather make this quick. So how do you want to handle it? Do I need to torture you to tears before I get my answer, or will you just roll now?"

His eyes stayed down, but he started to tremble. It probably wasn't a conscious decision, but an uncontrollable twitch of all his nerve endings. He might even shit himself, he looked so pale.

"Keep in mind that one of your potential victims is my woman—and I'm getting justice for that."

Rocco opened the briefcase he'd brought with all the gadgets inside, the jelly infused with gasoline so it'd stick to his face before we lit it on fire, the pliers and screwdrivers, bamboo shoots for the fingernails, the hammer that would slam down on his ball sack.

"By cutting off your dick."

"I'm—I'm not going to talk."

"Oh, you aren't?" Rocco said. "Good, you just made my day." He grabbed a hammer and spun it in the air before he caught it again.

"Yeah, Rocco loves this shit. Learned a lot of good stuff during his time at MI6."

"You—you won't hurt my family. So . . . you can't make me talk."

It was a leverage I would never have, leverage that would make all these transactions go quicker. But I'd never stoop to that level, no matter the stakes, because I was better than them. "Rocco, I'm going to handle this one."

"Aww, come on," he said. "I brought all my good shit."

"I know, I know," I said. "I'll let you play with him when I'm done. Cut off his pants and give me the jelly. I'm gonna burn his sack off first."

~

I stepped into the other room and made the call. "I got him to talk. Send everyone to the address I'm about to text. Meet you there."

I headed back into the room and found Vladimir pantsless and slouched over in the chair, his face stained with tears. "Gonna head over and raid the place," I said to Rocco. "Meet me at the Pantheon when you're done."

"Oh, it's gonna be a while." He grabbed a golf club that leaned against the wall and spun it around his wrist.

"I—I told you what you wanted to know," Vladimir said breathlessly.

"And thank you for that," I said. "But you touched my woman, so the fun's not over."

"I told you everything!"

I ignored him and looked at Rocco. "Make it good, all right? Because it should be me . . . but duty calls."

"I'll cut off his dick before it's over, don't worry."

"I told you what you wanted to know!"

"Thanks," I said. "See you over there."

We raided the facility, but there was no one to save. The victims were already corpses, and most of the dead had been cremated, so there were no remains to return to the families. We rounded up every asshole in that place, all fifty of them. About a dozen of them were security, and some were nurses and doctors who performed the operations, while the rest were other staff who did everything else.

We gathered all of them together, and a handful of them were women. A couple of them doctors.

"Put everyone in the van except the girls."

The guys were dragged away and put into the vans parked outside. The girls were left in a group in the center.

I didn't kill women, regardless of their crime. It felt like a contradiction to my principles, and it was blood I didn't want on my hands. I fully admitted it was sexist, because women could be just as evil as men, but I didn't have it in me.

But that didn't mean I let them go. "Let the police know they're here. Let's head out." They were all handcuffed around the wrists and the ankles, stuck on the floor. A few of my men stayed behind just to make sure there was no one we'd missed in the building who could let the prisoners go. "Enjoy your life sentences, ladies."

~

We blocked off the different streets that led to the plaza outside the Pantheon. Spectators were welcome to watch, but they just couldn't get close in case someone was in the wrong place at the wrong time.

Forty or so men were dropped onto the cobblestone outside the ancient building with pillars made of Egyptian stone. Once they were accounted for, we pulled out the pulley systems and prepared the executions.

Bound by their hands and feet, all they could do was lie there and wet themselves, cry, or try to console one another.

I stood and watched, watched my men work to prepare forty-two nooses.

My phone rang, and I checked the name to make sure it wasn't important—or it wasn't Aurelia.

It was President Barsetti.

He already knew.

I took the call and didn't speak.

"Are you out of your fucking mind, Constantine?"

"Why do you think I got the job?"

"There are people watching."

"Good. Let the enemies of Rome see what happens when you violate the Roman Republic."

"Constantine—"

"With all due respect, this is not your jurisdiction, Crow. *It's mine.* This is how I run my city. This is how I make the rats run back into the sewers. This is how I protect my people. You may not like my tactics, but I'm the reason tourists continue to come, why people walk the streets at two in the morning—because they know I keep those streets safe. The only thing I should be hearing from you is *fucking thank you*." I hung up the phone.

Rocco came to my side. "Barsetti?"

"Yeah."

"He'll get over it."

"Vladimir?"

"Bled out. Wrapped him up and threw him in a dumpster."

"Good."

The men started to grab the assholes and tighten the nooses around their necks. Some of them tried to fight, but all they could do was wriggle like a slug. Most of them begged for their lives, asked for mercy.

I felt nothing.

"Anyone else?" he asked.

"A couple girls. Let the police handle them."

He nodded in agreement.

All forty-two of them were hoisted up, and they started to choke the second their feet left the ground. Kicking and swaying, pointlessly trying to survive when there was no way to do so.

I stared at them all—like Christmas ornaments hanging on the tree.

Most of them were dead within a minute or less, but some of them lasted longer, turning blue in the face and swinging hard in the hope the rope would snap. Then it was down to one guy . . . like a fucking cockroach.

I took a breath, growing bored as it continued.

Rocco crossed his arms over his chest. "He's really going for it, huh?"

I walked forward, pulled my gun out of the back of my jeans, and aimed at the spot between his eyes, making sure not to miss and damage the stone of the Pantheon. I pulled the trigger, hit my mark, and then he was dead.

I turned to the fountain, all of the people who were brave enough to watch from behind the barricades we'd put up. *"Touch my people and provoke my wrath. Hurt my city and provoke my rage. Attack the Roman Empire and your body will hang from the Pantheon to be feasted upon by crows."* I stepped away from the crowd of people and gave an order to one of my men. "Leave them up until their bodies start to rot."

Prologue IV

Constantine

I arrived at the restaurant and stepped onto the patio. The small tables were covered in white tablecloths, little vases that held a single rose. It had a slight view of the ocean over the cliff, the sea sparkling in the sunshine. The motorbikes and vans were audible from the other side of the restaurant, the city bustling with people coming and going.

Tommaso was already there, his men spread out among the other tables, enjoying their cappuccinos. The other guests in the restaurant didn't have a clue that they dined among Cosa Nostra.

Tommaso had ordered his coffee, and he sat with his legs crossed, his suspenders visible because his jacket hung on the back of his chair.

I came to the table and gripped his hand before I gave him a nod.

He smiled up at me. "Constantine, sit."

Took a seat across from him and relaxed in the chair.

"You look like you need an espresso."

"A double."

He chuckled, then slightly raised his hand to get the attention of the waiter. "A double espresso for my friend here."

We sat in silence until the waiter brought the little cup on the saucer. Then he returned to his job handling the other tables. I knew Tommaso owned the place, so everyone jumped to be of service to him.

I wasn't sure if they knew he was the head of the mob, but I thought it was pretty obvious.

"Giovanni told me how you handled that deal last night. Impressed—as always."

We were supposed to make an exchange with a dealer last night. We'd already agreed on the amount, but my intuition told me it was a setup. When we got there, the product had been swapped with a fake, and they had snipers on the roofs.

But I had snipers on their snipers, and once they were taken out, I snapped all of their necks.

"I've worked with Harold for many, many years. Never expected him to go back on his word like that. How did you know?"

I gave a humble shrug. "I've always been good at reading people."

"And when did your intuition pick up on his treachery?"

"A couple weeks ago," I said. "I was doing a drop with Alfonso, and I spotted him across the street at Leonardo's."

His eyes narrowed. "We're his dealer."

"Exactly. I think Leonardo suggested to cut the middleman out of the deal, and then that planted an idea in his mind . . . a ridiculous one. It was just a hunch without sufficient evidence, but I never give people the benefit of the doubt. I trust my instincts—always."

He gave a nod. "If your intuition were a racehorse, I'd put my money on it."

I grabbed the little espresso and took a drink. "Thank you, Tommaso."

He took another drink of his cappuccino before he got the attention of the waiter. "Let's eat. I'm starving." The waiter was there in a flash. "I'll have the catch of the day—extra lemon."

I handed over the menu without looking at it. "I'll have the same."

"Would you like that cleaned?" the waiter asked.

"No," I said.

Tommaso gave a nod in approval. "He'll clean it for both of us." When the waiter walked away, he said, "I like a man who can prepare his own food."

"That's what a life in the restaurant business will do to you."

"How's your family?"

"Good. My ma was happy I came up for a visit." I'd been in Palermo for two years now, and I knew it was the right move for me. A new city with new people, a chance for me to be something other than a cook and a fisherman. My mother never asked me to come back, never complained about losing me at the restaurant, and let me find my own path in life. Isabella and I could finally be in the same room together. I'd moved on, and I got the impression she had as well.

"Does she know what you do down here?"

I gave a shrug. "I've never outright said it, but she's a smart woman."

"She must be made of something stronger to allow both of her sons to get mixed up with Cosa Nostra."

"I think raising twin boys has made her realize there's only so much she can do."

He chuckled. "Smart woman."

"Yeah." I missed her. Missed everyone in Taormina. This place felt like home, but not in the way Taormina did.

"So does your mother know that Edric has joined the Skull King in Florence?"

I gave a slight shake of my head. "I highly doubt it. Not that she would know who that is . . . or what it means."

"Between you and me, I'm glad Edric moved on to other things. He was always a stubborn hothead. But you . . . you're easy. Think with your brain instead of your ego. If you say you're going to do something, you do it. Simple as that."

I'd started as a low-level henchman when Tommaso first brought me on, but I quickly proved my worth because I learned fast. Showed my value and my loyalty. When our enemies put hits on us, I never took off. I always stood my ground with those who wouldn't betray Tommaso, and that got me promoted to the top of the organization almost overnight. I even took a shot for Tommaso once, and luckily, it was just a bullet graze.

"You're one of us. He was always . . . temporary."

I never said anything bad about my brother, even when he deserved it, but I didn't get upset when people voiced their poor opinions. To be fair, Edric earned each and every one of them. "I haven't seen him in a while."

"Well, I have work for you in Florence, so maybe you should stop by and check in."

"Yeah? Haven't been there in a while." Tommaso deployed me to lots of places—Florence, Rome, Milan, Athens, Paris—all to be his personal liaison when a conversation was important enough but he couldn't be there himself. All on his dime, so it was a free trip for me. Not that I needed any handouts anymore. My pockets were lined with cash these days.

"You think you'll settle down someday?"

The question was so random and unexpected, all I could do was stare.

"You know, take a wife." He pulled a cigar out of his front pocket and lit up.

"I don't know. Not really on my mind." Not even in the slightest. And not because Isabella broke my heart, but because I simply lacked the desire. I was just riding the waves of life at the moment, not sure where they would take me.

"You don't want kids and all that?"

"I don't think beyond tomorrow, if I'm honest. Why?"

"Well, I think you would be a good match for my daughter, Aurora."

Both of my eyebrows shot up in shock and disgust. "Isn't she like seventeen?"

"Jesus, not now," he said. "But in like ten years. You'll be almost thirty-five, and she'll be twenty-five. A good time for a man to settle down. I want my daughter to be with a man, you know. Not a hot-headed fuckboy. Someone who's not afraid to do the shit everyone's too scared to do. Someone who will take a bullet for her."

I didn't let my reaction get the best of me, understanding he'd just paid me an immense compliment. The boss thought I was good enough for his daughter, thought I was good enough to be his son-in-law. "We'll see if I'm alive in ten years first."

Tommaso chuckled, and I successfully averted that awkward crisis. "I think you will, Constantine."

It had taken me a long time to get over Isabella. It wasn't until we'd been broken up for eight months that I'd slept with someone for the first time. The heartbreak was hard to carry, because she was the only woman I'd ever loved and I'd really thought she'd be my wife. It wasn't something you just brushed off like it meant nothing. But as time went on, it got easier . . . and easier. There'd been a lot of different women in my life at that point. Sex had become transactional. Hard to imagine ever feeling that way ever again, and I suspected I probably never would.

The waiter brought our dishes a moment later, and I cleaned one fish and placed it in front of Tommaso before I cleaned mine. Then we began to eat.

"I'm worried Edric is gonna get himself killed over there." I said it more to myself than to Tommaso. A confession that kept me up into the night sometimes. Cosa Nostra might be a gang of criminals, but they were also a family, a big family business that ran a lot of operations. But their crimes didn't really have any victims. But the Skull King . . . whole different enterprise.

"You should be worried." Tommaso never minced words with me.

That was one of the reasons I liked him.

"All I ever hear is the Skull King's a psychopath." He cut into his fish, which was soaked in spices and butter and lemon. "It's the reason we don't do business in Florence—even if it's outside his jurisdiction. We've already got so much shit on our plate that we don't need his bullshit. I'm all about striking fear into your subordinates and your enemies, but he strikes fear into everyone for just being alive."

"Edric hasn't said any of that."

"He's probably never in the room with him. A foot soldier."

"Said it was a big pay advance."

"The Skull Kings have a much bigger territory, so even a foot soldier might have more opportunities there. For his sake, I hope he doesn't move too much. I would tell you to talk him out of it, but now that he's in . . . I don't think he can ever get out."

Prologue V

Constantine

I arrived in Florence, checked into the Four Seasons, and then finally met Edric in the bar downstairs. It was a large room with low lighting, couches and chairs spaced out everywhere, and he was seated in the corner with a stiff drink already on a coaster. He looked a little more like me these days with the tattoos he'd added to his arms. He'd clearly started lifting more, too, because his arms were thicker. His eyes lit up at the sight of me. "There's my bro." He stood up and embraced me, our palms coming together before we gripped each other tightly and let go.

We got comfortable at the table, and the waitress immediately came over and took my drink order.

"Four Seasons, huh?" Edric asked. "You really are Tommaso's favorite."

I'd moved up quickly with Cosa Nostra, and I wondered if that was the reason Edric left. He didn't want his failure to be compared to my success. My brother was the one who'd gotten me in with Cosa Nostra, but he'd quickly turned into an outlier because he was too stubborn to listen. The only reason sense wasn't beaten into him was because Tommaso didn't touch him out of respect for me.

In the end, I thought it was good that Edric left. I just wished he'd gone somewhere else. "How are things here?"

"No complaints." He was in a short-sleeved black T-shirt, the black ink on his arms visible and spaced out. It had taken a long time to fill out my arms completely, which was why I started when I was young. It was an expensive endeavor too. So Edric seemed to have begun that long process. "Money is good . . . pussy pie is even better."

"Pussy pie?" I asked.

"Yeah, try a slice while you're here. I can introduce you." He waggled his eyebrows. "So, how's the gang?"

"The same," I said. "Harold tried to double-cross us . . . got his head blown off."

"I never liked that guy."

"Yeah, me neither," I said. "Tommaso suggested an arranged marriage between me and his fifteen-year-old daughter."

"What the fuck did you just say?"

I chuckled. "Wish I'd said something different."

"No way."

"He said when she's twenty-five and I'm almost thirty-five. When I'm done sowing my oats. Still fucking weird, though."

"Really fucking weird," he said. "What'd you say?"

"Didn't really say anything. Kinda backed out of it and changed the subject."

"Damn, he fucking loves you, though. Thinking you're good enough for his daughter."

"He only feels that way because I took a bullet for him."

"You got shot?"

"Kinda, not really." I tugged up the sleeve of my shirt to show the mark where the bullet grazed me. "It was a graze. I'll add ink and cover it."

"Don't commit to that marriage. There's still a lot of time for her to get ugly."

I chuckled. "She could end up being the most beautiful woman in the world, and I still wouldn't be interested."

"Because of Isabella?" he blurted.

"No," I said with a scoff. "I would just never do an arranged marriage. And I don't like the age gap either."

"You're the first man in history to say he doesn't want a younger wife."

"Younger is fine, but ten years is too big of a difference. We won't have anything in common. We'll be in different seasons of life—"

"Why do you need to have anything in common to smash?"

"If she's my wife, then we're going to do more than smash."

He shrugged and took a drink.

"This is a stupid conversation."

"So you do want to get married?"

"No, I don't *want* to get married. But if, by chance, I met someone that I'd burn the world down for, then yeah." But the odds of that were a million to one. In my line of work, I didn't meet a lot of spectacular women, and a lot of spectacular women wouldn't want to get mixed up with someone like me.

"Good."

"Good?"

"I'd always hoped that the Isabella thing didn't permanently fuck you up."

Not permanently, but it sure fucked me up for a *long* time. "Life goes on. She's seeing someone now."

"Does that bother you?"

"No. I'm happy for her." I knew she'd struggled to move on as much as I did. Friends would tell me she'd go to the beach alone, pick up extra shifts because she wanted to stay busy instead of sitting around. We both processed our heartbreak, but she also had to process her guilt.

He nodded before he took another drink. "Seeing anyone now?"

"No. You?"

He smirked. "Kinda."

"Kinda?"

"Yeah, it's complicated. Forbidden, taboo, all the good stuff."

"So she's married."

"Yep."

I didn't bother to admonish him, just shook my head. I'd only slept with a married woman once—and that was because she lied to me. When I found out the truth, I blocked her calls and moved on. I was pissed that she'd lied, but I was also pissed that she'd made me complicit in an affair I wouldn't have been a part of if I'd known otherwise. Call me old-fashioned, but I didn't mess around with that. "So you like the Skull Kings?"

"Like I said, can't complain."

"Have you met him?"

"Who?"

"The Skull King."

"Oh, Darius," he said. "No, I haven't *met* him, but we've been in the same room together. And I know him pretty well based on reputation . . . and what I hear."

"Then I'm sure you've figured out he's a psychopath."

"And what the hell is Tommaso?"

"An ass—but not a psychopath."

"What are you saying, Con?"

"I don't know . . . I worry about you."

"You worry about *me*?" He placed his hand over his heart. "Me?"

"I just hear a lot of bad shit about this guy."

"But no one fucks with him."

"No, but he fucks with everyone—and you could be next."

"And you think Cosa Nostra is better?" he scoffed.

"Cosa Nostra sticks to their lane. We mediate disputes, we push product across borders, influence sea trade, bribe judges and officials to lean our way on certain matters, and we only physically harm those who cross us. And we're bonded to each other, loyal like a family. But the Skull King . . . he's only out for himself."

"If you think Tommaso isn't out for himself, you're delusional."

"Darius traffics women, undercuts his partners, lets the city go to shit because he doesn't care about it or the people who live there. Tommaso at least has a deep love for Palermo and Sicily, which is why petty crime is lower than anywhere else in the EU. Under Darius, crime flourishes—because he's getting a cut of it all."

"Which is why I have a job, Constantine."

"You can have a job with Cosa Nostra—"

"I'm not fucking doing that."

"So you'd rather participate in these horrific crimes?" I asked incredulously.

He sat back in his chair and crossed his arms, looking elsewhere as he thought of his answer. It was strange to watch him, to see myself and my own reactions like I was looking in a mirror.

"I'm not going to be the lesser brother. I'm not going to live in your shadow. You know how many times a day I hear how great you are and how shitty I am? I hear the way people talk about me, that you should have absorbed me in the womb so I never would have been born. So, no fucking thanks." He shook off the emotion in his eyes and took a drink. "Rather work in a place where no one has a clue I'm a twin."

"Edric, I can help you—"

"Did I say I needed your help?" he snapped. "I don't fucking need your help, Constantine."

"Well, I'm worried about you. You shouldn't be involved with an asshole like that. Cosa Nostra is the right fit for us and our values."

"Your values."

"No, we have the same values, Edric."

"No, we fucking don't," he snarled. "Because I don't give a shit about the women he traffics. I see them all the time, and I feel fucking nothing. I'm fucking his wife, and I feel nothing. You and I are not the same, Constantine—and don't you ever forget it."

I was stunned into silence, my brain so overloaded with shock that I couldn't process all the details he'd just shared. "What the fuck did you just say?"

"He uses the women to process drugs and puts them in whorehouses."

"What if that were Beatrice? What if she went on a trip with her girlfriends and ended up in the wrong place at the wrong time? And she's stunning, so we both know she wouldn't be processing drugs." I felt sick saying that out loud, but I needed fighting words to get through to him. "She'd be drugged and raped for the rest of her life."

"I didn't say I agree with it—"

"These are not our values, Edric. Cosa Nostra isn't a fucking nonprofit, but they aren't monsters. You are better than this. Don't sit there and say you feel nothing because, yes, you fucking do. I know you do."

He tightened his jaw and looked down at the table. "I broke up you and Isabella."

"And you felt like shit about it and still do. You are not him, Edric. You feel remorse and guilt and empathy. You are *not* a psychopath."

"You did call me a narcissist."

"A narcissist is not a psychopath. And you aren't a narcissist either, because you care. You care about me and your family, okay? I'm sorry I said that."

He moved his arms to the surface of the table, hunched forward slightly.

"We've both made good money. Let's open a business together."

"So I can run it into the ground?"

"Keep that attitude, and you're going to manifest your worst fears, Edric. And for the other thing you just said . . . *are you out of your fucking mind?*"

"Yes."

"Yes?"

"I fully admit I've lost it with this one."

I was shocked the Skull King even had a wife. Didn't seem like someone who would even entertain marriage.

"We crossed paths, one thing led to another, it just happened."

"Does anyone else know?"

"I don't think so."

"Then end it. *End it now.*"

"It's complicated—"

"Your life is literally on the line. It's not that complicated."

"She didn't want to marry him. It was an arranged marriage sort of thing. She doesn't love him but he's obsessed with her, and . . . we just connect. She's not just some woman I'm sleeping with."

"Jesus Christ, Edric. You're doing it again."

"Doing what again?"

"You only want what you can't have. Isabella and now this woman. You don't actually give a damn. You like being able to play house without having to pay the mortgage. You like the intimacy without the commitment. Because you know it can't go anywhere. Because you know it's doomed. But in this case, you aren't doomed—you're dead."

He dropped his face into his hands and ran his fingers deep through his hair. "Yeah . . . maybe you're right."

"End it and leave the Skull Kings."

"I don't know if I can leave."

"If he doesn't even know who you are, you can probably slip out. Cosa Nostra will protect you if there's trouble."

"They won't do shit for me."

"But they'll do it for me," I said. "So tell me you're going to end it."

His face was still in his hands.

"Edric."

He gave a sigh and finally straightened. "Yeah, I'll end it."

"Edric."

"I said I'll fucking end it."

Prologue VI

Constantine

I sat in the car, all the lights off because I'd been sitting at the curb for hours.

Finally, my target left the closed restaurant and got into his Bentley.

I watched him drive up the street before I fired off a text. On the move.

When his taillights started to fade, I started the car and pulled onto the road. The road he was on came to a three-way stop, and I took another street so I'd come out on his left and look less conspicuous.

When I got there, he'd just finished his pause at the stop sign, then continued on his way.

I turned right and pulled in behind him.

Then my phone rang, and I saw Edric's name on the screen. I ignored his call and directed it to voicemail because I was busy.

But he called again. "Jesus, what?" I answered the call and put it on speaker. "I'm busy right now, Edric."

"He knows, and he's coming to kill me," he said breathlessly, like he was literally sprinting down the street.

I immediately pulled the car over, abandoning the operation in the blink of an eye. "All right, I'll get there as fast as I can. What's your move?"

"I don't fucking know. Run and hide." He hung up.

I immediately called Tommaso, who probably wasn't even awake right now. It was one in the morning, and he usually sent the rest of us out to do these kinds of operations. But he answered and spoke normally. "What is it, Con?"

"The Skull King is about to kill my brother, and I need your help."

"My help?"

I pulled back onto the road and headed to the airport, where our stash of planes was parked. "You know I wouldn't ask if I didn't have to." I wasn't enough of a force to oppose the Skull King. He'd cut me open and hang me to bleed in his meat locker.

"I warned you—"

"I told him to get out, but he didn't listen."

"Then that's not my problem, Con. He made his decision."

"Well, I'm headed to the airport because I'm not going to let my brother die. So if you don't want me to fucking die too, then you better help me."

~

It was less than an hour flight there, but it was even quicker than that because we were able to just take off and push the engines faster than air traffic controllers would normally allow—but no one was on duty at the moment.

We landed in Florence, had our connections pick us up in SUVs already loaded with guns, and we headed into the heart of the city.

I'd been calling my brother ever since we landed, and he hadn't answered once.

"This might be a recovery rather than a rescue," Tommaso said honestly.

It was one of those times when I didn't want honesty. "He might have just dropped it."

"Dropped it after they grabbed him?"

"Shut up, Tommaso."

"I'm sticking my neck out for you, so don't you fucking tell me to shut up." He turned to the driver. "Go to their headquarters. Whether Edric is there or not, we need to speak to the Skull King."

I didn't have a better plan, not when I couldn't talk to my brother. "Can you call him?"

Tommaso sighed as he looked at me.

"Call him."

I didn't have Darius's number, and even if I had, he'd have no idea who I was. He wouldn't listen to me.

"This is a really fucking stupid idea, Constantine."

"I know."

"Then I want something in return for this."

"Name your price." I'd give him every fucking euro I'd earned if he helped me get my brother back.

"Marry my daughter when she turns twenty-four."

That was his request? "Are you out of your fucking mind?"

"That's my price."

"She might not even like me."

"I'm sure she will, Constantine."

"I might not like her."

"Does any man like his wife?" he demanded.

"I would fucking hope so."

"We got a deal or not?"

"No. I can't promise that. What if I meet someone?"

"Then have a mistress."

"I'm not that kind of man."

"Which is exactly why I want you for my daughter."

"Tommaso, you're fucking crazy. The answer is no."

"Then swear to me you'll consider it, when the time comes."

"We're talking, like, nine years from now. What if I'm already married?"

"That's fine, but you won't be," he said. "You want me to put my life on the line, that's what I want."

"Jesus fucking Christ, fine."

He extended his hand to shake mine. "I know you're a man of your word."

I shook it, potentially trading my future for my brother . . . who might already be dead.

He pulled out his phone and called the Skull King. It rang and rang.

Shit. "Call him again."

Tommaso repeated the call, but the same thing happened. "What did Edric do to piss off Darius?"

I didn't want to say. If I told the truth, none of them would help me.

Tommaso continued to stare at me. "Con, what did he do?"

I shook my head. "I—I don't know." I lied. Went against everything I believed in and fucking lied . . . just for a chance to save him.

~

The Skull Kings operated out of a large villa that used to be an apartment building. They'd taken it over and renovated it. Darius occupied it as his primary residence, with a militia of men to guard him.

I assumed his wife lived there too.

We arrived, and Tommaso asked for an audience with Darius—said it was a matter of life and death.

If I'd been the one to make that request, I would have been denied.

We were escorted inside, into a large foyer that was mostly empty space except for the couches arranged around the enormous hearth that was dead and cold. Chandeliers hung from the ceiling, their lights set to low, and there were old paintings on the wall that seemed to be left there by the previous owner.

We'd barely stepped inside when the double doors were thrust open with enough force to make them smack against the walls. Nearly flew off the hinges. Shirtless and enraged like a bull, the Skull King entered, a man of immense girth and strength, with eyes that were pitch black like the underworld. "Life and death? What could possibly be life and death when no one lives or dies in this city without my say-so?" He screamed like we were the ones who'd had an affair with his wife, and then he stopped when he looked at me.

It took less than a second for him to understand. "It's his life that you've come to plead for." He moved closer to us, a behemoth of a man who was six and a half feet tall, with so much muscle he must eat a cow every day to maintain his strength. He moved to me, ignoring everyone else like no one else stood in the room. "I should kill you too—just for the fucking likeness."

"Name your price, and I'll pay it."

He stepped closer to me, attempting to taunt me with his size.

I wouldn't be intimidated, not when my brother's life was on the line, my twin, the person I'd shared more life with than anyone else.

"Are you married?"

I hadn't expected that question. "No."

"Then there is no price you can pay." He stepped away. "Your brother is dead. But I'm glad you're here because I'd love for you to watch." He nodded to one of his men who stood by the door.

"There's gotta be something you want—"

"I want his come out of my wife's pussy." He turned back to me with a quick spin, moving his enormous mass with ease. "And her mouth. And probably her ass too—because she's a fucking whore."

Tommaso immediately turned to look at me—and the accusation was fierce.

"Well, she *was* a whore. Snapped her pretty little neck."

Jesus Christ.

A moment later, two guys dragged Edric inside, his wrists and ankles bound in zip ties. His face was already bloody, like he'd taken a serious beating, and he was dropped like a sack on the carpet.

I didn't look at him for long. My eyes focused on Darius.

Darius started to pace the room, swinging his arms across his chest like he was about to step into the ring and fight to the death. "Unbind him. I'd like to watch him run . . ."

The guys came over and cut the zip ties.

Edric struggled before he stood up, like he already had a ton of bruises underneath his clothes. His eyes glanced at Tommaso and the others, but when they found mine, they stayed.

I stared back, fucking terrified this was the last time I'd ever look at my brother.

Darius walked over and punched him in the back of the head so hard he flew straight to the carpet. He barely caught himself before he smashed his face into the floor. Then Darius grabbed him by the ankle and jerked him back. "You thought you could stick your tiny dick in my wife and get away with it?" He lifted him and slammed his head down hard into the carpet.

I moved forward.

"Fucking suicide . . ." Tommaso hissed at me under his breath.

"Name your price," I begged. "We'll kill your enemies with guns or trade. We'll do jobs for you for free. We'll pay you millions—in case. Whatever you want, I swear to you I'll make it happen—"

He stomped on my brother's knee, and the pop was loud like a gun.

"Ahhhhh!" My brother screamed, and I'd never heard him scream like that.

The Skull King stared me down like a lion on the hunt for prey—like I was next on his list. "I don't like your fucking face." He moved back to my brother and lifted his foot, staring right at me like I was the true recipient.

"Please." I raised both of my hands, begging for the first time in my life. "Whatever you want, I swear I'll make it happen—"

He stomped on his other knee, and there was another pop.

Edric screamed again, the anguish making my ears ring.

Tommaso moved in front of me and grabbed me by the arm. "There's nothing we can do."

"He's still alive—"

He shoved me back. *"There's nothing we can do."*

"Ahhhhhh!" My brother screamed when another bone snapped.

"I'm not going to leave him here."

He shoved me again. "Don't do this to yourself. We need to leave while we still can."

"Here comes the spine." Darius moved over my brother and raised his boot above his stomach, ready to paralyze him.

"No!" I pushed past Tommaso and ran forward.

The Skull King slammed his boot down—and the scream made me sick.

I lost my footing and fell forward, heaving with tears that came from my soul. I tried to crawl forward, but Tommaso and the guys grabbed me and started to drag me away.

The last thing I saw was Darius stomping on my brother's face over and over, smashing his skull into pieces, his brains flying out . . . while one of his men rolled in an oil drum to shove the remains into when he was finished.

The corners of my eyes blackened, my vision was blurred, I was so sick I felt my dinner come back into my mouth. I was literally dragged out of there by Tommaso and the others, yanked out to the street, and then I collapsed and threw up all over myself.

"Come on, move." Tommaso grabbed me by the arm and forced me forward, forced me into the back of the SUV, and told his men to take off before the Skull King came after us. "Go, go, go. Straight to the airport."

I threw up again, lying on the floor of the SUV, staring at the back of the driver's seat.

"Jesus Christ, you almost got us all fucking killed, Con."

I breathed and I heaved, stuck with the final memory of my brother . . . being broken into pieces. I didn't care that Tommaso and the others were in the car. I sobbed. Sobbed my fucking heart out.

Prologue VII

Constantine

I was incapacitated for two weeks.

In my villa, day after day, sleeping on the couch because that somehow felt more comforting than the seclusion of my bedroom. I didn't tell my mother or my sister what had happened. If my mother couldn't get ahold of Edric, she would call me and ask what my brother was up to.

So I still had some time before she knew.

Tommaso didn't ask me to show up for work. Didn't text or call. None of the guys did. I was either shunned from Cosa Nostra for putting them at risk, or he was giving me space to process . . . process the fucking horror.

I couldn't sleep because I dreamed about his snapping bones and his agonizing screams. It played over and over in my head, jerking me awake and reminding me it wasn't a dream . . . but a memory.

Someone knocked on the door, and I didn't flinch from where I sat on the couch. Just stared at the wall like I hadn't heard it. I hadn't ordered anything.

The knock sounded again. "Con, open up."

It was Tommaso. "It's open . . . I think."

He let himself inside the apartment, moved past the entryway, and joined me in the living room. He stood there and stared at me.

I showered sporadically, changed my clothes every few days, but I was cloaked in a depression so thick it felt like I was being choked every single day.

He examined me for a while before he took a seat in the armchair. "I won't bother asking how you're doing. It's pretty fucking clear."

My chest hurt with every breath I took.

"Have you told your family?"

All I could muster was a shake of my head.

He nodded in understanding. "You knew what Edric did. You lied to me."

"Yeah." I didn't care if he shot me in the head. Death would be a blessing. Living with this memory would be the curse.

"We all could have died."

"Yeah."

"You aren't even going to apologize?"

"No. At the time, all I cared about was saving my brother. So, no, I'm not fucking sorry. If you're going to kill me, just fucking kill me already."

He propped his arm on the armrest, his closed knuckles against his cheek.

We sat there in silence for a while.

"Look, I'm sorry this happened, but it's not your fault, Constantine."

My eyes shifted to the floor, the joints in my shoulders creaking from the weight of my guilt.

"I know you're used to cleaning up his messes, but you need to learn his messes are not your responsibility. He made the decision to join the Skull Kings when I advised him not to, and then he made the idiotic decision to fuck Darius's wife when there are plenty of brothels he could have visited instead."

"You're saying he deserved that?" I asked incredulously. "Who the fuck deserves that, Tommaso?"

"If someone fucked my wife, I'd do the same."

"No, you wouldn't," I snapped. "Maybe you'd shoot them—"

"That motherfucker would be dead, Constantine. And you're blinded by your familial love from seeing what's right in front of you. There are men in this world who make it no matter what's thrown their way—people like you. And there are people who are born a fuckup and will die a fuckup—and that's your brother."

"Fuck you."

"You know it's true. Even if the Skull King let him go, he'd get into some new trouble six months later. Always something. One idiotic decision after another—in perpetuity. And you need to understand that it's not your responsibility to fix that—to fix him. You were nice enough to forgive him for what he did to your fiancée. I certainly wouldn't have done that."

It didn't matter if everything Tommaso said was true. Edric was still my brother. The only person in the world who was more like me than anyone else. Losing a twin was more than losing a brother. It was losing yourself.

"I'm sorry to watch you go through this. You know I love you like a son, Constantine."

My eyes stayed on the floor, too numb to accept any kind of love right now.

"You always covered for him, always stuck out your neck for him, and he just held you back."

My eyes started to smart with tears. "That's not true."

"He was a fucking burden that you carried your whole life. You told me, when you were growing up, whenever he had a presentation in school, you pretended to be each other so you could do his presentation as well as yours. When he got into trouble too many times with your parents, you took the fall to lighten the load. You were a good brother to him, Con. You tried to save him, but there was nothing you could do. Forgive yourself. Relieve yourself of this burden."

I blinked, and two tears ran down my cheeks. I didn't care if he saw. "I have to get his body back."

"Con . . ."

"I can't leave him there. I need to bury him."

He gave an irritated sigh. "As shitty as Edric was, he wouldn't have wanted you to risk your neck a second time for him. He's done. He's dead. Let it lie."

"What am I supposed to tell my mom?" I straightened and looked him dead in the eye. "I need to bring him home."

"You're going to get shot in the fucking head, Con."

"So fucking be it." Angry tears burned the corners of my eyes.

He released a sigh as he dragged his hands down his face. "It doesn't change anything—"

"What if this were your brother? Your sister? Anyone you love?"

"You've seen what he's like, Con. You show up there, he'll literally rip your head off."

"Not if you come with me."

He released a loud scoff. "Oh sweet Virgin Mary, are you out of your mind?"

"Come. Don't come. I'm going either way."

He dropped his face into his hands and released a frustrated sigh. "Sleep on it—"

"No. Give me his number."

"You don't want to be on his radar. We were lucky enough to get the fuck out of there."

"I'm doing this, Tommaso—whether you help me or not."

"What about your mother, Constantine? She's gonna be devastated when she learns her son is dead. But how much worse would it be if she found out *both* of her sons were dead?"

Guilt flushed through me when I pictured her in my mind. "I still have to do this, Tommaso."

He released another irritated sigh. "Fine."

His eyes flicked back to mine. "If you go alone, you're dead. So we have to come along."

"You don't have to. This is my choice."

"And my choice is for you not to end up in an oil drum yourself, so . . ."

We arrived in Florence the next day.

Tommaso secured a meeting with Darius, and my hand should have been trembling with nerves, but I was fucking still. Grief made me invincible because I feared nothing. Edric's stupid decisions got him killed, but I could have done more to stop him. Could have called and checked in. Could have made sure that he broke things off before Darius found out. But I was too busy with my own shit.

We arrived at their villa, a sprawling estate not far from the Duomo. We were frisked before we checked in and then led to a different room from before. This one had a throne made of stone—with human skulls carved into the rock.

And he sat upon it, dressed in jeans, boots, and a T-shirt, slouched sideways like a king bored with his own responsibilities.

The large room looked like it used to be a ballroom because of the size. Now there were tables placed everywhere, with men occupying the chairs. Sort of reminded me of the gambling room at the Villa de la Sirenuse in Palermo.

The numbness from the grief faded when I looked at him.

Replaced by rage.

Bloodthirsty rage that would never be satisfied—even with his death.

Darius stared at me from his throne, eyes locked on mine with the same intensity as last time. Hostility simmered under the surface and slowly boiled to the top. He clearly hated me for a crime I didn't commit. "You came all this fucking way, and now you have nothing to say?" His voice boomed as he straightened in the chair, going from a state of calm to madness in a split second. He made a fist and slammed it down on the stone armrest—hit it hard enough to make a thump so distinct it sounded like wood. "Speak." Then he was on his feet, a behemoth in size and power, the statue of Apollo that had come to life. "Or should I just rip your tongue out now?"

"I want my brother's body back—and I'm happy to pay you for it." I kept it brief and straight to the point because his presence was so intolerable. I had no weapon on me, so if I wanted him dead, I'd have to do with my bare hands. We were the same height, but my size was no match for his. He was like a fucking gorilla.

He turned to one of his men and gave a nod that was as good as a verbal order. Then he returned to his throne, sat down with his knees wide apart, back to looking bored.

A moment later, the oil drum was brought out on a dolly and placed next to his chair.

"Was thinking about making it my nightstand. Put my lamp on there, some other shit. A fucking piece of furniture."

I couldn't control my expression. Couldn't control my breaths. All I could do was stand there and be stabbed by his words.

"And that's what he'll remain. Forever my prisoner, floating in chemicals to preserve his flesh and bone, his tomb holding my gun while I fuck my favorite whore on the bed." He smiled at me, like the horror on my face was the finest hit of cocaine. "Should have told Tommaso that over the phone." He gave a shrug. "But I thought this would be more fun—and it was." Sick pleasure radiated from his eyes, and then he gave a quiet chuckle like this was all fun and games.

"Name your price," I repeated. "I'll pay whatever you want—"

"You think I need money?" He was on his feet again and then striding toward me, his behavior unpredictable, volatile. He came right up to me. "Do I look like I need money to you?" He yelled right in my face. "Your piece-of-shit brother came in my wife's mouth, and he will spend the next sixty fucking years as my nightstand. When I'm old and shit with a maid wiping my ass, he'll still be my nightstand. When I'm buried, he'll be buried with me—*because that motherfucker is mine.*"

"We understand," Tommaso said. "We'll be on our way—"

"I'm not leaving without him." I held the Skull King's stare, his face just inches from mine, and saw a beast instead of a man.

"Constantine."

Darius suddenly shoved me hard in the chest.

I stumbled back only slightly, prepared for him to hit me.

"I don't fucking like you, you pompous little cunt." He came for me again. "I don't like your face. Maybe I should shove your body in with his so I can have the set. Because your fucking face . . . *I hate looking at it.*" He seethed as he stared me down, a gorilla about to beat his chest and rip my face off.

Tommaso moved to me and grabbed me by the arm. "Let's go. Now."

"I can't—"

He grabbed me by the neck and shoved me back. "Are you really going to make me die for you? After everything I've done for you?" He tried to speak in a whisper, but the room was silent, so every word was heard. Accusation and resentment burned like the waves of heat across the desert. "We tried, Constantine. It's done."

I didn't want to give up the fight, but I knew there was nothing I could do—at least at this moment. I gave a nod in agreement.

"Good." He grabbed my arm and escorted me out—like I might change my mind.

I lied to my mother, told her he'd been killed in a car accident, arranged the funeral, and made sure it was a closed casket so she would never know what really happened. That was the least I could do for her.

My sister was a mess. Everyone was devastated.

I'd had more time than anyone else to process his death, but because I'd witnessed the way his body was broken, I seemed to be doing the worst. I couldn't comfort my mother because I felt unworthy to even touch her. I didn't save my brother—and I didn't even bring his body back.

We had everyone at the house afterward. It was the first time my mom had hired a caterer instead of cooking herself.

I couldn't stand the voices of everyone there, didn't want the company of a single person, so I made my way outside, sat on the ground with my back against the wall, looking at the lights of the city my brother would never see again.

Isabella must have come looking for me, because when she found me on the ground, she took a seat beside me, in a black dress with sleeves, her heels left in the house somewhere.

I held an empty beer bottle in my hand, finishing it a long time ago but unable to remember to throw it away.

She glanced at the side of my face for a while. "It wasn't a car accident, was it?"

I continued to stare at the lights, my eyes filling with tears. I took a painful breath, then shook my head.

Her hand reached for mine, and she squeezed it, releasing a sniff.

I blinked, and the tears streaked down my cheeks. I cried in front of her without restraint. I couldn't cry in front of my mother, had to be the man of the family since I was the last one left. My father had clutched his chest and gone down in the kitchen, dead before he hit the floor. And now my brother floated in an oil drum.

I was all that was left.

"Con . . ."

"I—I tried to save him. But—but I couldn't."

She squeezed my hand harder. "It's okay, it's okay . . ."

"I watched him die." I started to cry harder. "I watched him die . . . and I couldn't stop it."

~

A week after the funeral, I went back to work.

"You ready, Con?" Tommaso asked when he sat on the couch across from me in his study. "It's okay to take more time."

I shook my head. "Thank you . . . for everything you did for me. And for coming to the funeral."

He gave a nod. "When I said I loved you like a son, I meant it."

"I know." He'd shown me more affection than my own father ever had. Stuck out his neck for me in a way my father never would have. We were only about fifteen years apart in age, but we were in very different seasons of life.

"I hope you find peace, Con."

I shook my head. "No. I'll never let this go."

He continued to watch me.

"There's nothing I can do about this now. But someday . . . I'll come for him."

He rested his arms on his knees, his palms slowly sliding back and forth across each other.

"Someday I'll be the most powerful man in Italy—*and I will fucking come for him.*"

Prologue VIII

Constantine

The only reason the Pantheon had survived all these centuries was because the pope had turned it into a church. Everything else had been pillaged and abandoned, the Roman Forum somewhat preserved because of the lake of mud that had submerged it all this time. That made the Pantheon special, because even the floors were original. It was almost completely intact—even the bronze doors that still worked to this day.

And that was why the council conducted their meetings there, in the moonlight from the open arch in the ceiling, accompanied by Raphael's coffin buried under the slate of glass. There were five chairs in the front, occupied by each aristocrat on the council.

The first was the president of Italy, Crow Barsetti. The second was General Farina, the head of the Italian military. The third was Chief Romano, the chief of the police force, the fourth was Dr. Conti, the leading archaeologist and historian of ancient Rome. And the fifth was none other than Pope Zephyrinus—my uncle.

"I've submitted my records and proof of my lineage through reputable ancient texts and genetic testing—as confirmed by Dr. Conti. Emperor Augustus had a daughter named Julia, and if the succession of power hadn't been grossly misogynistic, she would have had the throne. I'm the last living descendant of the first emperor of ancient Rome—and therefore, the Roman Empire is mine. I will serve the people of this country, and I will protect them with my life. I will work with the president and the pope, and together, we will ensure the prosperity of the Roman Empire. Do you accept?"

After several seconds of silence, they all looked at one another, convening in my presence even though they'd already had their discussions in private.

"What do you seek?" General Farina asked.

"Everything I just said," I said. "My time in Cosa Nostra and my other unsavory connections have made me a powerhouse in this country. I will police criminal enterprises by my own laws—and I will protect innocent people from their ways. Women and children will be safe. Innocent men will be safe. I would gladly give my life for this country. The crime has become rampant. There's graffiti on every single building, even the damn obelisks. The Skull King has poisoned the rivers with his criminality and destroyed this beautiful countryside. I seek to restore it—to rebuild the empire."

"But are your ambitions truly that altruistic?" Pope Zephyrinus asked.

My eyes shifted to my uncle.

"Because there can be no peace in war. With your newfound power, will you use it to destroy the Skull King—your blood nemesis? Or will you put the people and the empire first?"

The men stared at one another before they looked at me once more.

"You must remember, Constantine," the pope continued, "that the blood of emperors may run in your veins—but so does the corruption. Rome had kings before the republic, and then they had the greediest leader of all—Julius Caesar. The emperors were a chance to turn over a new leaf, but like all men who seek power, they're easily corrupted. Can you look us in the eye and prove you're different?"

My uncle didn't care about the same blood that ran through our veins, clearly. "The best way to protect Rome and the country is to eliminate the Skull King. He's vile, evil, and a parasite to our society."

"I believe the best way is through peace," the pope said. "I believe you're capable of restoring this city to its previous glory. I believe you will protect your people from the crime that has infected our veins. I believe your heart is good. But I also believe that your hatred for Darius has poisoned your good intentions."

It'd been two years since my brother had been killed. Two years since I'd had to return to Taormina and give my mother news no mother should ever have to hear.

"I believe you won't stop until vengeance is yours, Constantine."

"I will not deny that his death is what my heart truly desires." I wouldn't lie for anything—not for a woman, and not for a position. "He deserves to die for what he's done to Florence, but more importantly, for what he's done to me." It was easy to argue that my brother deserved what he got, but I would never feel that way. There was nothing he could ever do to make me turn my back on him. Alive or dead, he was still my brother, still my family—and I would not stop.

"An outright war with the Skull King would not only be expensive, but deadly," President Barsetti said. "The police and military have done everything they can to rid the city of him, but he's too strong and too well guarded. He has access to weapons and bombs and has everyone in his pocket . . . no way to know exactly who. A truce of peace is the only course of action."

"Spoken like true cowards."

"That is our condition, unanimously decided among the five of us," President Barsetti said. "We'll instate you as Emperor Constantine II of the Roman Republic—but only under a declaration of peace between you and the Skull King. Italy is no place to have a civil war."

It fucking disgusted me. These last two years, I'd tried to find a way to destroy Darius. Cosa Nostra wouldn't help me. None of his enemies in Florence was willing to openly oppose him. My only course of action was to seize the power of the emperor and use that to make my move—but even that had been taken from me.

"Upon your word of peace, power will be granted," President Barsetti said. "And you will serve the Roman Republic."

It wasn't what I wanted. But just because it didn't happen today or this year or next year didn't mean that it wouldn't happen someday. That the opportunity wouldn't present itself and I'd take that shot. "Then I give you my word—I agree to the truce."

I looked out the enormous window behind his desk that faced Saint Peter's Square. Stared at all the arches and the statues erected on top, one of the seven wonders of the world—in my humble opinion.

Rome was mine to serve and protect, but that responsibility felt hollow.

"I know it's not what you wanted, Constantine. God doesn't always give what you want—but what you need."

I turned away from the window and looked at Pope Zephyrinus, who stood there with his hands together in his billowing robes, a perpetual warmth to his eyes despite the dark subject of our conversation. "The Skull King harms and murders innocents, and your response is to let him."

"That is not my response," he said. "But every war fought is paid in blood, and you don't know whose blood that will be. Will it be yours? Will it be your family's? Or will it be thousands of innocent people who happened to be in the wrong place at the wrong time? Wars can be won without guns. Victory can be earned through conversation and diplomacy."

I rolled my eyes—at the fucking pope. "The Skull King strikes you as an expert in diplomacy? No offense, Father, but you're out of your element with this."

"Perhaps," he said. "But he already took your brother. And if you provoke him, he'll take everyone else. Are those consequences that you can accept?"

I turned back to the window again. I thought of my mother and my sister . . . of my aunts and uncles and cousins . . . and Isabella. It wouldn't be hard for him to figure out what she'd meant to me at one point in time.

There was a quiet knock on the door, and then one of the staff poked their head inside. "Father, President Barsetti is here to speak with you."

"Of course," he said. "Show him in."

A moment later, President Barsetti entered the pope's chambers, in his dark-blue suit with a black tie, his shoes so shiny the sun seemed to reflect off the leather. He greeted Pope Zephyrinus with the type of handshake that remained firm. Then he slid his hands into his pockets and looked at me.

I stared back.

"I know you disagree with our decision, but in your heart, you know we're right—"

"In my heart, I think you're a fucking coward, Crow Barsetti."

The pope remained idle, standing there and blending into the background.

President Barsetti gave no reaction. "I know more about this sort of thing than you realize, Constantine."

"Really?" I challenged. "From your comfy armchair in your office? With your fancy political science degree from Oxford? Oh, I'm sure you're the leading expert in kingpins . . ."

He continued to stare at me. "My family has been in Tuscany for several generations, and my roots are not steeped in the vineyards of my grandfather's estate, but in the blood of the people who have been killed with his arms. My father was a hit man in his day, and a lot of my relatives built their wealth by illegal and sinister means. I know about the Skull King, and I know his predecessor and his predecessor before that. Some of them were good, ruled by a code of decency. But Darius, he's the vilest man ever to sit upon the throne. My mother worries for me every single day."

I hung on to his words because this was a chapter of his book I hadn't read.

"I'm not a coward. But the Skull King is more powerful than the rulers who came before him. There's never been a Skull King who has usurped power from the police and the military. And Darius's reach is further and deeper. I could organize a hit on his headquarters since he doesn't exactly hide his location, but he's threatened the families of so many people that several people would leak the plan before I could even execute it. It's happened before, and it'll happen again."

"I get it's complicated, but letting him destroy Florence is not the answer."

"And I think engaging him in a civil war is not the answer either, Constantine."

The pope approached us. "It's the words from our hearts that bind us, not divide us. Perhaps the right words could be said to Darius . . . and there would be civility."

Not in a million fucking years.

Like the pope could hear the words in my head, he said, "Peace is always the answer, son—*always*."

"If you don't declare a truce with him, he'll come for Rome," President Barsetti said. "The Roman Empire fell once—and it could fall again. We both know he's capable of taking more than Florence. He could kill me and put in a minion in my place, and then the republic would truly fall. You have to remember we're fighting for more than this city, but the country, the people."

"He's right, Constantine," the pope said. "The fate of Rome is in the hands of us three."

~

I crossed the busy street and approached the outdoor terrace of the restaurant in Palermo, which had stunning views of the sea. At a table placed away from all the other guests, oblivious to who he was, sat Tommaso, putting out his cigar in the crystal ashtray.

When I entered the restaurant, he smirked widely at me but didn't rise to greet me. "Look who it is . . . Emperor Constantine."

I moved into the seat across from him, relaxed against the metal back of the chair, and rested one ankle on the opposite knee, the most relaxed I'd ever been in his presence, because he wasn't my boss anymore.

Technically, I was his boss now. "Con is fine."

"Wow, so humble." He smiled, then gestured for the waiter to run over like an obedient dog. "A drink for my friend."

"An old-fashioned is fine."

"Right to the good shit," Tommaso said in approval.

The waiter brought the drink and left. Didn't ask if we wanted to order, like he knew this was a business meeting.

"So how's business been?" I asked.

"Same. Bodhi got taken out."

"Oh damn. What happened?"

"Friendly fire."

"Who shot him?" I asked, my eyebrow raised.

"A new kid. Had to put him out to pasture. Can't have a moron like that on the payroll."

"Yeah." I would have just fired him, but I wasn't around to make that decision.

"Look, Con. I've already heard about the initiatives you've been implementing. The tariffs we have to pay and the rules we have to follow to be compliant with your regime. And I think you know exactly what my stance is on the matter."

Tommaso had been more than a boss to me, a friend, but that familial comfort between us was displaced by tension. Now we sat on opposite sides of the table, two different players in a deal.

"You know we're already compliant with your regulations. We've never dabbled in the violent shit you're worried about. You know how much we love pussy, so women have never been our victims."

"I wouldn't have worked for you otherwise."

"Exactly," he said. "But if you think I'm paying you ten percent, you've got another thing coming."

I smirked. "I knew you'd say that."

"Then you also know I'm fucking stubborn and I'm not going to change my mind."

"You know I can't play favorites."

"But you should honor loyalty. Con, you were nothing when you showed up in Palermo. Just a mama's boy who made good arancini in the kitchen of his family's restaurant. I made you into a man." He gestured toward me across the table. "This. This is all my doing."

"A little bit dramatized . . . but okay."

"And you remember what I did for you with Edric. I could have let you die, but I didn't."

"And you already made me pay for that with your ridiculous request to consider marrying your daughter."

"Well, I still think that's a small price after what I did for you."

I released a sigh. "If anyone finds out I've given you a free pass, it'll be hell."

"Then let's not tell anyone."

"I'm sure most people know Cosa Nostra are my roots. Might suspect it."

"You know how I'm a good liar, Con." He grabbed his wine and took a drink. "If they can't follow the money trail with their own eyes, they'll never know. And if someone becomes suspicious, we'll do the dance until they look the other way. Sounds good?"

"I have a better idea. I can't let you focus on your own interests here in Sicily but remain under the Roman Republic. So, you need to contribute, and if you don't want to do that monetarily, then I have something else for you to do."

He cocked his head. "I'm listening."

"A lot of people want me dead, and a lot more people are going to want me dead. My whole world is here in Taormina. My ma, my aunts, uncles, cousins, friends, everyone. Protect them, and I'll consider that your ten percent."

He stared me down across the table as he considered what I asked, taking his time processing it. After a minute or two, he finally gave a nod. "I think that's a fair compromise. We won't let you down, Con."

"Thanks, Tommaso."

"I'll never forget the way your mother cried at your brother's funeral. She's a good woman. And she makes a killer lasagna."

"She does," I said proudly.

"No one will touch a hair on her beautiful head. That's my promise to you, Emperor Constantine."

Chapter 10

Aurelia

When I watched the news, I saw the coverage of the Pantheon. Constantine and Rocco and their men were never shown, but I could tell it was their doing. Vladimir and his cronies who operated the black market transplant enterprise had been killed, and the others at the facility had been arrested.

A couple weeks ago, this would have freaked me out, but now I accepted it.

It came with the territory.

The last time I'd talked to Con, he came by the apartment afterward, fucked me like some kind of booty call, and then left.

I didn't mind that one bit. I didn't even have to get out of bed. All I did was lie there and get some fabulous dick and then went right back to sleep. It was great.

I worked on my laptop at my dining table, going through all the edits that needed to be cleaned up. I'd had a wedding last Saturday, and those were the worst because of the sheer number of photos I had to process. I considered charging more for those events just so I would get hired for them less often.

My phone lit up with a text from Constantine. In the neighborhood. Can I stop by?

Is this another dick delivery? 🍆

Would you like it to be?

Yes—always.

I was gonna take you to dinner . . . but that works too.

I smiled, then put the phone back down. I had hundreds of photos that needed to be edited, but now, all I could think of was the sexy man about to walk through my front door in a couple minutes.

He arrived ten minutes later, letting himself in because I left the front door unlocked. He commanded the room the second he stepped inside, a mammoth of a man, filling out his T-shirt with his hardness. His eyes did a little dance at the sight of me, similar to the way Medusa looked at him when he came home—like I was his whole world. "Hey, sweetheart."

"Hey." I rose to my feet, my cheeks warm from the flush that rippled through my body.

He scooped me up like he always did, and my body moved with his like it expected it. He carried me into my bedroom, laid me down on the queen bed, and after he undressed me, his big dick was inside me . . . and I was in heaven.

This was the position he always took me, his heavy body on top and doing all the work, while my only job was to fold and twist like a pretzel and just take it. Take his dick and come around it until he was finished.

He rolled off me, then immediately started to get dressed. "Hungry?"

I rolled onto my stomach and lay there. "And a little sleepy."

He gave my ass a playful smack. "Keep lying like that with your ass out and see what happens."

"Really gonna fuck me in the ass right now?"

He turned to me, his shirt in his hands, about to be yanked over his head. "Is that a challenge?"

I stared.

He stared back.

I decided not to call his bluff and got dressed.

~

He took me to a nice place close to the Pantheon, Armando al Pantheon. Our table was outside, so we had a view of the impressive monument. It would have been a beautiful sight—if the bodies weren't still hanging there.

It was a little chilly, so I wore tight jeans, boots, and a long-sleeved top with a deep cut in the front. If I were fully covered, he wouldn't care for that. Something needed to be on display, my tits or my ass. He was the opposite of a controlling guy who liked all the goods hidden away. If anything, he was proud.

And no one was going to fuck with me because then they'd have to fuck with him—and that just wasn't going to happen.

I tried not to stare at the bodies that moved slightly when a breeze came through. "You remind me of a cat who wants to show his owner the mouse he caught."

He grinned. "You thought I brought you here to show you that? Nah, I just like this place."

"How long are they going to stay up there?"

"Until it starts to smell." He got the attention of the waiter and ordered wine and an appetizer for us to share, which told me he was pretty hungry because he usually just waited for the main course.

The waiter brought the wine, and Constantine took a big drink before he stared at me again. "What are you in the mood for, sweetheart?"

I looked at the menu. "There's a spicy pasta that looks interesting. What about you?"

"I usually get the chicken."

"Not the steak?" I teased.

He gave a slight smile. "It's their popular dish here. Pretty damn good."

"Then I'll try a piece."

When the waiter returned with the bruschetta, Constantine ordered for the both of us.

I thought I would be too disgusted by the dead men hanging from the Pantheon to have an appetite, but it didn't bother me much. Guess I was used to being the girlfriend of a violent crime-lord emperor.

I took a piece of bruschetta and had a couple bites.

He finished his in a single bite, then stared at me the rest of the time, just watching me eat like it was as entertaining as a football match. "So, the dick delivery didn't bother you?"

"No," I said with a laugh. "My door is *always* open."

A handsome smirk moved over his face. "It'd be nice if you were there every night I came home."

"Yeah, wouldn't that be nice." There were four pieces of the bruschetta, so I took another one, the olive oil and the tomatoes so scrumptious. I hadn't eaten much today. Didn't have any groceries in the kitchen, and I'd been stuck to my computer most of the time.

"It would be nice," he said. "So how about you move in with me?"

I'd just gotten the last bite into my mouth when he asked me a question I hadn't anticipated whatsoever. It was an awkward exchange because my mouth was full and I desperately tried to get it down.

All the while, he just grinned wider and wider like this was hilarious.

I finally swallowed. "Are you serious?"

"I'm always serious." He took a drink of his wine.

"Just to make booty calls more convenient?"

"Come on, that's not the *only* reason." He wore the most handsome smile, a grin that lit up his entire face, making him irresistible. "It's a *big* reason, sure."

"Constantine, I can't tell if you're joking."

"I'm not joking." He turned serious and dropped his smile. "I planned on asking you tonight before the dick-delivery jokes. This relationship is pretty fucking serious now, and I want you home with me. I don't have my guys watching you—as per your request—and that's just not working for me anymore."

"You can have your guys watch me if that makes you feel better."

"I want you to live with me. I want you in my bed. I want you there with me always."

I'd literally met him six weeks ago—and now he wanted me to live with him. The craziest thing about it? *I wanted to say yes.* Wanted to jump headfirst into this man's ocean. My apartment was fine when I moved in, but now I felt out of place whenever I was there . . . like it wasn't home.

"I know it's fast—"

"Yes." I should have second-guessed Enzo a million times and I never did, but I knew I shouldn't second-guess Constantine ever. Was it too fast? Yes. Was this fucking crazy? Yes. But I didn't have one foot out the door anymore. I'd put all my chips on Constantine the moment I got him back. "I want to live with you."

The grin that stretched over his lips . . . to die for.

"I hate my apartment anyway."

There was a twinkle in his eyes, a warmth that rivaled the summer heat in August. There was a softness there too, a masculine gentleness he seemed to show only me. He rubbed his jawline with his fingers like he wanted to map the smile that seemed permanently carved into his mouth. "Attagirl."

~

I packed a bag, and he took me to his place afterward. Medusa greeted us when we walked inside, and as always, Constantine stopped everything he was doing to give her a rubdown and a kiss on the head.

I loved seeing him with her. I'd heard that you could judge a person's character based on how they treated animals—and that meant Constantine had a heart of gold. She was a big dog to share our bed, but I'd already formed a connection with her the second our eyes met, so I didn't mind.

I carried my bag to his closet, and when I came out, Medusa had already jumped on the bed. "I guess I should introduce you to my friends."

"Damn right you should."

"But you're going to have to tone down the emperor thing."

He chuckled. "What do they think I do?"

"Personal security, like what you said in Taormina."

"Why not just tell them the truth?"

"Well, they'd probably think I was lying. And if they believed me, they'd probably be terrified."

"Whatever you want to do, sweetheart." He started to undress, more of his hard body and black ink revealed as he got undressed. I'd never cared for tattoos either way, but his were absolutely gorgeous against his skin.

He tossed his clothes aside, then got into bed.

Medusa methodically got in the middle to make sure she kept us apart.

"Baby girl, sleep on the couch tonight." He spoke to her like she could understand what he said.

She kept her chin on the top of her paws.

"Baby girl." He deepened his tone. "Mommy and Daddy need their alone time."

She released a quick sigh before she left the bed and jumped on the couch.

"Wow . . . she understood you."

"It's not the first time I've had to ask." He pulled back the sheets and patted the bed beside him. "Now get that fine ass over here."

I undressed down to my thong and one of his T-shirts and got into bed.

Like an animal, he was all over me, grabbing on to me and pulling me hard. He released a growl against my collarbone before he kissed my neck, before his big hand pulled my little thong free. Like he hadn't taken me before dinner, he moved over me and in me, sealing his dick in my airtight vault. "Fuck, sweetheart . . ."

Constantine's driver, Roberto, pulled over outside the restaurant so we could hop out.

"Nervous?" I asked as he took my hand.

"No," he said with a smirk. "Should I be?"

"Well, I'd be."

"I'm good, sweetheart." He continued to smile as he opened the door for me.

We walked inside, and I found my friends seated together at the table. It was Cindy, Bethany, and Danielle. Cindy still wasn't herself since Timothée had left . . . at least, that's what she believed. I'd known Bethany since secondary school, and Danielle was another photographer I'd met in the business.

And I swore—all of their jaws dropped.

Their eyes were glued to him as he came closer.

Utterly transfixed by his beauty, they just stared like morons.

"Constantine," I said, even though he clearly didn't need an introduction.

"Almighty God," Bethany said under her breath but loud enough for everyone to hear.

"That's Bethany," I said as he shook her hand. "And then Cindy . . . and Danielle."

"Nice to meet you all," Constantine said with that smug grin, fully aware of their rapt attention. Then he pulled out the chair for me, and once we sat down, his hand immediately moved to my thigh under the table.

The three of them continued to stare.

"Guys, I already showed you his picture," I said, wanting the drooling to stop.

"But we thought you did something with AI," Danielle said.

"Or you took another guy's picture," Bethany said.

"Thanks," I said sarcastically. "I know he's out of my league, but he's real."

"Come on, sweetheart." He gave my thigh a squeeze under the table. "Look at you."

My friends stared at him, then stared at me, probably completely beside themselves that this man was treating me like a queen. I was beside myself every single day because I couldn't believe it either.

After a long bout of silence with lots of staring, Danielle spoke. "So . . . do you have a brother?"

He smirked. "A sister."

"You know what," Danielle said, "I can make that work."

Constantine left the table when he got a phone call. He stepped outside to take it.

"Sweet baby Jesus," Bethany said. "You're the luckiest bitch alive."

"I know," I said. "But I also wonder if it's karma . . . after Enzo." Maybe the universe felt bad for what had happened to me and decided to send something good my way. Good . . . as in unbelievably good.

"Then I pray some man cheats on me." Bethany put her hands together and said a quick prayer under her breath. "Please, please cheat on me . . ."

"Speaking of worthless cheaters," Danielle said. "I'm pretty sure Enzo and Luna aren't together anymore."

"What makes you say that?" I asked. It'd been a clean break with Enzo and me. We didn't have any mutual friends. He kept his friends, and I kept mine. So it wasn't like anyone kept in touch.

"The stuff he's posting," she said. "I'm not sure if he knows I still follow him or if he *wants* me to know he's single so I'll tell you, but he's alone in all his pictures. He'll take a picture of a coffee cup at a café or himself alone on a hike. Sometimes him with his friends, but Luna isn't there."

That information made me feel nothing—and it felt so fucking nice. I didn't care either way. Didn't care if they broke up or got married. It'd only been six weeks, but it felt like six months. "He came by the apartment and told me he'd made a mistake with Luna . . . and he was sorry."

"Uh, why didn't you mention this piping-hot tea?" Bethany demanded.

I shrugged. "I don't know. Guess I forgot?" Guess I just didn't care? "Wasn't sure if he'd try to make it work since I wasn't an option or it just wasn't going to work out, no matter what. Maybe she was the one who left. I don't know."

"What an idiot," Danielle said. "Blew up his entire life for some married woman with two kids . . . and once reality set in, he tried to run. He abandoned you and then tried to abandon her. Such a worthless scumbag."

I shrugged. "Yeah, guess so."

"Guess so?" Danielle asked. "Shouldn't you be more upset about this? Or at least happy? Spiteful? Smug?"

"Have you seen the man I brought in here?" I looked over my shoulder and saw him in the window, still talking on the phone. "This is the man in my bed, and you ask why I'm not upset about Enzo?" I gave a laugh as I waved off their comments. "Yeah, I'm good. Constantine actually asked me to move in with him."

"Oh really?" Cindy asked. "What are you going to say?"

"Already said yes. I know it's been like six weeks, but I was with Enzo for two years and he left me for a married woman. So . . . fuck it."

"Sorry about that phone call," Constantine said when we got home. "I had to take it."

"Didn't bother me. Gave us time to talk about you." I smiled before I moved to the couch to slip off my heels. Medusa jumped on the couch next to me the second I sat down and put her paw on my thigh.

"Yeah?" He slipped off his watch and put it in his closet before he came back out, already shirtless. "Good things, I hope."

"Oh, *definitely* good things. Told them I'm moving in with you."

"Yeah?" He smiled like my commitment to the decision made him happy.

"I told them I know it's fast, but I just don't care." I put my heels to the side, then petted Medusa for a while, feeling bad for getting up when she'd just jumped up to be with me. I rubbed her behind her ears, and her eyes softened like that was her favorite spot. "They said it seems like Enzo and Luna broke up, based on the stuff he posts."

"Didn't see that coming a kilometer away." He dropped his jeans and stood in just his boxers, his legs muscular with dark hair over his thighs and calves. His chest and stomach were mostly free of hair except for a few curls right in the center of his sternum. "How do you feel about it?"

"I don't care either way. It's hard to believe I was so upset about the whole thing six weeks ago." Now I had a new life and a new man and a dog . . . and I didn't know who that woman used to be. I didn't understand why she'd settled for so little. Why she'd cried over a man who was vastly inferior to Constantine in every way.

Constantine walked over and took the seat beside me, leaving Medusa on the other side. Even though I hadn't said anything to relay my emotion or my gratitude or relief, he seemed to know it was there. "Because now you're the woman you were always meant to be—*my woman*."

Chapter 11

AURELIA

I packed up my things in my apartment, which were mostly just my clothes and other belongings. None of the furniture was mine, and I didn't feel remotely sentimental about parting with it. This had been a refuge when Enzo kicked me out of my own home and had someone replace me, so I would always be grateful for that. It was the start of something new, when Constantine came into my life and pushed my walls down until he made his way in. But I was ready to move on.

Ready to move in with Constantine.

A part of me worried that moving in with him too quickly might ruin what we had, because from what I'd gathered, he'd never lived with a woman before. Maybe my constant presence would be too much. Maybe the proximity would ruin the magic. But I trusted Constantine wouldn't have asked unless I was truly welcome there.

I was organizing a few things in a box when I got a text message from Armand.

Hey, Aurelia. How are things?

Armand was Enzo's best friend, so this was weird. The more time I was around Constantine, the less of a filter I had. I just spoke my mind and cut through the bullshit. We've been broken up for six weeks, so why the fuck are you texting me now? I liked Armand when Enzo and I were together, but once that relationship was over, so was the friendship. A harsh reality, but that was just how it went.

I know I should have texted you before.

Yeah, probably. Peace out.

I've been meaning to reach out to you for a while, but it was complicated. Could we meet for a cup of coffee?

Nah.

Please, Aurelia. I wouldn't ask if it weren't important.

I'm not your friend, Armand.

I know it seemed that way, but that's never been the case. I've worried about you this entire time, and Enzo and I aren't even friends anymore.

Whoa, that was news to me.

Come on. A cup of coffee. Please.

I should just ignore his messages, but the fact that they weren't friends anymore did intrigue me. Fine. I've got an hour, but then I've got to get back to packing.

Packing? You're moving again?

Yep. Moving in with my ridiculously hot boyfriend.

I met Armand at the café. I went ahead and ordered my coffee and took a seat, because like hell was I gonna wait for him. He hadn't done anything to me, but he must have known that Enzo was sneaking around behind my back and chose to be loyal to him—which meant he was no friend of mine.

Armand arrived, and instead of ordering something inside, he immediately took the seat across from me.

I was glad he didn't try to hug me.

I was in a T-shirt and shorts with sneakers, and sunglasses on my nose, even though the sun wasn't directly in my face. I took a drink of my coffee, then returned it to the saucer. "Long time no see, huh?"

"Yeah." He had the humility to look down as he released a sigh. "I knew about Luna for a couple of months before you broke up—"

"Before he left me for her—in Taormina—and kicked me out of our apartment."

"Yeah." At least he admitted it. "I just wanted you to know I gave him shit about it the entire time. Told him he was making the biggest mistake of his life and he should end it while he still had a chance to salvage his relationship with you. He didn't listen, obviously. It was like he was bewitched or something."

"Damn, she must have a nice pussy."

His eyes widened at what I said.

Now I really did sound like Constantine.

"Honestly, I don't know what he ever saw in her."

"So you met her?"

"I stopped by the apartment to return something, and she was there . . . it was awkward."

"Where was I?"

"At work."

"Ugh, that's fucking disgusting."

"I know, I know. He and I caught up later, and he told me what was going on. And I hated him for putting me in this position. Because we all loved you, still do, and then we were wrapped up in this lie. We felt like shit."

"But not shitty enough to tell me."

"Yeah, I regret that."

"Actually, I'm glad you didn't." Because I wouldn't have ended up in Taormina and met Constantine. "That was where I met him."

"The guy you're moving in with?"

"Yeah."

"It's probably not my place to say, but is this just a rebound situation?"

"Nope, it's definitely not." I grabbed my phone. "Let me show you what this hunk of a man looks like." When I unlocked my phone, Constantine texted me.

Is he bothering you?

My heart gave a jerk when I read that message, wondering if he was nearby or the men who tailed me day and night had informed him of my lunchtime coffee date. But I was glad he'd learned from his past mistakes and didn't bombard me and bark at Armand until he left. No, he's an old friend.

Constantine didn't text me again.

I pulled up one of Constantine's pictures and showed Armand. "Look at this man."

Armand glanced at the screen before he looked at me again. "I mean, he's not bad to look at."

"Oh, come on. You know he's a high-quality piece of man meat." I put the phone aside. "You can be straight and still recognize it."

"Well, I'm happy for you."

"Thanks. When Enzo left me, I was at my lowest point. But now I realize that needed to happen for me to find where I really belong. I know I've given you a hard time up until this point, but there's really no hard feelings between us."

"Yeah?"

"Yeah," I said with a nod. "It's complicated when your best friend is a cheating asshole. If one of my friends did that, I'm not sure what I'd do either. Feel like shit for the guy getting cheated on but afraid to destroy your friendship—and it's a choice you shouldn't have to make in the first place."

"That's exactly how I feel about it."

"Then why aren't you friends anymore?"

He shrugged. "I know what he does in his personal life and in his business to an extent, but I just didn't look at him the same after that. I told him this was all a mistake, and he snapped at me and said some things he couldn't take back. I just didn't know him anymore, so after he moved in with Luna, I kinda just dropped him. Some of the other guys did too."

"Damn." I actually felt a little bad for Enzo. Just a *little*, though. "I heard he and Luna broke up."

"Really?" he asked, both eyebrows elevated like this was really a surprise.

I shrugged. "The girls stalk his socials. He's been posting a lot of pictures of himself alone. And he did stop by my place a couple weeks ago and told me it was a mistake, and he was sorry about the whole thing. So yeah, I'm not surprised it ended."

"Bet that felt good."

"Eh, not really," I said. "I've moved on."

"This guy sounds like the real deal."

"Oh, he is. His name is Constantine."

Now that the conversation seemed finished, he sat there awkwardly, glancing at the street and the motorbikes that passed before he looked at me again. "I know this is kinda weird, but I'm gonna go for it anyway . . . what do you think about us being friends?"

"Really?" I couldn't help but smile.

"Yeah. We all thought you were the coolest chick ever."

Something about that compliment made my heart squeeze. Enzo had made me feel so unwanted for so long, and now I really knew it was his problem and not mine. That even people in his camp truly cared for me. That I wasn't as worthless and replaceable as he made it seem.

"I honestly wondered if Enzo had a brain tumor because of how ludicrous it was."

"I still don't know what happened."

"She was his superior and complained about her marriage. They had chemistry, and he just got lost in the forbidden aspect of it all, I guess. Why it wasn't just a onetime fuckup is beyond me—not that that should have happened either."

"Yeah."

"We all make mistakes, I get that. I wouldn't have judged him if that was all it was. But lying to you for, what? *Months?* Keeping you on the hook while also exploring this other relationship . . . it was just sickening. I kinda hate him for making me complicit in the bullshit."

All the animosity I had was completely gone. I felt like I got a piece of myself back. "Yes, we can be friends."

"Yeah?" he asked with a smile. "We're all going out on Friday night. You wanna come?"

"Depends. Can I bring Constantine?"

"Of course."

"You seeing anybody?"

"I was for a while, but it kinda just fizzled out," he said. "Does Constantine have a sister?"

"He does and she's beautiful, but she lives in Taormina."

"Damn."

"Might be for the best, because you wouldn't want to date any of his relatives."

"Why?"

Because he's kinda psycho . . . *sometimes.* "He's just a bit protective, is all."

~

Instead of me driving my motorbike around, Constantine's driver chauffeured me wherever I needed to go. After I finished my lunch with Armand, he took me back to my apartment, and I continued to pack up my stuff for another couple of hours.

When I was done, the driver came upstairs and loaded it into the back of the Range Rover, and then he drove me across the city, where I could meet my client for a sunset shoot. They were family portraits, probably to be used in an annual Christmas card. Once I was done there, the driver took me back to Constantine's place.

It was a little strange to be driven everywhere, but it was nice not to fight traffic or squeeze my motorbike between cars or worry about parking at every stop. I just hopped out of the back seat, and the driver continued on.

He drove me behind the large gates to Constantine's estate, and when we pulled around the fountain, the security guys opened the back and began unloading everything. In the distance, at different spots on the property, I could see the armed guys carrying machine guns. Every corner was guarded by a dozen of them. There weren't any in the house—as far as I knew—so that was a relief.

Because the men weren't allowed in Constantine's private corridor, they placed everything to the side outside the mahogany doors. It wasn't much, just a dozen boxes of my whole life packed up.

It'd been a long day, so I didn't care about putting everything away tonight. I headed into the corridor with my sight set on the double gold doors, but then I heard Constantine's voice come from the study.

"The maximum extension for tariffs is seven days—with twenty percent interest. You already know this, so why are you asking me?" There was a pause as he listened, but then a moment later, he continued. "I don't give an exception to anyone, not a single person for a single reason, so take the extension with interest or don't." He seemed to hang up, because it went silent.

Medusa must have heard my footsteps because she left the study and moved into the hallway, beelining right for me. She ran toward me, did a little jump in the middle of it, and then came right up to me.

I got down on one knee exactly as Constantine did and gave her a good rubdown. "Hey, honey. Missed you too."

When Constantine heard me, he left his desk and stepped into the corridor, wearing nothing but gray sweatpants.

Oh mother of God.

Enormous and cut with the pants low on his hips, he was utterly delicious. With the dark ink on his beautiful skin, the shadows between the different segments of his thick muscles, he was like a mixture of a bull and a man.

And he was mine.

Then he smiled, and if I had been wearing a dress instead of jeans, my panties would have slid right off. "Hey, sweetheart."

It was the little things he did that made me feel special. Like the fact that he left his desk and came to me all the way in the hallway. He always made an effort, showed his enthusiasm, made my importance known. "Hey."

I got to my feet and moved over to him.

His hands were on my ass as his lips feasted on my mouth, feeling me up right off the bat. When he finally let me take a breath, he stepped back and headed back into his office. "Just finishing up some calls, then we'll have dinner."

"Okay." Medusa and I followed him into his study, the most beautiful room in the house, in my opinion. But then again, I'd only seen a fraction of the place. "Are we having dinner in your room?"

He sat behind the desk. "*Our* room. And yes, unless you have something else in mind."

"Nope. Just want to make sure that's what you'll be wearing."

A ghost of a smile moved over his lips before he grabbed his phone. "And what will you be wearing, sweetheart?"

~

We didn't make it to dinner. Once he stepped into the bedroom, he took me on the edge of the bed and filled me with two loads back-to-back. It was for the best, because I wouldn't have been able to enjoy my food if I hadn't rubbed one out beforehand.

This man turned me into a horny teenager.

Dinner was served, and we ate together at the table in his private dining room. Medusa was given her dinner at the same time, so she ate out of her bowl on the raised silver tray that was set about a foot from the floor so she didn't have to bend her head so low to eat.

Spoiled dog.

Our dinner was salmon, rice, and white asparagus.

"No steak tonight?" I teased.

"I told Elio to substitute fish a couple nights a week."

"This is the best salmon I've ever had. You don't like it?"

"Let's just say . . . it's not steak."

I chuckled, then continued to eat.

He ate with his arms on the table, the muscles bulging even when he was relaxed. I noticed he ate most of his calories during the day, but at night, he cut his portions way back. He had a big breakfast and a heavy lunch, and then another lunch before dinner. Which made perfect sense, considering the sheer amount of muscle attached to his bones. "Tell me about your friend." His tone wasn't accusatory, so there didn't seem to be a hint of jealousy there.

"His name is Armand. He's actually Enzo's best friend . . . or he *was*."

"Then why did you have coffee with him?"

"At first, I was kind of a bitch and dismissed him."

"Cutting someone off doesn't make you a bitch."

"Well, he just wanted to apologize for not telling me about Luna. The apology seemed sincere. He said he cut Enzo out of his life because he just couldn't stand what he'd done to me. Said he didn't want a friend like that."

Constantine gave a nod. "You are the company you keep."

"He said the other guys had cut Enzo out too. Then he asked if we could be friends."

He took another bite of the salmon and sat back in the chair as he finished it. "Not to sound like a dick here, but does he actually want to be friends? Or does he want a chance to take his best friend's girl?"

"He actually wants to be friends," I said with a chuckle. "I told him about you right at the start of the conversation. Showed him your picture and everything because I wanted him to see how hot you are."

"Is he gay?"

"No. But come on, any straight man would know you're hot."

That handsome smirk moved onto his lips.

"You'd be the first one to say Rocco is hot."

"He is hot," Constantine said automatically.

"See?" I said. "I wanted him to know I'm doing just *fine*. He said he was happy for me and asked if we could be friends. That he was bummed that Enzo fucked it up because they all really liked me, which is really sweet. Then he asked if I wanted to hang out with him and the guys on Friday night."

"And what did you say?"

"I said yes and asked if I could bring you. He said yes," I said. "I'm so over that relationship, but it's really nice to know that I mattered to some people, even if I didn't matter to Enzo."

Constantine digested all that information for a while before he gave a nod. "Where are we going?"

Prologue IX

Constantine

The plane landed in Catania, and the driver picked me up. It was an hour's drive from the airport to Taormina. I'd been the emperor of the Roman Republic for two years now, and that time had flashed before my eyes. I had to hire a crew to serve me, had to build the infrastructure, had to come in hard and fast so all the assholes knew I was a force to be reckoned with.

As a result, I hadn't been home in two years.

I should have visited more, should have been there for my mom while she spent the last years grieving, but I'd been grieving too. And staying busy was the way I coped. My endgame was always the death of the Skull King, but I had to play it right.

I agreed to stay with my mom even though I would have preferred my own space, but I knew it meant a lot to her to have me there instead of at a hotel, so I let her have her way. The driver dropped me off outside my childhood home, and I carried my bag over my shoulder before I knocked on the door.

I heard a muffled scream from inside the house. She was probably working in the kitchen to make me all my favorite meals. I wouldn't be surprised if she dropped whatever she was holding when she heard me at the door.

A minute later, she opened it and screamed. "My boy!" She launched into me and squeezed me hard, her face buried in my chest. For a petite woman, she had serious strength, and she literally squeezed the air out of my lungs.

"Ma, can't breathe . . ."

She released me, then cupped my cheeks, looking up at me with the eyes of a puppy. "Oh, my son . . ." But then her eyes changed as she looked me over. She took a step back, examining me with a critical eye, looking at me from head to toe. "You're—you're so *big*."

Nearly a hundred pounds of muscle bigger. I'd hired a nutritionist and a chef and hit the gym twice a day—no exceptions. Didn't matter if it was my day off or if it was a holiday, I still hit the weights.

I looked forward to the day Darius and I crossed paths.

I came into the house and dropped my bag in the entryway. "Been working out."

"And I was worried you wouldn't be eating enough."

"Nope, definitely been eating, Ma."

"You're so sexy. Big, sexy man."

"Ma."

She moved into me again and hugged me tightly. "Oh, I'm so happy my baby is home. You have no idea how much—" Her voice broke, and she started to cry, cry like she'd been holding it in for a long time. "How much I missed you."

~

She put five platters of food in front of me. An entire pan of meat lasagna, arancini, a seafood platter with red shrimp, octopus, and fried calamari, an entire pizza, and then, of course, the cannoli.

No way in hell could I eat all this. "Everything looks good. Thanks, Ma."

She sat across from me with her coffee, fully prepared to just sit there and watch me eat.

I purposely hadn't eaten anything at all that day because I'd known this was coming. I served a little bit of everything onto my plate and started to eat.

"How are things in Rome?" she asked.

"Good. Busy."

She didn't ask for specifics, like she'd rather not know.

"I wasn't sure if you were going to come. Isabella told me you RSVP'd, but I still wasn't sure."

Isabella was getting married tomorrow, and she'd invited me to come. I wasn't sure if she actually wanted me there or not. It was complicated, a damned-if-you-do, damned-if-you-don't kind of situation. My mother would have been pissed if I hadn't been invited, but she also pitied me for being obligated to go. "Wouldn't miss it." I took a few bites of the food, my mother's home cooking that I missed often, but the subject made me lose my appetite.

My mom continued to study me, her sharp gaze piercing my flesh. "You okay, baby?"

I nodded. "Yeah, Ma."

Her eyes continued to cut into me deep.

"If you ever really love someone, you always love them. So, I guess . . . it kinda hurts." It'd been six years since we'd broken up. I'd been with a lot of other women, but no one who made me feel the way she did. No one who made me want to settle down. No one who made me . . . feel something.

I was close with my mom, but I didn't share every thought and feeling that came into my heart. But when I really felt lost and couldn't find my way back, I turned to her. "Sometimes I wonder if I made the right decision. Maybe I was too hard on her. Maybe I was too harsh. Maybe I should have given her another chance." I would have been married for years, stayed in Taormina, and Edric wouldn't have joined Cosa Nostra and would still be alive. I'd probably have a couple of kids by now.

One shitty night had drastically changed our lives forever.

My mom released a quiet breath and brought her hands together. "You made the right decision, Constantine."

My eyes looked at the platter of food that would take me days to eat. And of course, she'd make me take leftovers, even though that would be a nightmare on a plane. "You think so?"

"I know so."

My eyes lifted to hers again.

"Because when you meet the one, you won't have to wonder. You'll know with every fiber of your being that you can't live without her. You'll know that you would burn down the entire world in her name just because she asked you to. I love Isabella, but I know she's not your person, Constantine. You wouldn't have lived without her these last six years if that were the case."

Prologue X

Constantine

I took a week off from work and headed to Taormina. I'd been making more of an effort to visit over the last two years. It'd been six years since Edric had died, and my mother finally seemed to be in a better place. The pain of losing a son would never go away, but at least now it was manageable. She'd taken some time away from the restaurant, but now she was back in the office every day, running her little empire in Taormina.

I was happy to see that.

I was in a better place too—but revenge didn't sleep.

I would kill Darius—someday.

When I came for a visit, I stayed in a hotel now. I told my mother I needed my space, and she let me have my way. Now that she wasn't utterly heartbroken, she was okay being alone at the house.

I hung out with my friends and cousins, hitting the beach and the town, feeling right at home. I spent the day jumping off the rock with my cousin Antonio and other friends, taking turns doing backflips and belly flops, acting like kids when we were grown-ass men.

When we made it back to the beach, we ordered drinks and pizza and ate in our cabana.

"What's going on in Rome?" Antonio asked.

"Work. That's about it," I said before taking a bite of the mortadella pizza with pistachio pesto.

"Done with Cosa Nostra?"

"We keep in touch, but I do my own thing now." My occupation was an open secret. Everyone kind of knew about it, but no one asked too many questions. They knew my life had changed, that I had a lot of money now, based on my home and my clothes and my own plane, but no one treated me differently.

That meant a lot to me.

"Seeing anyone?" he asked.

I shook my head. "Not seriously, no." My life was a carousel of women, different ones hopping on while old ones hopped off. I didn't have to work for it either. It just happened. I was fit like a bull, rich like a billionaire, and attractive like a celebrity, so I really didn't have to do anything. But I never shared that information. Didn't want to brag.

The beach was full of locals and tourists, all enjoying the sun and the waves. The bar was packed with people, and the weather was perfect, without a cloud in the sky. Antonio watched the TV in the cabana for a while.

Francesco nudged him in the side. "Tell him about Isabella," he said under his breath so I wouldn't hear.

But I did. "Tell me what?" I asked in a normal voice.

Antonio tossed his slice of pizza back into the box then wiped his hands clean on the napkins. "She's getting a divorce."

"What?" I blurted. She got married two years ago. I didn't know the guy, only saw them together at the wedding, but they seemed happy. Isabella and I didn't talk at all at the wedding. I kept my distance out of respect. Sometimes when we were close together, that tension was still there, and the last thing I wanted was to make her special day complicated. I assumed she didn't feel that way about me anymore, but it was still complicated. "What the hell happened?"

"She caught him fooling around on her."

I went absolutely still at that information. "What the fuck did you just say?"

"Some girl he works with at the bank," Antonio said. "Isabella found their texts and then tailed him one day. Caught him red handed."

"Yeah, fucking asshole," Francesco said. "Hasn't come around since."

"She moved back in with her mom," Antonio said.

"When did this happen?" I asked.

"Couple weeks ago," Francesco said. "I'm surprised your mom didn't mention."

Oh, I know exactly why she didn't mention it.

My appetite was done for, and the beach day was ruined. I got up and pulled on my shirt.

"What are you doing?" Antonio asked.

I started to walk out of the cabana. "I've gotta check on her."

Her family owned Levante Gelato Artigianale, one of the most famous spots in Taormina for gelato, so when I called and texted and got no reply, I assumed she was there. I headed down the main street until the very end where it was located.

Her family was like family to me, and my family was like family to her, so when I walked in, I headed straight to the back instead of taking up the worker's time. I went past the storage shelves to the office in the rear. I could see her through the open door, working on her laptop, hair thrown up in a bun like she didn't care.

That wasn't like her.

I stopped in the doorway. Whatever she was working on had so much of her focus she hadn't heard me. "Hey."

She flinched at my voice, did a double take, and then released a sigh.

Her phone was right there, so she'd chosen to ignore me.

"Scared the shit out of me, Con."

A chair was positioned against the wall, so I pulled it up next to her desk. "You okay?"

She took a breath, and then she blinked several times in a row, like she wasn't the least bit okay. All she could muster was a shake of her head.

My hand reached for hers.

She took it like it was a life raft. "The worst two weeks of my life."

"Yeah."

She sniffed, and then her eyes started to flood with tears. "He's such a piece of shit . . . I can't believe he did this to me."

"Men suck," I said honestly. "Ain't shit."

She gave a pained chuckle like it was a joke.

"I'm serious."

"I know you are." She sniffed again. "And that's why I love you, Con." She pulled her hand away from mine and wiped her tears, patting the corners of her eyes dry. "I didn't see it coming. We'd been married for only two years, a hot piece of ass came along . . . and that's all it took."

"You aren't supposed to see it coming—because it shouldn't come at all."

"I'm just glad it happened before we had kids. Then I'd be stuck."

"You wouldn't be stuck."

"I wouldn't be married to him, but I'd have to share my kids with him forever."

"Yeah."

She stared at the corner of the desk.

"Why didn't you take my call?"

"Because . . ."

I waited for her to say more, but she never did. "Because why?" I pressed.

"Because I deserve this for what happened with Edric. Karma is real, and she served justice."

It was the most ludicrous thing that had ever come out of her mouth. "Issy, look at me."

"No." She kept her eyes on the desk, the tears bubbling again.

"Issy."

The tears came free before she lifted her chin and looked at me.

"You did *not* deserve this. No one does."

The tears were like slow rivers that traveled down her cheeks.

"The situations aren't even comparable, Issy. And even if they were, I still wouldn't want this to happen to you."

She gave in to a quick burst of tears. "Because you're such a good guy, and I hate myself every day for losing you."

"Issy . . ."

She dropped her face into her hands so she could cry with some sort of privacy.

And I just had to listen to it.

"You never would have done this to me," she said between the breaks in her fingertips. "You never would have hurt me. And now look at me. Divorced before I'm thirty. Living eight years in the past because that's the last time I was truly happy."

"Issy," I said gently. "I know it's hard right now, but I promise you'll be happy again someday. This is a bump in the road, not the end of your story. You'll remarry, and he will be the one you were supposed to be with. And you'll have kids, and he'll never hurt you. And you'll wonder why you had to wait so long to find him."

"Con, I want you." She dropped her hands, her cheeks red, her eyes puffy. "It's always been you. It'll always be you. It's been eight fucking years, and I can't escape you. Guys have come and gone, but you're the one who stays in my heart. You'll always be the one who got away."

Now I was the one who avoided her gaze. "You're just upset right now—"

"I'm upset that one stupid mistake cost us our happiness. One stupid mistake has kept us apart for almost a decade. Can you look me in the eye and tell me you've loved anyone since? Or have ever come close?"

My eyes stayed on the desk.

"Con."

"No, I haven't." For the first few years, the women were a distraction from my heartache. Then they turned into a playground. Then they turned into a blur of good sex but meaningless nights. No one ever meant a damn thing to me, and I didn't know why. Even when I was ready to be with someone, there was no one.

"Then why not?" she asked through her tears. "Why can't you just give me another chance? You really think I would do something like that again? I was a twenty-one-year-old girl who made a mistake—"

"Issy, we can't keep rehashing this conversation like it's still on the table."

"But why is it not on the table?"

"Because."

"Because why?"

"Because I meant what I said before." That she wasn't the one. But I didn't want to say the words. Didn't want to cut her down even more. Didn't want to make a difficult time wholly unbearable.

She looked away as if I'd slapped her.

I clenched my eyes shut, hating myself for saying what she didn't want to hear.

She was quiet for a long time, her tears fully stifled and eyes dry. "I'm tired of asking and begging, so I'm not going to do it anymore. But think about it, Con. Think about the love that's still here. The love we still have for each other after all this time."

I opened my eyes and looked at her again.

"You're always there for me, and I'm always there for you. That is not normal for two people who've gone their separate ways. That's not normal for people who wanted to spend their lives together."

I knocked on the door to the apartment.

It took a minute for him to answer. There were footsteps, and then the shift of the bolt out of the lock. Then he opened the door and stared at me, like it took him a moment to remember my face. "Constantine, right—"

I punched him so hard in the stomach, he fell to the floor, hand over his stomach, heaving like I'd knocked the life out of him.

"Get up." I stepped into his shitty apartment and shut the door behind me.

He continued to struggle to breathe.

"Get up." I grabbed him by the T-shirt and forced him up. I waited until he stood on his two feet before I shoved him hard into the wall. He bounced off like a fucking tennis ball, then collapsed again. "Fuck with my family, you fuck with me, asshole."

I was in my hotel room, sitting on the couch with the football game on. I'd ordered room service, had a stiff drink with dinner, but I didn't really care about the game. My mind was lost somewhere in the past, full of self-doubt.

Wondering if I'd been wrong all this time?

As if she was literally thinking the same thing at the same time, Isabella texted me. I'm in the lobby of your hotel . . . if you want to get a drink.

A flush of heat moved through me, setting my body on fire, burning me to the bone. It'd been a long time since anything had actually meant something. I'd met a lot of wonderful women who were smart and funny and endearing . . . and nothing.

I knew this was a bad idea—a really bad fucking idea.

But maybe one more night would finally put an end to this story. Maybe the closure would help put it behind me. Maybe a piece of me was still here, and that was why I couldn't move on with someone else. *One night—and then it's done.*

~

I intended to stay in Taormina longer, but after my night with Isabella, I knew I needed to leave. I grabbed my bags and left her there in the hotel. Then I caught my flight, headed home, and returned to reality.

When I took my phone off Airplane Mode, she'd blown it up with messages.

Sneak out first thing in the morning? Smooth . . .

And that's it? We're just never going to talk about it?

Con, I thought you were better than this.

I didn't reply, not when I was annoyed like this. I might say something hurtful.

When I got home, Rocco called. "Sorry to call when you're visiting family, but we've got a couple issues here in Rome."

"I'm home. Just got back." I spoke to him from the back seat as my driver took me to my villa.

"Oh? Thought you were there for another five days?"

"I was, but then some shit happened."

"Let me guess . . . Isabella."

"Right on the money."

"I'll swing by in a couple hours."

"Bye."

~

I still didn't text Isabella back.

Even when Rocco came by around dinnertime, I continued to ignore her.

We sat together on the outdoor patio while my staff served us dinner.

"Normally when you come home from Taormina, you're in a good mood." He grabbed the bottle of wine and refilled his glass.

"Yeah, not this time." My phone was on the table, and I saw Isabella's call come in from there.

I ignored it, then temporarily blocked her because I knew she would just call and call.

Rocco saw it. "Oh, this should be good."

I told him about Isabella's divorce, the fact that I beat her ex unconscious in his apartment and left him there, and then our hookup.

Rocco gave a slow nod. "And you're ignoring her now because . . . ?"

"I left without saying goodbye."

"That'll do it."

"I didn't mean to be a dick, but I told her it was a one-night thing, so . . ."

"And you think she believed that?"

"Guess not."

"And how do you feel? I know she's always been a big part of your life."

I took a breath, all the things I wanted to say popping into my head but never leaving my mouth. Then I let it out. "Shouldn't have happened. I fucked up."

"At least it gave you closure, right?"

"No, not really," I said honestly. "Just opened up old wounds—unnecessarily."

"I don't get it, Con. You obviously love this girl, but you won't be with her. I know she fucked up, but it's been eight years."

"I can't really explain it. It's complicated."

"Maybe she's calling because you put her ex in the hospital."

"Based on her texts, she doesn't know about that yet."

"Shit, maybe he's dead."

"Hope he is." Fucking asshole.

~

Later that night, I called her.

She answered before the first ring ended, like she'd been waiting.

I said nothing.

She said nothing.

I expected her to immediately start shouting and ripping into me, but that didn't happen.

She eventually sighed. "Um, I'm sorry I blew up your phone earlier."

An apology?

"I just . . . wasn't myself. Upset that I only had a piece of you when I wanted the whole thing."

"I told you it was just one time, Issy," I said gently.

"I know, I know. But fuck, I still love you." She said it more to herself than to me, full of sincere, unbridled emotion.

I said nothing.

"You put Will in the hospital . . . but still won't give me a chance."

So, she did know.

"Why, Con? Why do you do this to us?"

"Because I want a woman who knows me so well that she knows when my twin is impersonating me. I want a woman who runs to me with her problems instead of plotting to hide the truth. I want a woman who doesn't carry on an emotional affair in front of me like I'm too stupid to figure it out. Who takes advantage of unwavering trust. I want a woman who didn't drive my brother to Cosa Nostra and then further away to get himself killed. I want a woman who doesn't divide my family but makes it stronger. That's what I want, Isabella—and that's not you."

Prologue XI

Constantine

It'd been a year since I'd last seen Isabella.

We hadn't talked since I'd ripped her to pieces over the phone. She didn't say a word when I finished. Just hung up. I didn't mean to do it, but I fucking nuked our relationship—or what was left of it.

I blamed her for my brother's death, and even though I meant it with every fiber of my being, it was the most fucked-up thing I'd ever said. She didn't deserve it and I should apologize for it, but I didn't want to open the box that finally felt shut.

I returned to Taormina, nine years after Isabella and I broke up, and walked to Rosticceria Da Cristina after it opened for the day. I'd texted my mom after I checked into the hotel, and she told me she was at the office.

I walked inside and immediately caught up with the boys behind the counter. "My ma driving you crazy yet?"

"Only every day, man," Georgio said. "It's not even the high season yet, but it's already busy. Gets busier every damn day."

"Yeah, I know how that goes."

We continued to catch up, talking about the restaurant, sports, recent events on the island, the last eruption of Mount Etna. The second I showed my face, I knew it would make it back to Isabella. My mom would mention it to her mom, and since neither of them knew what happened last time I was here, they wouldn't hesitate to tell her.

I wasn't sure if it would provoke her or if she would continue to pretend I didn't exist.

Then I felt this stare on the side of my face, scalding like a hot pan and deep like a knife. I didn't even check my peripheral before I turned to look at who stared at me so hard through the window.

My eyes immediately locked with the green eyes the color of vines . . . with the sparkle of an emerald. There was something mesmerizing about them, something unique even though I'd seen green eyes a hundred times. Something within the color struck me . . . the longing . . . and the sadness.

My vision drew back and took in the rest of her, beautiful brown hair around her shoulders with a gold chain around her throat. She was dressed in just cutoff jean shorts and a deep-blue tank top with sneakers, but she was fucking gorgeous.

God fucking damn.

And she was alone.

She didn't look away right away, even when she'd been caught, as if she couldn't stop staring at me the way I couldn't stop staring at her. As if time stopped for both of us. Even though she was seated, I could tell she was tall, with long legs for days, every part of her body slender and toned like she was on her feet a lot.

"Con?"

"Hmm?" I kept my eyes on hers.

"Did you hear what I said?" Georgio said. "Your mom is thinking of opening a third location."

"She said what?" I turned back to him when the news caught me by the midsection. "She can barely keep up with the two."

He shrugged. "That's what she said. Look, I'll show you the plans." He headed to the office, and I followed behind with the others. He went to her desk, opening the folder that sat there. "She applied for a loan and everything."

I flipped through it, and while I was disturbed by my mother's idiotic business plan, I kept thinking about the woman outside.

What if she left and I didn't get a chance to talk to her?

What if I didn't even learn her name?

I shut the folder. "I'll talk to her about this. Make sure this gets canned." I walked out of the office and left them there.

"Con, where are you going?"

"I gotta take care of something real quick." I rounded the corner and came back to the front of the store. People were already there, waiting to order. I looked right past them and out the window to where the woman with the green eyes had been sitting.

But she was already gone.

~

A couple days later, I had dinner at my mother's house, then headed back to the hotel. I walked past the double doors and the valet outside, moving around the glass walls that surrounded the outdoor bar, and then headed to the indoor bar, where a pianist played in the corner. The lights were low, the bar was busy, and I found a table against the wall.

I texted Antonio. I'm at the bar if you want to meet up.

Cool. Be there in fifteen minutes.

I set down my phone, and the waiter came over to take my order. Then the strangest feeling came over me—the sense I was being watched. It was the same stare I'd felt days before, through a glass window, warm and purposeful. I didn't let myself get hopeful, knowing the chances of it being *her* were slim to none.

But I looked up—*and it was her.*

In a little black dress with seashells on the straps, her curtain of dark hair over one shoulder, her eyes smoky with the way she did her makeup.

I was fucking hypnotized.

Jesus Christ, those eyes . . . do shit to me.

And again, they looked sad. Intense, but sad. A little empty too.

It was the first time in my life when I felt paralyzed. Even face-to-face with the Skull King, I didn't hesitate. I stood my ground, thought quick on my feet, reacted with lightning speed. But with her . . . *I couldn't fucking think.*

The waiter dropped off my drink, but I didn't look away. She broke eye contact and shifted her gaze somewhere else.

I followed her stare, seeing a woman get up from her group of friends and then head toward me.

My eyes went back to her, and I saw it all in a flash. The disappointment, the urgency, the fight-or-flight . . . and then the defeat. She turned back to her drink, got the attention of the waiter, and signaled for the check.

The woman helped herself to the free chair beside me. "Hi, I'm McKayla."

My eyes were on the woman at the other table. The most beautiful woman in this bar, in the whole fucking village, honestly, and she pivoted her body away from me like she didn't want to watch me pick up someone else.

She didn't fight, like she wasn't a worthy opponent.

"Did you hear me?" McKayla asked.

I just told her the truth. "Sorry, already got my eye on someone else." I grabbed my drink, crossed the room, and then sat in the chair across from her.

She hesitated before she looked at me—like she didn't expect this.

Up close, I could really see her eyes now, see that they were even more beautiful than I realized. And I saw the cacophony of emotions in them, like she wanted me there . . . but didn't believe she belonged there.

I could read people well—my intuition was off the charts—and despite how insanely sexy she was, I could tell this woman didn't have an ounce of confidence.

And all I wanted to know was why. "Constantine."

Her eyes continued to study me from behind guarded walls, but the longer I sat there, the less timid she became. "Aurelia . . ."

Chapter 12

Constantine

Over the course of a couple days, Aurelia unpacked her stuff and incorporated it with my belongings. Because she had no furniture, her entire life was in a dozen boxes. Clothes, shoes, accessories, mementos.

I'd never lived with a woman before, but I was happy to share my space with her. Happy to know she was safe when I wasn't around, that when I came home from a long night, she'd already be waiting for me in bed, that Medusa had her favorite woman to keep her company. And I liked how easy it was.

I asked her to move in, and she said yes—just like that.

She'd had cold feet the entire beginning of the relationship, had a million reasons why it wouldn't work, but then she'd turned a corner when she lost me. And it'd been great ever since. She was one hundred percent in this with me, and we finally felt like a team.

When I got out of the shower, I stood at the vanity for a while and stared blankly at my reflection. Didn't really see my face or my eyes. I pictured my brother's face instead, the last time he'd looked at me as he lay on the floor—before Darius broke his knee.

I heard his screams and I closed my eyes, but that didn't make it stop. My brother had been dead for seven years, and there were times when I thought the grief had passed . . . and then it lunged at me like a pissed-off viper. Sank its fangs into my flesh and poisoned me.

A soft hand landed on my bare back. "You okay?"

My eyes snapped open, and the screams were silenced. My hands left the edge of the vanity, and my spine straightened. "Yeah." I cleared my throat and looked at my pale face again before I reached for my razor.

Her eyes shifted to the mirror, looking at me in the glass.

I put the preshave lotion over my chin then turned on the electric razor and got to work, getting rid of the dark hair that had grown across my jawline.

She continued to stand there like she didn't believe me.

I was a shitty liar. "I don't want to talk about it." I focused on my own face as I kept shaving, feeling her stare just the way I'd felt it at Rosticceria Da Cristina. I continued and she stayed, but I refused to look at her.

"There's only one thing you don't like to talk about."

I turned off the razor, then leaned over the sink as I splashed water onto my face. I stared at the bottom of the basin as the last drops slid down my face. Then I grabbed the towel I used in the shower and scrubbed away the water and the residue from the lotion. "I have to see someone tonight that I really fucking don't want to see."

A hint of confusion moved over her face, like she wondered if her guess had been dead wrong.

"But there's no way around it." I left the sink and walked out of the bathroom to the closet to get dressed. I put on my jeans and T-shirt, along with my watch. I left the handgun on top of the dresser and stepped back into the room.

Aurelia sat on the edge of the bed with Medusa lying on her stomach beside her. Her makeup was gone like she was already ready for bed. She did her nighttime routine after dinner, and her eyes looked pretty even when they were tired. She had a healthy and predictable sleep schedule, starting to get grouchy around ten in the evening. Polar opposite of mine—which was all over the fucking place. "I'll be back in a couple hours. Don't wait up for me." I moved to her and gave her a quick kiss. I didn't fuck her before or after dinner. I'd been in a sour mood since I'd started my day.

"Be careful."

I headed to the front door. "It's not me I'm worried about."

~

I arrived in Vatican City, and like everyone else who stepped onto the grounds, I had to go through security. But there were more security steps this time than there'd been in the past—probably because of the occasion.

I was escorted by security to the Apostolic Palace, and when I entered, I found Pope Zephyrinus seated on the couch, fully dressed in his robes and glasses. "Hope it's not too late for you." I approached him and extended my hand.

He rose to his feet and took it, patting the back of my knuckles with his other hand. "God doesn't work on a schedule, and neither do I. Hope you're well, Constantine."

I shrugged. "Eh."

He gave a nod in understanding. "This moment will pass."

"And then it'll come back . . . until I kill him."

He didn't admonish me for the confession. Nonjudgmental as always. "I enjoyed meeting Aurelia a few weeks back."

"Yeah, she was a bit awestruck by you."

A little smile moved over his lips. "I can tell she makes you happy."

"She does," I said. "I hope you'll marry us when the day comes."

"It would be my honor to bless your union—when the day comes." He smiled, then gave my arm a playful squeeze.

I smiled back.

Then the joy was sucked out of the room when the door opened. "He's here, Your Holiness."

Showtime.

"Send him in," Pope Zephyrinus said. "Thank you." He was over a foot shorter than me, shorter than Aurelia, so he had to lift his arm high to give my shoulder a comforting squeeze. "You'll make it through."

"We'll see."

A moment later, he came into the room like a fucking storm cloud. A darkness so intense it drove away the shadows. He sauntered into the place like it was his own, took a scan of the space even though he'd been there before, and then he stopped before us—his eyes locked on mine.

I stared back, his dark eyes morbid like the underworld. I could see the devil in those eyes, see evil like no other. A man without a heart, a soul that had already been taken by a demon. He cared for nothing and no one—except power.

The stare went on for several minutes. Minutes of the most intense silence ever known to humankind. I was so angry I couldn't feel my face, had no idea how my expression looked when I stared at the man I wanted to break with my own hands.

Years had passed since we were last in the same room together. Since then, I'd changed, bulked up to his size, so now there were two mountains in that room. I worked hard every single day, lifted once in the morning and then again in the late afternoon. Continued to train, continued to keep my reflexes sharp, continued to prepare for the moment I'd finally kill him.

I didn't know when that moment would come, but I believed in my heart it would someday.

Pope Zephyrinus stood between us, blanketed in our shadows. "Welcome, Darius." He extended his hand.

Darius struggled to take his eyes off me, hostile like I'd been the one to kill his brother. But he possessed some inkling of manners when he turned to the pope and took his hand. "Thank you for having me, Your Holiness."

"Of course." He gestured to the couches on the rug. "Let's have a seat." He moved to the armchair in the center of the two couches.

We went right back to our death stare.

Darius's eyes left mine to do a quick check of my body, clearly noticing my change in size since we'd last crossed paths. "Good, you aren't a vegetarian anymore." He turned his back on me and walked to one of the couches. Took a seat, knees wide apart, forearms on his thighs in a position that would allow him to jump up instantly if he wanted to. "Oh, and your brother says hi."

I hesitated because the jab stung even though I'd been prepared for it. I fortified my mind with all the armor I could muster, but it still wasn't enough to dull the sting. I inhaled and brushed it off as I took the seat across from him, the coffee table between us, surrounded by bookshelves and artwork from the Renaissance.

"Got something to say?" It came out as almost a bark. Probably would have been a shout if the pope weren't there. "I came all the way down here. You better have something fucking good to say."

"Mind your manners when you speak in the presence of the Holy Father," I said calmly.

Pope Zephyrinus raised his hand slightly and shook his head, excusing the classless behavior.

Darius went quiet then, but his jawline was tense like he had more to say but was smart enough not to say it. My response hadn't even been offensive, but this man couldn't tolerate any kind of criticism at all.

"It's come to my attention that arms are getting into the hands of our enemies through Florence." I came right out and said it. "I've already had intelligence from MI6 that a terrorist attack is imminent somewhere in the EU. I'm concerned that the two events are connected. A treaty has been signed with the EU through the UN not to sell any types of weapons outside our allies. I'm afraid someone in your jurisdiction is violating this agreement."

His stare didn't change at all. He continued to look at me like he hadn't heard a word I said.

I waited for him to say something.

The pope looked back and forth between us.

I realized nothing would come. "Have you nothing to say?"

"Thank you for the information. Are we finished here?"

"No, we aren't finished," I snapped. "Because you need to stop whoever is doing this . . . or stop doing it yourself." My gut instinct was always right, and judging by his indifferent reaction to this information, not only did he know about the sale, but he was a part of it.

"Sounds like you're trying to tell me how to run my country." He moved forward slightly, farther off the couch, his fingers stitching together. "Which is none of your fucking business."

"It is my business when it affects everyone else. When it directly violates an international agreement. You can conduct whatever nefarious activities you wish, but not at the expense of innocent people."

"I can do whatever the fuck I want, Constantine."

"You already make money hand over fist. Just sell to a different buyer. You still get your money, and you can do the right thing for the first time in your goddamn life—"

He slammed his hand down on the coffee table and made it tremble. "Mind your manners when you speak in the presence of the Holy Father, asshole!"

The pope raised both of his hands before we went for each other's throats. "Gentlemen, let us be civilized. Remember, this is a discussion, not an attack."

"Country before profit, Darius," I said. "Money is important, but there are things infinitely more important."

"God, you're such a pussy. Little vanilla ice cream bar sitting there covered in little nuts."

The pope gave a sigh.

"Your spine is as weak as your brother's, which is why I was able to snap it in half so fucking easily—"

"I'll fucking kill you—"

"Then do it. You think a couple protein shakes is enough to take me on, pussy? I didn't like your face the last time I saw it, and now I fucking hate looking at it. See the same pussy eyes that thought they could look at my wife's cunt and get away with it—"

"Enough." It was the first time I'd heard my uncle raise his voice.

Darius scooted back on the chair, withdrawing from his rage.

"This conversation has gone as far as it should," Pope Zephyrinus said. "Constantine, you've let Darius know about the rising tensions among enemies of Europe and the catastrophic consequences of an arms deal. And Darius has received this information. That is the most progress we're going to make here."

The Skull King had so much power, he couldn't be challenged—even when it could make us vulnerable to an outside attack. We had our disagreements, but I assumed there was one thing we would be united on—fighting against enemies of our country.

But I was fucking wrong.

Darius rose to his feet and addressed the pope. "Thank you for your time, Holy Father." Then he let himself out.

I stayed seated on the couch, my hands clutched tight, my eyes on the surface of the coffee table. Rage pumped in my heart so forcefully, I could feel it beat against my ribs. The corners of my eyes were red instead of black. My hands ached to snap every joint in his body that held his bones together.

My uncle stared at me for a while. "It's done, my son."

"It's never done—not for me."

Chapter 13

Aurelia

Constantine was not himself—*at all.*

He was at work all the time, and when he was home, he chose to be in his study . . . even though he didn't seem to be working. When I snuck a peek at him, he just sat there and stared at one of the walls . . . lost.

Whenever I tried to talk to him, he wasn't interested in having a conversation.

He wasn't even interested in sex.

I was buck naked when he came home one day, and he didn't even look at me before he hopped in the shower.

Every time I asked him to talk to me, he said he didn't want to. But the moment never passed. He just became colder and more distant . . . and kind of an asshole. It got so bad that I took his phone when he was in the shower, found Rocco's phone number, and then texted him from my phone.

Hey, it's Aurelia.

Everything alright? He sounded just like Constantine.

Constantine hasn't been himself in a week, and I don't know what to do about it. He won't tell me what's bothering him.

Yeah . . . he's been in a dark place.

I don't know what to do.

I don't think there's anything you can do. Need to let it run its course. Just remember, it has nothing to do with you and his obsession with you hasn't changed. It's just masked by an ugly cloud of depression.

I was relieved it had nothing to do with me. I'd assumed that was the case, but now that a full week had come and gone, I wasn't certain anymore.

Be patient.

Yeah, I'll try.

Elio set the table for dinner, and we ate in his dining room. We were seated across from each other, but Constantine didn't look at me one time. Just focused on his food or his wine or the window. It was like I wasn't even there.

"Con."

His eyes immediately flicked to mine—probably because I'd never called him that before. Everyone else he knew did, but I always loved his full name, the way it sounded, the power in its length.

"I'm sorry you're going through a hard time right now, but I wish you would confide in me."

He was only halfway done with his food, but he set down his fork like his appetite was long gone. He propped his elbows on the table, hands together at his chin, the defeat still heavy in his gaze. "It's not that I don't feel like I can talk to you about this. I just literally don't want to talk about it." He swallowed, as if just acknowledging his source of heartache was enough to destroy him.

"You forget that I've lost someone too. That the grief comes and goes depending on the day and the season. You also forget that I also had an absent father. But in my case, he didn't even try."

His eyes dropped momentarily, his fingers interlocking a little tighter.

"I'm sure my loss is different from yours, but I'm sure it hurts the same." I didn't expect him to perk up immediately after I broached the topic, but I didn't necessarily expect him to share his heartache either. I just wanted to address it since he was clearly unable to cope with it on his own.

He lowered his hands to the table and inhaled a deep breath before it came out slowly. He stared at his hands for a while, no longer looking like the big, strong man who had flashed his killer smile every few minutes. He looked worn and withered, like a leather couch that had been in a house for forty-five years. "I met with the Skull King last week. We're having some international-security issues."

This was not how I expected the conversation to go.

"And I have to sit there and look at his fucking face . . . and not kill him."

"Why do you want to kill him?"

His eyes stayed on his hands, and he drew another heavy breath. "Because he killed my brother." His voice came out quiet, so quiet it seemed like he didn't want to share that with me. "Seven years ago. And I watched him do it."

Oh Jesus . . . "Babe." My hand reached for his on the table, held on to it like I was his life raft . . . when he was actually mine.

He stared at my hand as it gripped the top of his. Then he changed his position, sliding our fingers so we were locked together. "I tried to save him, but I couldn't. So I stood there and listened to my brother scream for mercy as all the bones in his body were broken . . . and I stayed, even though I couldn't do anything, because I didn't want him to be alone. I still remember the last time we looked at each other . . . and his stare . . . he knew he was gonna die."

I continued to grip his hand.

"They stuffed him in an oil drum right in front of me."

I'd lost my mother, but our loss was not the same. I'd watched her die in her sleep, on the maximum dose of morphine, so high she didn't even know she was dying. Just faded away, until her lungs stopped inflating. This . . . this was a whole different kind of traumatic.

"I returned a few weeks later to get his body back, but Darius wouldn't give it to me. There was no amount of money he would take."

"Why did Darius kill him in the first place?"

He continued to stare at our joined hands. "Because my brother had an affair with his wife."

"Oh shit." Now the violence and the pettiness made sense.

"A part of me . . ." His voice caught, and he paused to swallow before he continued. "A part of me thinks . . . he deserved it . . . and that makes me feel worse. Not deserved it because the punishment for infidelity is murder, but because he knew exactly what the Skull King would do to him if he got caught . . . and he did it anyway."

I didn't know what to say, how to comfort him. It was just so horrible.

"But I'm still going to kill Darius anyway. I don't know how or when . . . *but I fucking will.*" That was when he took his hand from mine. When he pulled it back to his side of the table and lifted his gaze to look at me. "He has so much power that he's untouchable, but he became that way because everyone was too scared to provoke him . . . and they know he's a fucking powerhouse. He's a traitor to his own country, and I still can't do anything about it."

I didn't know what to say to that either.

"My mom thinks my brother died in a car accident. She visits his grave every morning, not knowing it's just an empty coffin. She's gotten better through the years, but she's never been the same."

"Understandably."

"He left Taormina for Palermo when I refused to speak to him after he kissed my girlfriend. I didn't know what he was doing there at the time. My mother begged me to talk to him, said that family was more important than this *disagreement*, so I went there to work it out. Found out he joined Cosa Nostra, and it just took off from there. So I know this is even more fucked up, but . . . the reason I still resent Isabella after all this time is because if that hadn't happened, my brother would still be alive. I blame her for it, and every time I'm triggered, I just start to hate her again."

Now I understood why he'd spoken to her so viciously on the patio. This was a woman he wanted to marry, but he treated her with so much resentment, like she'd done something more egregious than kissing his twin brother by mistake. When I said I wished he were normal and he dropped me, that honestly felt like a bigger crime. But he forgave me so easily and never mentioned it again. He didn't strike me as the kind of man to hold a grudge, but he'd held this grudge against her for a long time. "If one thing had been different . . . everything could have been different."

His eyes dropped again. "I know that this happened because my brother decided to fuck Darius's wife. That it was entirely his stupid decision that led us here, but I still feel that way."

"It's okay to feel all these things, Constantine. Grief is complicated and cyclic. When it returns, sometimes it's worse—and sometimes it's better. I'm sorry you've been through all this . . ."

He continued to stare at the table, and then he spoke like he hadn't heard me. "We would have stayed in Taormina and continued to work at the restaurant. I would have been married and had a couple kids. My mom would be happy. But then I realize . . . if all that had happened . . ." He lifted his eyes and looked at me again. "I wouldn't have met you. And I just can't imagine my life without you, sweetheart."

After that conversation, Constantine was himself again.

He took me out to dinner, bent me over his desk in his office, woke me up when he came home from work at three in the morning by shoving his big dick inside me.

Back to normal.

I had a shoot in the morning, and he texted me and asked if we could meet for lunch afterward. The driver dropped me off outside a restaurant with an outdoor patio. He was already there, seated under the shade of the umbrella in a dark-gray T-shirt and a dazzling smile.

"Hey, sweetheart."

"Hey." I walked to where he was seated, but he didn't stand up for me like he normally did.

He pulled me onto his lap and kissed me, his arms scooping my legs up like I weighed nothing. Naturally, he moved his hand to my ass and gave it a hard squeeze before he let me go. "How was your shoot?"

"Boring." I moved into the chair across from him.

"You don't have to work. You know that, right?" He grabbed the menu and gave it a look.

It was true. I didn't need money. I didn't pay rent, and I didn't need groceries because I'd never even set foot in his kitchen. The only time I spent money was when I hustled around the city and needed a coffee or a sandwich. "I like my job. I just don't like infant portraits. Hard to get a good picture when they're screaming at the top of their lungs."

"Well, I wouldn't describe that as boring," he said with a chuckle.

"Stressful, then."

"Then maybe you should only take the jobs you want since you don't need the work anymore."

I'd never asked him to support me. He'd just started doing it . . . like we were married. "Maybe. But you never know where a word-of-mouth recommendation will go. I photographed this wedding and her uncle was a politician, and that led to a huge job six months later."

He flipped the menu over and looked at the other side. "Keep it in the back of your mind."

"I'm happy to pay rent and contribute to other bills—"

"Sweetheart, stop." He grinned wide. "Trust me, you pay your way."

"Hey, I suck your dick for free."

"But if you're good at something, never do it for free, right?" He winked, then looked at the menu again.

He pulled off that wink so well. So handsome and smooth.

"What are you getting?" he asked.

"Maybe the salad. I already ate breakfast."

When the waiter came over, Constantine took over the conversation as always. He ordered our drinks and our lunch and then handed over the menus.

He moved closer to the table, elbows on the surface. "What else is new?"

"Other than you being so fucking hot, not much."

He smirked. "But that's not new, sweetheart."

"A bit arrogant, but you can pull it off."

"Oh, I know I can." He continued to smile as he fished his phone out of his pocket. "It's Beatrice." He took the call and put it to his ear. "Hey, sis."

I wasn't sure what she said on her end. I pulled out my own phone so I didn't just sit there and stare at him as he continued to talk.

"How are the monkeys?"

Monkeys? She had pet monkeys?

"Tell them if they give you any more shit, Uncle Con will straighten them out."

Ohh . . . his nephews.

"Yeah, things are good. At lunch with Aurelia right now." He listened to her for a bit. "Yeah, Aurelia's here. You want to talk to her?"

My heart rate spiked because I *knew* she didn't like me. *Please say no. Please say no.*

"All right, I'll let you go. Food will be out soon. Love you." He hung up and set the phone on the table.

I did like that he said *I love you* to his sister . . . and said it first.

"She said she had to go," he said. "One of the boys had climbed onto the counter to grab a cookie from the jar."

I nodded. "It's okay, Con. I know she doesn't like me."

His eyebrows furrowed, and he sat back in his chair and crossed his arms. "Why would she not like you?"

"Well, she was kinda cold when we met at the house."

"She was?" he asked in surprise.

"Yeah, but I totally get it, she and Isabella are friends. It's complicated." I didn't take it personally. If you hoped your best friend and brother would end up together, of course you wouldn't like *the other woman*. But they'd been broken up for almost a decade, so I wasn't sure why she hoped they would reconcile. They'd even slept together again, and they still didn't work it out.

Constantine cocked his head the other way and continued to stare at me, continued to stare *hard*.

"It's not a big deal. Don't worry about it."

But he continued to look at me in a way he never had before.

"Maybe she'll come around. Just needs some time." I didn't want him to be angry at his sister. She couldn't help the way she felt. She couldn't compromise her loyalty if her best friend was in pain.

But he continued to stare me down . . . like he was mad as hell.

Chapter 14

Aurelia

The drive home was spent in silence. His anger was palpable.

I started to wonder if it was directed at me instead of Beatrice.

We were dropped off at the front, and the walk inside the villa to the stairs and to the third floor felt like an eternity. When we reached the corridor, Medusa ran down the hallway to greet us, but she halted halfway.

Constantine had made a quick hand gesture, and it seemed to be a command for her to heel.

She darted into the study and jumped on one of the couches.

"Constantine?"

He took the lead and stepped into the bedroom.

His anger was like a cloud of smoke that suffocated us both. Every breath burned my lungs. I stared at his back as he moved away from me and ignored me. Everything had been fine at lunch. He'd smiled brighter than the sun, and now, he was a living earthquake. Every step shook the earth. The world trembled at his feet. "Constantine—"

He turned to me with a quickness that showed his strength, strength I forgot he had because he was always delicate with me. *"How did you know it was Isabella?"*

It took a second for the terror to strike me. To realize the hand I'd shown without thought. I'd known it was Isabella since the beginning, and the occasional times he'd spoken of her, that was exactly who I pictured. I didn't even realize he hadn't referred to her by name.

"Because my mother didn't say her name. My sister didn't. So how did you know?" He was furious exactly the way he'd been in my apartment after Enzo left, the moment before he'd walked out on me and everything we had. Red in the face, cords popping in his neck, he looked deranged. *"Answer me."* He didn't yell at me the way he had with Enzo, but it was pretty fucking close.

I didn't want to tell him that I'd eavesdropped on their conversation, but I knew not to lie. For Constantine, a small lie to mask the truth was infinitely worse than any crime. "When—when you had me over for dinner at your family's house, I noticed your sister was a bit cold to me and I didn't know why. And then I noticed the woman she was with. Everyone was drinking and laughing and having a great time, but they looked so miserable—"

"And you just figured out it was her?" he asked incredulously. "Walked up and asked for her name?"

"No." I wanted to tell him off for cutting me off, but he was so mad I didn't dare make it worse. "I went into the house to help your mom, and you two were talking on the patio . . . and I could tell there was tension there."

"But my mother wouldn't have told you that—"

"Let me finish, Con. This is the part of the story that makes me look really bad, so let me just get it over with."

He crossed his arms over his chest.

"I noticed there was an open window near where you were standing, so I walked over there and listened." I closed my eyes because it sounded so much worse when it came out of my mouth. I'd violated his privacy and eavesdropped like a nosy bitch. I kept my eyes closed because I didn't want to see his pissed-off reaction. "I heard everything you two said. I know that you slept together like a year ago. I know there's this tension between you that doesn't go away. I know she's still sorry . . . after all this time. And the reason I didn't tell you is—"

"Why?" he snapped. "Why the fuck did you sit on this for so long?"

I opened my eyes and saw him staring at me with pure disgust—and it killed me. "Because you told her you were worried about me seeing the two of you together and you didn't want to fuck it up. You didn't want to have to explain *why* you were talking, and I didn't want to put you in that position by telling you. And honestly, we didn't need to talk about it. Because I wasn't upset you used to be with her and I didn't care that you were talking and I didn't care that she still wanted you—because I don't blame her."

He was still livid, his face the color of lava.

"I'd feel the same way if I lost you. Whether it's nine years or nineteen, I would never get over you. I would never move on. I have no ill will toward her at all, because I don't blame her."

He'd stopped yelling at me, so maybe that was a good sign.

"I'm sorry I eavesdropped on your conversation. That was wrong. I know."

He continued to stare.

"And I'm sorry I didn't tell you. I just didn't want to make a problem that didn't exist in the first place. I'm not jealous . . . just empathetic."

"You still could have told me. Could have told me you knew about Isabella and you felt bad for her. But you sat on it while I tried to find the right time to tell you about her."

"The right time?" I asked. "You've mentioned her indirectly several times. That would have been the moment to tell me, but you didn't. I walked into that party having no idea your ex-fiancée was there. So were you ever *really* going to tell me?"

He got fired up again. "You're really going to try to flip this on me?"

"I'm not trying to flip anything, but I waited for you to tell me it was Isabella, so then I could tell you I already knew. Let's not pretend we weren't both keeping secrets for the preservation of this relationship.

We'd only known each other for a few days the night of that party, so we didn't know where it was going to go. We didn't know I'd be living with you six weeks later. So let's just . . . take a beat here."

He was still pissed off. It was written all over his face.

"I said I was sorry, Constantine."

He stepped away from me, like he was done with the conversation.

"Con."

He moved for the door.

When I realized this conversation was over, I broke. "Please don't leave me." I was right back to the woman I used to be, weak and pathetic, begging him to stay the way I'd begged Enzo to stay. But this time, I was the one who'd fucked up. "I said I was sorry." The tears were instantaneous because I'd lost Constantine once before, and that week nearly killed me. Now I was about to end up like Isabella, missing a man I could never have again, hoping for a dream that would never come true. "I'm really fucking sorry. Con, please don't go." I followed him into the hallway and burst into tears. *"Please."*

He spun back around when he stepped into the corridor, eyes full of a rage that was even worse than it'd been a second ago. "I'm fucking mad as hell right now and I need some damn space—but I'm not leaving you."

The relief was so strong I couldn't hide it. My hands automatically cupped my mouth as I took a breath. My eyes closed, and rivers of tears ran down my cheeks. Gratitude of epic proportions struck me like a mound of bricks.

I looked at him again through my hazy vision. I probably looked like a fucking mess with the tears and blotchy skin and the breaths I couldn't control.

"For the last nine years, I've wondered if I made the right decision about Isabella. If I was being too harsh on her, if I expected too much, if I could drop the resentment so we could move on and be happy. When she got married, it fucking hurt, and when we slept together again, it just ripped open old wounds. She haunted me like a fucking ghost, and

I worried that I'd thrown away the person I was meant to be with. But then you know what happened?" He stepped closer to me, angry eyes locked on mine. "*You.*"

I swallowed, new tears springing to my eyes for a whole different reason.

He formed a fist and put it to his chest, right over his heart. "I met you, and all those doubts disappeared—*because you're the one*. You're the one I've been waiting nine years for. My mom told me that one day a woman would come and I wouldn't be able to live without her. That I would burn my world to the ground just because she asked me to. And she was right—because I fucking love you—"

"I love you too," I said breathlessly, more tears pouring down my cheeks. "I love you so fucking much."

His eyes flicked back and forth between mine. "This is it for me. You're it for me."

"Constantine . . ." Even though I was an ugly mess, I moved into him, rose on my tiptoes, but I didn't have enough height in my flats to reach his lips.

But he lifted me like I knew he would, scooped his big arms under my ass and pulled me to him.

I hooked my arms around his neck, and I kissed him differently than I had in the past, let all of me pour into him, let my heart and soul release in the kiss. "I love you," I said between our kisses. "For the rest of my life."

~

I couldn't believe this was my life.

I couldn't believe this man was mine.

He was still asleep next to me, his smile absent while he dreamed, his entire face relaxed as he continued to rest until almost noon.

I loved the view, but it was hard not to touch him.

Medusa sat up from the couch and looked at me like she needed to go out.

I put my finger to my lips to tell her to be quiet, then snuck out of bed before I silently got dressed. I snuck out of the room with Medusa, and we left the corridor and took the stairs to the bottom floor. We stepped out into the garden, and she immediately pranced around to find a spot to do her business.

I walked with her down the path through the trees, glancing around at the private estate that looked like it'd been preserved since ancient Rome. In the corners far in the distance were the armed guards, but I just stayed in the center and close to the house to avoid them.

A pool was hidden from view by the trees, so I walked down the path to look at it, the dark-blue tile along the edges, the loungers around it. I decided to take a seat in one of them and enjoy the sight of the water while Medusa continued to enjoy the outdoors. She found a patch of grass in the sun and lay down so she could bask in the warmth.

I wasn't sure how much time passed, but then I heard his voice from behind me.

"There you are."

I turned to see him standing tall in nothing but his black sweatpants, the dark ink everywhere, that beautiful smile on his lips. His eyes shifted behind me to look at Medusa on the other side of the pool. "She must really like that sun spot because she's not even getting up to say hi to me."

I got to my feet to kiss him. "Morning."

"More like afternoon." He squeezed me to him and kissed me, his big hands making their way up my dress like my ass was a magnet for his palms. "Sorry I slept so long."

"You're fine. I would have stayed in bed, but Medusa needed to go out."

"Thanks for taking care of her."

"She's kinda my dog too, now."

He smiled at me. "More than kinda." He gave me a gentle spank before he sat on the lounger and patted his thigh.

I made myself comfortable across his lap.

He was big enough to be a chair, handle me just fine. "Beautiful day."

"Really is." I hooked my arm around his neck and kissed him again, just because I could. "Love you." I said it just because I could say it. Said it because I knew he would say it back.

He smiled like he fully understood. "Love you too, sweetheart."

I dug my fingers into his hair, touching him far more than I ever had, feeling like he was fully mine. "Do you have work today?"

"I have work every day. But I'm gonna blow it off."

"And do what?"

"You—obviously."

"Ooh, works for me."

"Then we'll go out for a nice dinner."

"Or we can stay in for a nice dinner."

He chuckled. "Even better."

When Medusa got too warm, she left the sun and moved around the pool toward us.

"Hey, baby girl." He petted her and rubbed her around the neck. Then he gave her distinct pats on the flank—like she was built solid. "Now I gotta keep two women happy every day."

"Good luck with that."

"One likes sex, and the other likes hamburgers."

"Well, I like sex *and* hamburgers."

That adorable smile moved onto his lips again. "And that's why you're my woman."

Chapter 15

Constantine

"What the fuck is wrong with your face?" Rocco asked as he stood across the table from me.

"What?"

"You've been smiling for like fifteen minutes straight. It's fucking weird."

I scoffed. "Fuck you, asshole."

"What are you so happy about?"

"Aurelia."

"She suck your dick for the first time—"

"Are you trying to get me to punch you in the face?"

He gave a quiet chuckle. "You make it so easy, Con. May as well put a big red button on your forehead that says Aurelia on it."

"Your woman should be your big red button."

"Seriously, tell me what you're so happy about. Because last time we spoke, you were in a pretty dark place." He moved to the open chair and dropped into it, shutting the laptop in front of him even though he hadn't been using it.

I'd had to look my brother's killer in the face and play a game of diplomacy. It felt like a betrayal to him and to my family. The guilt choked me from the inside out. But then a fight with Aurelia changed all that. "Aurelia said she loved me." The smile crept back at the memory, the way she didn't let me finish saying it first before she cut me off.

"I thought you guys were long past that."

"I was trying to take it slow."

"*Slow?*" he asked. "She's living with you and you're dropping the L-word, when you met six weeks ago."

"What can I say? When you're in love, every day feels like a week." It'd been a whirlwind, a tornado that lifted me off my feet. I'd spent the last decade questioning the decisions I made, the path I took in life, jumping from bed to bed and woman to woman.

"By that math, then it would be a year, which is still pretty fast."

"Asshole, you're supposed to be happy for me."

He grinned for a moment before the smile faded and the seriousness crept in. "Come on, you know I'm happy for you. I like Aurelia and think she suits you well. Just like to tease you a little bit."

I pulled out the chair and sat across from him, the place a mess with old take-out meals, devices, guns, and grenades. Constant clutter because there was never time to organize the space, not when there was so much going on all the time. "Thanks. Means a lot to me."

He gave a nod. "Gonna ask her to marry you?"

"Yeah." I knew I would. Had no doubt about it.

His eyebrows rose slightly, like he was surprised. "Now?"

"I don't know when, honestly," I said. "I'm happy where we are right now."

"And how do you think this will affect your work?"

"Affect my work?" I asked in slight surprise.

"Surely it must have crossed your mind already." He sat back in the chair, hands together as his elbows propped on the armrests.

"I told her from the beginning that I'm never walking away from this. Not if I get married, not if I have kids. And she's not the type of woman to try to change my mind either. She was shaken up by what Pierre did to her, but she bounced back pretty quickly. I think she can handle it."

He gave a nod. "Yeah, I think she can handle it too."

"She's it, man," I said as I gave a slight shake of my head. "I'm almost thirty-five, so I started to wonder if she was out there. But she was in Rome the whole time, right under my fucking nose." I'd spent time with a lot of beautiful women who had a lot to offer, but whatever I was looking for just wasn't there. Whoever said you couldn't choose who you loved was right on the money, because I'd been ready to settle down for a few years and felt absolutely nothing for every woman and every fling. I wasn't sure exactly what made Aurelia stand out to me, but whatever it was got me the second I saw her.

My phone started to ring in my pocket, so I fished it out and glanced at the screen, my instinct always going to Aurelia in case she needed me. My priorities had already changed drastically if she was the first thing I thought about every time my phone went off. But it wasn't her. It was one of my guys in Florence. "Roger, what's going on?"

He skipped the small talk and pleasantries. "Been a lot of movement here, Con."

It was a vague message, but it made my heart drop like a stone.

"Tanks, Hummers, the Skull Kings are making big moves—and they're headed south."

My eyes went to Rocco across the table.

He was absolutely still, focused on me like he could hear the words over the line.

I put Roger on speaker and set the phone on the table. "You're on speaker. Rocco's here. Know anything else?" I asked, hunching over the phone as I scooted closer to the edge of the table.

"No," Roger said. "But it's a massive operation. All hands on deck, it seems."

Rocco continued to stare at me.

I stared back. "Let me know if you hear anything else." I hit the red button and hung up.

"The arms operation was either a distraction or the gesture of an alliance," Rocco said.

"So an attack is coming from the east and the north . . ."

"Possibly. Perhaps he gave those arms in exchange for helping him take Rome."

"Or he's just pissed that I called him out for being a traitor, so he's coming for me."

Rocco nodded. "Either way, he's coming for Rome."

I nodded in agreement, and instead of launching into action, I thought of the two people who mattered most. "I need to move Aurelia and Medusa to a safe house. You prepare for the attack."

He was already out of his chair and across the room.

I got to my feet because I couldn't sit still with all the adrenaline knotted in my stomach. It was after midnight when I called Aurelia, and I hoped she'd answer. Otherwise, Elio would have to wake her up. It rang a couple times, and she didn't answer. "Pick up the phone . . ."

After the fourth ring, she finally answered. "Constantine?" she asked in a tired voice.

"Sweetheart, I'm about to come at you with a lot, so listen carefully. Pack a bag and get ready to leave. My guys are moving you and Medusa to another location."

That yanked her out of sleep in record time. "What's happened?"

"I don't have time for this. Do as I say."

She didn't ask me again. "Okay."

"Love you."

"Love you too," she said quickly.

I hung up, told my guys to move the girls, called the security at the Vatican so they could discreetly move the pope in case he was a possible target, and then prepared for the moment I'd been waiting for.

To finally kill Darius.

Chapter 16

Aurelia

I jumped out of bed and pulled on a pair of jeans.

Medusa seemed to know that something serious had happened, because she never got up when I peed in the middle of the night or when I doomscrolled on my phone because I couldn't sleep. But she jumped off the bed and stood beside me—like she was guarding me.

I pulled on my bra and a top, not caring what I wore or if it matched. I slipped on a pair of flats, my heart racing so fast it made me dizzy. Constantine gave me no context in his phone call, but I assumed something bad had transpired if he felt pressured to move me somewhere else. The place was already surrounded by a wall, tall and thick like the one around the Vatican, and armed guards were everywhere.

If it wasn't safe here, where was it safe?

I shoved my essentials into a bag and zipped it closed—and that was when I noticed how hard my hands shook. I didn't know where Constantine was. I knew he was okay at the moment, but how long would that moment last? Who had threatened him enough to make him move me?

I looked at Medusa, who was still seated beside me. "He'll be okay . . . he'll be okay."

She continued to stare at me with those dark-brown eyes . . . eyes that reminded me of Constantine.

I took a breath before I got to my feet and threw the bag over my shoulder. "Okay, let's go. I'm guessing they'll pick us up outside." We left the bedroom and stepped out of the golden doors into the hallway. We were only halfway down it when we heard it.

The sound of gunshots.

A lot of gunshots. Automatic weapons, hundreds of rounds passing through the barrels in just a few seconds. It was hard to know where it came from because the palace was enormous, but if I could hear it so well . . . that wasn't a good sign.

"Shit."

Medusa released a low growl as she stared at the door at the end of the corridor.

"Fuck, what do we do?"

She growled again, baring her teeth as she stared down the door.

"Think, think, think." I could call Constantine, but if someone had hit the palace, he probably already knew about it. I had to survive long enough for him to get here. "I need a gun." I dropped the bag and headed back to the suite, knowing Constantine had stuff in the closet.

I made it back into the bedroom and stepped into the walk-in closet. I flicked on the light and looked around frantically, opening the drawer where he kept his watches, trying to open the locked safe in the back. I felt like there was a gun around all the time, and then when I actually needed one, there were none to be found. "Maybe his nightstand." I headed back to the bedroom and opened the top drawer of his nightstand. There it sat, a large black handgun. I picked it up, felt the weight of it in my hand, and checked the safety to make sure it was off. I had no idea if it was loaded and didn't know how to check, but I assumed it was.

Medusa came back to me.

"Okay, we'll just lie low—"

There was more gunfire, and this time, it was loud. Loud enough that I nearly jumped out of my skin. Medusa didn't bark, but she released a vicious growl as she turned back to the door.

I dropped down and squatted by the bed, dropping the gun on the rug beside me as I gave a loud cry in sheer terror. The only reason the sound of gunshots was getting louder was because they were coming closer, and they were getting closer because they were coming for me.

This was what Constantine warned me about. The price I had to pay to be with him.

He promised nothing would ever happen to me, but I had to fight like he wasn't coming. Had to buy him enough time to get to me. Because I knew he was rushing through the streets that very moment to stop whoever had come for me.

"Come on, Aurelia." I picked up the gun again and rose to my feet before I headed to the double golden doors. Medusa was in the hallway, looking down the corridor, growling and baring her teeth like she was prepared to take them all down by herself.

"Medusa, get over here." I looked at the double gold doors, the ones that were so heavy I could barely move them. "They won't be able to get through these. Come on."

To my surprise, she came right away.

And then I heard voices in the corridor, like they'd rounded the corner at the end of the hallway.

"Oh shit." I set down the gun and started to push the doors shut, using my entire body to make the doors that weighed tons creak shut. It was like moving a car in neutral, except I couldn't get any momentum because the doors were on hinges instead of wheels.

"Anyone home?" a guy taunted from down the hallway. "Empress?" he mocked.

These were not the kind of men I wanted to face. That gave me a burst of energy, and I finally got the doors shut in the center. I threw the handle and enabled the lock before I scooted back and grabbed the gun again. "That should stop them . . . right?" They had to be bulletproof.

And the lock was concealed within the golden metal, so there was no way they could shoot it.

Medusa stood at the door and growled louder, her stance tense like she was prepared to rip someone's throat out.

I was so glad she was there. I couldn't imagine doing this alone.

Then I heard the spray of bullets on the other side, machine guns firing against the golden doors. Even with the barrier between us, it was so loud I couldn't hear my own scream. I covered my ears to protect my eardrums before I crawled away.

Medusa came with me.

I crawled to the threshold of the bedroom, then looked back, seeing the dents form in the metal from all the bullets.

Then the sound stopped.

"Please tell me it's over." Crouched on the floor like a bullet would fly over my head any second, I waited with Medusa, hoping Constantine and his men were on the other side, neutralizing the threat that came right to my door.

But then the gunshots resumed.

I covered my ears again and closed my eyes.

Guess they just needed to reload.

Minutes later, they did enough damage that one of the golden doors fell back and collapsed on the floor, the force so strong it literally shook the floors as if an earthquake had struck Rome.

I'd hoped Constantine would get there before they made it through, but I really was on my own.

"Empress, I'd like a word." I couldn't see what he looked like because I was still hidden around the corner, but his voice was deep like Constantine's—though it was far more sinister. "Come out on your own, or I'll drag you out by your ankle. Choice is yours."

Fuck, fuck, fuck.

What the fuck do I do?

I gripped my gun until my knuckles hurt, but it was useless against their automatic weapons. I didn't know how many guys there were, but even if it was just the guy who threatened me, I was still outmatched. I could tell from his voice alone.

"Was hoping you'd say that." His footsteps came as he stepped into the entryway with the round table in the center. He could have gone to the right, where the dining room was, but he seemed to somehow know I was to the left. His footsteps grew louder.

And then Medusa aimed to kill. She rushed him with a speed I'd never seen her use before. She jumped right on him and sank her teeth into his arm.

He didn't cry out, but he grunted from the bite.

I jumped from around the corner and fired my gun in his direction, not sure if I hit my mark because I'd purposely kept the lights off so it'd be harder for them to see. I fired several times, knowing one of those bullets had to hit my target.

He flung Medusa off him like a 150-pound dog weighed nothing—and she soared across the room until she hit the wall.

"No!"

She collapsed on the floor but didn't get up right away. She was alert and aware but disoriented.

I looked back at the man who'd thrown her like a Frisbee and saw he was enormous, like a mountain. But unlike Constantine, his strength was utterly terrifying. With dark hair and midnight-black eyes, he looked like a demon in human form. Just one look at him told me this man was pure evil.

He glanced at his arm, which was badly gashed and bloody, then shrugged it off and looked at me.

He looked at me like he fucking hated me. A snarled curl to his lip, vengeance in his eyes like I was the one who'd provoked him when he was the one who'd broken into my home.

I caught Medusa moving in the corner of my eye, seeing her try to get up but struggling to do so. When I looked at her fully, I realized her leg was broken, but she was still trying to protect me. Still growling. Still fighting the agony she must feel everywhere. Then she started to limp toward us.

My assailant pulled out his gun and aimed it at her.

"Wait, wait, she'll stop." I made the hand gesture I'd seen Constantine make last week. Some kind of sign that told her to heel.

Her growls quieted and she lay back down, but she continued to bare her teeth like she couldn't suppress her rage.

"She's not a problem. Just leave her alone."

He lowered the gun and gave me his full attention. "You do realize I'm going to shove my dick in your ass, torture you, and then kill you in the most painful way possible . . . *and you care about a fucking dog?*"

I inhaled a sharp breath and couldn't hide the terror that gripped my windpipe and didn't let go. I knew I was in trouble, but I'd been in trouble before with Pierre and his crew. Though, this . . . this was something else. "I'll go without a fight. Just let her go."

"Does it look like I'm worried about a fight?" He slipped the gun into the back of his jeans. "Drop the gun and let's go."

I could try to shoot him again—and not miss.

He stared me down. "You're out. But go ahead and try it. Every bullet you pump into me, your dog will get two."

Maybe most people wouldn't prioritize a dog over themselves, but she was more than a dog to me. She was one of us, making us a family of three. I'd never had a dog before, but I'd gotten used to her so quickly, napping on the couch with her even though she was way too big to fit. And the way Constantine loved her was the sweetest thing.

So I dropped the gun.

He moved over to me fast, grabbing me by the arm and shoving me forward like I would fight him the whole way. He tugged me hard like he wanted to rip my shoulder out of the socket. He flung me so hard that I fell to the floor. I wanted to scream in terror, but I kept my mouth shut and bottled it inside.

Then I finally felt a surge of hope when I heard what one of his men said.

"Constantine is here." He was one of four men who held an automatic rifle.

The man who'd thrown me didn't seem displeased by that information. He sauntered toward where I'd fallen in the corridor. "Good. Tell him to come alone or his whore dies." He continued to pace slowly, a mammoth of a man, muscles big and thick like Constantine's. Dressed in all black and laced-up boots, he paced across the rug.

I stayed on the floor, trying to be as invisible as possible.

When I looked back through the door, I saw Medusa limping toward me, still trying to get to me.

Tears flooded my eyes at the sight of her still trying.

I tightened my hand into a fist the way Constantine had done, trying to keep her alive and out of the fight. I mouthed, "Heel."

She stopped again, lay flat, and rested her broken leg.

We just had to hold on a little longer . . . until Constantine got here.

He would get us out of this.

I knew he would.

The man continued to pace slowly, the men remained alert, and then after what felt like an eternity, the sound of quick footsteps grew louder.

I knew Constantine.

He rounded the corner, then came to a stop at the end of the corridor, surveying the scene—me on the floor, Medusa hurt, the four guys with guns who would shoot our brains out if we moved wrong, and him.

The asshole who wanted us dead.

I had no idea what thoughts passed through Constantine's head, but he looked pissed.

Then he started down the corridor again, appearing unarmed, the only armor he wore his clothes and the muscle underneath.

I had no idea how he'd save us, but I believed he would.

The man who'd captured me stopped his pacing and stared him down as he approached. "You really think I'd start a civil war? You're dumb like your brother. All that pussy turning your brains into scrambled eggs. Well, my boot turned his into scrambled eggs, I guess."

Now I knew who he was—the Skull King.

Constantine kept his eyes on him, but he moved toward me.

"Whoa, slow down, Con." He took a step and moved between us, blocking Constantine's path.

Medusa gave a quiet whine as she looked at Constantine.

Constantine didn't look at her. Didn't seem to hear her. Then he made a fist and put it against his chest—silently telling me to be brave.

I lay still and tried not to cry.

Constantine only looked at the Skull King. He showed no hint of distress, even though he must have been a wreck inside. I'd seen a version of him that night when he killed Pierre and the others who'd tried to kill me. But this version was different because he was an emperor who faced off against a king. "Name your price."

The Skull King pulled out his gun and aimed it at me—all the while not taking his eyes off Constantine.

Constantine kept his closed fist to his chest, continued to stare down the man who put a gun to my head. "A bit unnecessary when I just asked you to name your price, Darius."

He cocked the gun—just to be an asshole.

"My brother fucked your wife, and your response is to kill mine?" His voice rose, the anger booming down the hallway. *"What the fuck do you want?"*

"Here are my terms—accept them and she lives."

Constantine continued his hard stare.

"And you also live. Because you're right. You didn't fuck my wife. But I still hate your face every time I look at it, so you go back on your word, and I will kill everyone you've ever known and loved. Understand me?"

He was utterly still, hand to his chest, eyes sharp. "Yes."

"Rome is mine. This palace you call home is mine. The Roman Republic will lose its emperor and have a king instead, and you will not interfere with my reign. Your men either join me or retire permanently—"

"Done."

Darius hesitated in obvious surprise.

I didn't expect it either. Didn't expect him to give up everything he loved . . . for me.

Darius continued to stare at him like he didn't quite believe it.

"We'll be gone by morning. You can have everything, and I'll disappear."

The stare-down from the Skull King was long and penetrative, like the two of them were in a poker match and one of them was bluffing. "Well, that was easy." It seemed to be over, but then he raised his gun again and pointed it at Medusa to shoot her. "Except one more thing. Your little bitch bit me—"

With superhuman reflexes, Constantine jumped in the way of Medusa, and his body jerked back hard when the bullet struck him.

"Oh my god!" I shrieked and rushed to him. "Constantine—"

Darius grabbed me by the arm and flung me hard to the floor. He walked over to Constantine, whose body completely blocked Medusa, his shirt stained with blood from the bullet that seemed to have hit him in the shoulder. "You took a bullet for a dog?"

Constantine showed no sign of pain, held himself up on his uninjured arm.

"Are you fucked in the head?"

Constantine stared up at him, his breathing slightly elevated from the pain or the loss of blood. "I agreed to your terms. We'll grab our things and head straight to the airport." He slowly pushed himself to his feet, then stood tall, the blood dripping down the ink of his arm and to his fingertips. Medusa got up behind him and started to limp toward him. "You know I'm a man of my word, Darius."

Darius returned his handgun to the back of his jeans, then nodded to his men. "You have three hours. My men will keep an eye on you until you're done. All calls and texts are prohibited. If you try, you'll all be shot—including your dog."

~

I rushed to him and went straight for his arm, yanking up the sleeve to see the visible wound and the blood that continued to pour out of it. "We've got to get you to a hospital."

He yanked the sleeve down again. "I'm not worried about it."

"You've been shot."

"Been shot before. It's fine."

"What?"

He blew off my concern and grabbed me hard by the arm. "Are you okay?"

"I—I'm fine."

"Did he hurt you?"

"No." He'd thrown me on the floor twice, but that was nothing compared to what he could have done. "But . . . Medusa tried to protect me. She bit him really good on the arm, and he threw her across the room and broke her leg." I started to cry, remembering the thud her body had made when it smacked against the wall.

Constantine grimaced, like that knowledge really affected him. He turned away from me to Medusa, where she stood balancing on her three paws so she didn't have to put pressure on the fourth. It was her right front leg. "Baby girl . . ." He knelt down to her, cupped her face in his hands, then kissed her forehead. He rested his lips there for a long time. "We're gonna get you better, okay? We just have to get out of here first. Stay here until we're ready." He kissed her again. "You did a good job protecting Aurelia."

I watched him comfort his dog while he bled out from the bullet he'd taken for her. Watched him give all of himself to everyone. Watched him sacrifice his whole world for the two of us.

He rose to his feet again. "Let's grab what we need and go."

I stared at his bleeding arm and then the calmness in his eyes. It was the scariest moment of my life, but it seemed like nothing to him. But I knew deep inside he was devastated by the price he'd paid for my life. "Constantine—"

"We don't have time." He cut me down like he knew exactly what I would say. Like he could see the guilt written all over my face.

He stepped into the bedroom and then his bathroom. He found the first aid kit in the back of one of the cabinets, popped it open, and got to work on himself. He grabbed a pair of tweezers and watched his movements in the mirror as he dug out the bullet and dropped it into the sink.

I just watched in horror, knowing only experience could have made him so good at that. "That's why you have so many tattoos . . . to hide the scars." More blood came from the wound when the bullet was extracted, but he already had the needle ready. Sutured himself up like it wasn't his first time either.

He didn't confirm what I said. Or maybe he hadn't heard it because his mind was somewhere else.

Once the wound was sutured, he wrapped it in gauze and secured it in place. He left the bloody mess in the sink for Darius to deal with later.

I would have offered to help, but he seemed to have it under control.

Then he went into his closet, opened a bag, and shoved a couple things inside—some watches from his collection, a few guns, some of his clothes, a picture album he had on one of the shelves.

Most of my belongings were still in boxes, so I took only the things that mattered, like pictures of my mom, my cameras and my laptop, some of my clothes and shoes. Just the essentials because we could only carry so much. Everything else was left behind.

Constantine hooked his bag over one shoulder and then hooked mine over the other. He walked back to where we'd left Medusa, who lay there panting as she struggled to tolerate the pain in her broken leg.

This place had been an oasis for me, but now it was the site of destruction.

Constantine knelt down and helped Medusa upright on three of her legs. Then he scooped her up into his arms and cradled her to his chest, a dog who weighed over one hundred pounds. He carried her and the bags like it all weighed nothing.

Chapter 17

CONSTANTINE

I left Aurelia and Medusa in the car and entered the Temple.

Soon, it would belong to Darius . . . along with the rest of Rome.

Rocco was already there, leaning against the table with his arms crossed over his chest, his face bruised like he'd gotten the butt of a gun. He had a bandage on his arm like he'd been cut or shot too.

I stopped before him, and judging by the look on his face, he already knew everything. A pained look full of potent disappointment. It was so palpable I could smell it in the air. I'd let him down. Let down everyone. Let down the republic.

"You're really going to leave?" he finally asked.

"I said I would."

"And you're really just going to give up? Let him take Rome. Let him take everything you've built." His voice rose as the anger got to him.

Mine became calmer. "I didn't have a choice, Rocco."

"But you have a choice now. Fight back."

"We both know I'm a man of my word. He beat me fair and square. Beat me so good I didn't even see it coming."

He continued to stare me down.

"After we met at the Vatican, he never left. Just fooled us into thinking he did. He knew I'd confront him about the arms deal that he *wanted* me to see." It was all a setup, and I fucking fell for it. He distracted me and then took the palace, knowing the battle would be over once he captured my queen.

The Empress.

"I don't care how we got here, Con. We need to figure out what to do next."

"I agreed to his terms—"

"Then break them." He straightened, then shoved me in the chest. "*Fight back.* The Roman Empire fell once, and now you're going to let it fall again."

I let him push me. Let him take out his rage on me.

"You said you would never let a woman change what you believe in. But now you're giving it all up for her."

"Change what I believe in?" I asked quietly. "So you think I should have just left her there to be raped and killed so I could take him down later? Let him kill my dog? *That's your solution?* No, I haven't changed what I believe in, but you sure have."

He moved back to the table, shaking his head slightly.

"I don't like this outcome." It killed me to walk away from it all. To accept all the consequences that would come later. How it would affect Rome and its people. "But I couldn't live with the other choice. I chose Aurelia, and I would choose her again a thousand times. You know the Roman Republic is built on my blood, sweat, and tears. You know I would die for it. But she's my Roman Empire—and I will defend her with everything that I have. I'm not fucking sorry for the choice I made. But I'm sorry that you're so fucking disappointed."

"He killed your brother, and you're just going to let him go."

I couldn't believe he said those words to me. Cut me deep on purpose, called me a coward without actually saying it. I would have punched him in the face or thrown him across the table if I weren't utterly demoralized enough as it was. "Go fuck yourself, Rocco."

~

We drove to the airport, and I chartered a private plane to Taormina.

It was almost dawn by the time we left. I carried Medusa onto the plane and made her comfortable on a large dog bed. I had been able to get some pain medication for her so she could relax before I got her the care she needed in Sicily.

I knew Darius had his men tail me all the way to the airport. Knew if I overstayed my welcome, that psychopath might change his mind and break every bone in Medusa's body and make Aurelia his new wife.

Aurelia continued to cast glances at me, her stare full of concern and worry, like she knew I was a broken vessel inside. I'd worked my whole life to earn this position, and I knew damn well I was the only one good enough to do it. It took all my strength to turn my back on it, my people, my country, and let a dictator seize it.

It would haunt me for the rest of my life.

~

When we arrived in Sicily, the first thing I did was take Medusa to the veterinary hospital. She'd been patient for hours, dealing with a broken leg with only the occasional whine because my girl was fucking tough.

I checked her in with the doctor, and after a couple x-rays, they realized her leg was broken in two different places. She needed surgery right away, and even though it was supposed to take a week to get her on the schedule, I paid a million euros to the surgeon to do it in the next few hours.

I wasn't going to let my girl be in pain for a fucking week.

I was dead fucking tired and emotionally drained, but Aurelia didn't ask me about it. She just held my hand or touched my arm or comforted me with her silence—like she knew I wasn't ready to talk.

Hours later, we got Medusa back, her leg wrapped up and her meds in tow, and I drove us into Taormina. Returning to this special place should fill me with joy, but for the first time, it filled me with pain. We didn't drive to the hotel where we'd met, but to my residence because the renovations had just been completed.

We pulled through the gates and around the fountain out front and then into the garage. The place was empty of security and staff because I hadn't told anyone I was returning to the house. They were still on their paid hiatus until my return. I'd been so busy with everything that had happened that notifying them hadn't crossed my mind at all.

I carried the bags inside, up the stairs to my bedroom, and then returned downstairs, where I'd left Medusa on the couch. She was still drowsy from the meds and clearly pain-free for the time being.

Aurelia sat beside her, gently petting the side of her cheek while she stroked her side, like a mother looking after her sick child. The compassion and concern she had for Medusa was clear as day.

I could see it written all over her face. "I'd take her upstairs, but she'll need to go out soon."

She kept her eyes on the dog she already loved like her own. "I'll stay with her, Constantine. You should shower and rest. I know it's been a hard day for you." She lifted her chin and looked at me.

"I think your day has been worse than mine." Cornered by Darius, with nowhere to go, she must have been utterly terrified. I'd crashed into two cars as I'd raced through the streets to get to her and didn't even stop to see if the passengers were okay. I'd run all the red lights and sped straight to her. Abandoned all my obligations and my men for her.

Her hand stopped moving over Medusa's fur. "I don't think that's true, Constantine."

~

It was late afternoon when I woke up.

I got out of bed, checked my phone on my nightstand, and saw at least fifty missed calls and a hundred text notifications. President Barsetti's name popped up multiple times. I set the phone on the nightstand as I sat on the edge of the bed, looking at the closed curtains over the window. The walls had been redone and repainted, and the hardwood floors had been replaced. Artwork was returned to the walls, and new furniture had been added. It was ready for me even when no one knew I was coming.

It was the first time in my life when I'd felt lost. When I'd lacked a purpose.

When I'd run from a fight.

The phone started to ring on the nightstand—President Barsetti.

I took a slow breath before I dragged my hand down my face. I grabbed the phone as I cleared my throat, then took the call. I answered without saying a word, letting him have the floor to eviscerate me with the fancy vocabulary he learned at college.

But he was quiet too.

I continued to hold my silence.

"Con, you know what will happen if you don't take the city back."

I gave a painful nod even though he couldn't see me. "Yeah . . . I do."

"Then we need to figure out a plan together."

My wrists were chained to my feet. I was restrained by my love for a woman. She was the single most important thing to me now. She didn't have my last name, but she was family to me. "You know I can't do that, Crow."

"The corruption Darius will sow into our fields will grow into weeds."

"And why is that entire responsibility on my shoulders?"

"Because you're the emperor, Con."

"I was. But not anymore."

"You would turn your back on us—"

"I had no other choice. He would have done unspeakable things to my woman. I betrayed my country for a single woman, and I'm not sorry about it. I'm not fucking sorry. The only thing I'm sorry about is letting him outsmart me, for not seeing the double play unfold right before my very eyes."

He said nothing.

"I told you years ago that he needed to be stopped. But you and everyone else were too scared to do anything. You enabled him to become this shadow over our country, and now his storm clouds will cover it from head to boot. This is not entirely on me."

He remained quiet.

"I'm a man of my word. Darius let Aurelia live in exchange for my exile—and I will honor that. I gave my all for my people every day, and now it's time for someone else to take up the torch. I've made my decision, and it's final. Good luck."

Chapter 18

Aurelia

I couldn't carry Medusa the way Constantine could, but I helped her off the couch so she could go outside and do her business. In the adrenaline of the moment, I hadn't taken in the beauty of Constantine's home at all. It was much smaller than the palace in Rome, but it was still a luxury property on the edge of the cliff, stunning views of the sea below, a large pool and a private garden with colorful flowers and trees. I wasn't sure if Medusa was allowed to do her business in the garden, but I wasn't sure where else she was supposed to go. Under the circumstances, I doubted Constantine would care.

We made it back inside, the seating area with three oversize couches and armchairs in front of a grand fireplace with an enormous TV on the wall. Paintings, art, and mirrors were already placed everywhere, like someone else had decorated his home.

Instead of making Medusa bend down to drink from her bowl, I lifted the bowl to her so she could drink without putting more weight on her front paw. She slurped down half the bowl, and then I lifted the other bowl that held food and helped her eat that.

I felt Constantine's presence before I heard his footsteps on the hardwood floor. There was an electricity to the air, a power in the walls of the house. I set down the bowl, then stood up to turn to him.

He was in just a pair of sweatpants, his face far less tired after adequate sleep, but his eyes were still hollow with sorrow. "How are my girls?" Despite the obvious heartache, he smiled. And it seemed like he meant it. He hooked his arm around the small of my back, and he kissed my hairline.

"Medusa is doing okay," I said. "She'll be out of commission awhile."

He knelt down and grabbed her face with his big hands and gave her a deep rubdown before he kissed her on the head. "I know you've got this, baby girl." He scooped her up and carried her to her dog bed on the floor so she could get comfortable. It seemed to be exactly what she wanted, like she was too tired to desire anything else. She lay there and closed her eyes. Constantine grabbed her bag of essentials and pulled out a stuffed Lamb Chop before he placed it beside her paw. The eyes were ripped out, and there was a hole where the stuffing had been yanked out of its chest, so clearly, it was her favorite.

Then he stood up again and came to me. "Elio will be here later today. I let the staff know I'm back, so we'll have our old routine."

He meant we would be serviced and pampered like royals again.

"I know it's not as spacious as my place in Rome—"

"Are you out of your mind?" It was a three-story villa just above the village of Taormina, a beautiful home like I could only dream of. "I love it here. I think I love it more, actually." This village felt like home away from home, the place where I'd met him and his family, stepped into his world.

He smiled slightly. "Good. I love it too."

~

I spotted Constantine outside, standing at the iron railing along the edge of his terrace. It was sunset, so the sky was a beautiful splash of pastel. He stood there in just his black sweatpants, the gauze still wrapped around his arm, his back covered in the ink that hid all the scars I would never know about.

I opened the glass door and stepped onto the terrace, an enormous patio that had a large pool along with a sitting area and a full dining table, like he entertained often. Strings of white lights were draped over the dining table and were illuminated, like he'd switched on the timer at some point.

His arms rested on the iron railing, and he looked out at the sea, a yacht parked near shore.

I came to his side, wearing a sweater because it was a bit chilly that evening. It was the end of June, almost July, and soon, the weather would be hot and humid . . . and a bit unbearable. My arms rested on the rail, my forearm touching his to let him know I was there.

He continued to look out at the water, his eyes sharp and guarded.

We'd been there for a few days, taking turns caring for Medusa, with the vet coming by for in-home visits to check on her. Elio took over the duties of the house, and our meals were prepared throughout the day. The floor below ground level was where the chef's kitchen was located, along with the washer and dryer and guest rooms for Elio and the staff, so Constantine and I stuck to the second and third floor and had our privacy.

Constantine hadn't mentioned what happened.

I didn't either, wanting to give him time to process it.

But it'd been long enough now, and the guilt was eating me alive. "I'm sorry . . . for what happened."

A sarcastic smirk moved on to his lips. "I'm the one who should be apologizing to you."

"You did nothing wrong."

"I let him outmaneuver me. I underestimated him. None of that would have happened if I hadn't allowed it to happen."

"You're being hard on yourself—"

"I wasn't there to protect you. And you have no idea what that man is capable of. When he found out his wife was sleeping with my brother, he killed them both. He's not like me. He doesn't respect or care for women."

"I'm okay."

"Thank god for that. But Medusa is hurt, and that kills me."

My hand moved to his arm. "The vet said she'll make a full recovery."

"Doesn't matter. She's my baby girl, and I should have protected her."

My hand moved up his arm to his shoulder, feeling the bandage there. "You saved her life." He'd taken a bullet for her when most men would have let their dog die. But he treated her like a person, like a member of his family. "And she'll be okay."

He continued to stare ahead, his expression the same, as if my words didn't have the desired effect. Everything I said bounced off him like heavy raindrops.

"I don't want you to give everything up for me. I know what the Roman Republic means to you."

"It's already done."

"Doesn't mean you can't—"

"Sweetheart." He pivoted his body and looked directly at me. "Yes, I'm devastated that this has come to pass, but I have no regrets about my decision. You are the single most important thing to me. The Roman Republic may fall—but you're my Roman Empire. I fight for you before I fight for anyone else."

I was moved practically to tears, watching a man choose me without hesitation. Watching a man sacrifice his world because he loved me more. I didn't know what to say. Didn't understand what I'd done to earn such loyalty and commitment.

"It's time for someone else to take up the torch. Someone else to fight for the Roman Republic. I've done my time." He stared into my eyes with quiet confidence. He'd only been honest with me, so I believed he spoke the truth, not just what I wanted to hear so I'd feel better about the situation. "A part of me wonders if all this came to pass so I would find you. And then I would settle down here next to my family and we'd live a long and happy life by the sea. If that's the ending to this story . . ." A smile entered his gaze as he looked at me before it started to reach his lips. "Then that's just fine with me."

OTHER WORKS BY PENELOPE SKY

Golden Retriever in Another Republic

Fifth Republic Series

The Butcher

The Carver

The Saint

Golden Retriever in a Mafia Romance

The Betrayal Series

It Kills Me

It Breaks Me

It Ruins Me

It Hurts Me

It Pains Me

It Destroys Me

Morally Gray Hero in Organized Crime

The Buttons Series

Buttons and Lace

Buttons and Hate

Buttons and Pain

Buttons and Shame

Buttons and Blame

Buttons and Grace

Morally Gray Hero That Doesn't Care About Boundaries

Skull Series

The Skull King

The Skull Crusher

The Skull Ruler

Arranged Marriage with Alpha Protector

The Wolf Series

The Wolf and the Sheep

The Wolf and His Wife

The Lone Wolf

Alphahole That Falls First

Banker Series

The Banker

The Dictator

The Tyrant

Alpha Male That Wants Revenge Through Arranged Marriage

Betrothed Series

Wife

Husband

Lover

Committed

First

Second

Forever

Lie

Secret

Truth

Morally Gray Alphahole

Lesser Evil Series

Lesser Evil

Better Man

Harder Betrayal

Golden Retriever Mafia Romance

Empire Series

Bartholomew

Barbarian

Morally Gray Antihero in a Romantic Thriller

Chateau Series

The Chateau

The Camp

The Boss

The Palace

Alpha Male Protector in a Romantic Thriller

Cult Series

The Cult

The Catacombs

Alphahole Captor Falls First

Queen Series

Protect Your Queen

Love Your Queen

Worship Your Queen

The Barsetti Clan from the Buttons Series Continues

Beyond Buttons Series

Buttons and Revenge

Buttons and Betrayal

Buttons and Devotion

Buttons and Power

Buttons and Despise

Buttons and Beauty

Buttons and Loyalty

Buttons and Blood

Buttons and Death

Buttons and Lies

Buttons and Deceit

Buttons and Hope

Buttons and Belief

Buttons and Desire

Buttons and Shadows

PENELOPE SKY WRITING AS PENELOPE BARSETTI

Morally Gray Alphahole Necromancer

Death Series

The Death King

Blood of Dragons

The Dragon King

The Dragon Queen

Princess of Death

Empire of Death

Alphahole Hell-Bent on Revenge

Forsaken Series

The Forsaken King

The Broken Queen

The Three Kings

Obsessed Golden Retriever Vampire

Dirty Blood Series

Bite The Woman That Feeds

Bite The Terror That Feeds

Bite The Power That Feeds

The Forsaken Vampire

The Broken Prince

Clash of Kingdoms

About the Author

Penelope Sky is an international phenomenon and multiple Amazon Charts, *New York Times*, *Wall Street Journal*, and *USA Today* bestselling author. She's best known for her dark romance, mafia romance, and romantic thrillers, and with books translated into dozens of languages around the world, she's sold more than five million copies worldwide. Sky also writes fantasy romance under the pen name Penelope Barsetti. You can follow and connect with the author on Instagram or TikTok at @penelopeskyauthor.